PRAISE FOR
THE PERFECT MAN NOVELLAS

"A very fun read.... Ms. Thompson's fans will be pleased, and anyone who is a true fan of contemporary romance fiction will also find it an entertaining piece."
—Book Binge

"Short and sweet and everything I hope for when reading a contemporary romance ... this book was like a dessert at the end of a meal. It was quick, light, and fluffy, and the perfectly sweet end to a day."
—Ramblings from This Chick

"Cute, quick, and romantic ... everything was described beautifully. I loved the author's writing style ... a must read."
—Jackie's Book World

"[The chemistry] is off the charts.... I have always enjoyed Ms. Thompson's writing and storytelling, and this is one of her best."
—Fresh Fiction

"Sweet and light and, above all, charming."
—BookCrack

continued ...

ALSO BY VICKI LEWIS THOMPSON

Werewolf in Alaska
Werewolf in Denver
Werewolf in Seattle
Werewolf in Greenwich Village
(A Penguin Special)
Werewolf in the North Woods
A Werewolf in Manhattan
Chick with a Charm
Blonde with a Wand
Over Hexed
Wild & Hexy
Casual Hex

THE
PERFECT MAN

Vicki Lewis Thompson

A SIGNET ECLIPSE BOOK

SIGNET ECLIPSE
Published by the Penguin Group
Penguin Group (USA) LLC, 375 Hudson Street,
New York, New York 10014

USA | Canada | UK | Ireland | Australia | New Zealand | India | South Africa | China
penguin.com
A Penguin Random House Company

Published by Signet Eclipse, an imprint of New American Library, a division of
Penguin Group (USA) LLC. *One Night with a Billionaire, Tempted by a Cowboy,*
and *Safe in His Arms* were previously published separately in InterMix editions.

First Signet Eclipse Printing, September 2014

One Night with a Billionaire, Tempted by a Cowboy, and *Safe in His Arms* copy-
right © Vicki Lewis Thompson, 2013
Prologue and excerpt from *Crazy About the Cowboy* copyright © Vicki Lewis
Thompson, 2014

ISBN 978-0-451-41931-6

Printed in the United States of America
10 9 8 7 6 5 4 3 2 1

For David Santa Maria,
the Perfect Man for my sister Karen

Acknowledgments

Many thanks to two of the Perfect Women in my life—my editor, Claire Zion, who came up with the idea for this book, and my assistant, Audrey Sharpe, who helped me make it happen.

Prologue

"To Paris!" Melanie Shaw lifted her margarita glass and grinned at her two best friends in the world, Astrid Lindberg and Valerie Wolitzky.

"To Paris!" they both echoed as they touched the salted rims of their glasses to Melanie's.

Melanie sipped her full drink and set it down carefully in front of her. Good tequila should be savored, not gulped, and Golden Spurs & Stetson served the best margaritas in Dallas. "I still can't believe we bought plane tickets today. We're actually going." She gazed across the round table at Astrid, her petite blond friend whose family had more money than God, and Val, a sassy redhead who was one of the best young lawyers in Dallas. "I mean, *Paris*. Do you realize we've dreamed about this since college? I can remember sitting in the sorority house late at night talking about this trip."

Astrid smiled. "Me, too. And it always had to be just us experiencing it for the first time together. Edward couldn't understand why I'd refused to go with him last spring. He didn't get that I was waiting until the three of us went."

"That's what I love about you," Melanie said. "You could have flown to Paris anytime, but you waited for us."

"Of course I did! Besides, I'd much rather tour Paris with you two than Edward." Then she blinked. "Did I just say that out loud?"

"'Fraid so." Val studied her over the rim of her glass. "You do realize that half the women in Dallas want your guy. Good-looking billionaires don't exactly grow on trees."

"I know." Astrid sighed. "I just . . ."

"I think Astrid prefers a Stetson-wearing man." Melanie winked at her. Astrid had defied her wealthy family's wishes and become a large-animal vet, a job that put her in constant contact with cowboys.

Astrid picked up her margarita. "Okay, I'll admit that Western wear gives a guy a certain rugged appeal."

"Doesn't it, though?" Melanie had been raised on a ranch and had dated cowboys almost exclusively. Her current boyfriend, Jeff, wasn't particularly adventurous. For instance, he had no interest in going to Paris. But he sure was pretty to look at. "I'll take a broad-shouldered cowboy over a billionaire any day."

"Why settle for one or the other?" Val glanced across the table. "As long as we're dreaming, why not order up a billionaire cowboy for each of us?"

"The best of both worlds." Melanie nodded in agreement. "The perfect man. Why not?"

Astrid raised her glass. "Billionaire cowboys for all. It's no more than we deserve, right?"

"Right!" Val said.

Laughing, they finished their margaritas and ordered another round. Tonight, with their long-awaited trip to Paris finally becoming a reality, nothing seemed impossible.

One Night with a Billionaire

MELANIE

One

I'm in Paris.

Melanie Shaw stared at the façade of Notre Dame as the deep-throated bells counted down the hour. Ten o'clock in the morning. Instead of mucking out stalls or riding the fence line at her daddy's ranch outside of Dallas, Texas, she was standing in front of frickin' Notre Dame. Amazing.

Her plane had landed two hours ago, and she still couldn't believe she had both feet planted in Paris, France. Only one thing could have made this moment better—if her friends Val and Astrid could be here with her.

They'd become friends and sorority sisters in college, and five years later, they were tighter than ever. A few months ago all the planets had been aligned for this trip. They'd found a killer plane fare and had spontaneously booked the trip. Then Val had been unlucky enough to get caught in a bomb scare during a concert. She'd suffered a broken arm and two broken ribs. Although those had healed, she now avoided crowds and wouldn't be traveling anytime soon.

Melanie had adjusted to having Val stay home. Astrid was a great traveling companion and they'd still have fun, even without Val. Then, a couple of weeks ago, one of Astrid's clients had developed a problem with a pregnant mare. With the mare's life on the line, Astrid had reluctantly canceled her trip, too.

Melanie had almost given up once her friends had bailed. The hotel they'd booked was way too expensive for her to handle alone, so she'd canceled that reservation. But she'd held on to her airline ticket because she couldn't bear to think of not going. An online search had yielded a cheaper hotel, although it was also far from the main attractions.

Her boyfriend, Jeff, had said she was crazy to consider traveling alone, but he wasn't about to go with her to someplace where he didn't speak the language. His provincial attitude had pounded the nail in the coffin, and she'd ended their relationship. It had been on the skids anyway.

Now that she was actually here, though, she'd better get busy and take some pictures with her phone. She'd left her suitcase with the hotel desk clerk because she couldn't check in until noon, but she had her backpack with all her sightseeing essentials crammed inside. Shrugging it off, she unzipped a side pocket and reached for her phone.

Without warning, the backpack was ripped from her hands. At the same moment, someone else shoved her from behind, knocking her to the ground with such force that the breath left her lungs.

"Hey!" A deep male voice from behind her issued a challenge.

She raised her head in time to glimpse a dark-haired man in jeans and a brown leather jacket dash after the thieves. Then folks who were obviously worried about her hurried over and blocked her view. An older gentleman helped her to her feet while two women clucked over her in what sounded like German.

She wasn't hurt except for a couple of scrapes on the heels of both hands, but if the guy in the leather jacket didn't catch the thieves, she was in deep shit. Her backpack held almost everything of value—her phone, both credit cards, and two hundred dollars' worth of euros. Her passport, thank God, was tucked in a pouch under her shirt, but thinking that she might have lost everything else made her sick to her stomach.

Members of the German tour group patted her shoulder as she stood up and dusted off her clothes. They offered words of comfort she couldn't understand but appreciated anyway. She made the effort to smile her thanks as she scanned the crowd for signs of a tall, broad-shouldered man wearing a brown leather jacket. He'd looked athletic, so maybe he'd be able to tackle the guys who took her backpack.

On the other hand, she didn't want some stranger risking his safety for her. At least two people had been involved in the mugging, which meant the guy was outnumbered, even if he should catch them. She crossed the fingers of both hands and waited, heart pounding from a delayed adrenaline rush.

At last she saw him coming toward her. His eyes were hidden by sunglasses, but his angry strides and the tight set of his mouth told her all she needed to know. Her hopes crumbled. The backpack was gone.

Despair engulfed her, but she was determined to thank him properly for trying. She hoped he spoke English. All she'd heard was his shout of *hey*, which might be one of those universal expressions used by everyone. She hadn't traveled enough to know if it was or not.

When he was about ten feet away, he shook his head. "I'm sorry, ma'am. They got clean away from me."

She gasped at the familiar accent. "Oh, my God! You're from *Texas.*" Hearing a voice from home made her want to hug him. She restrained herself, but the world brightened considerably.

"Yes, ma'am." He drew closer. "Are you all right?" He took off his sunglasses and gazed at her with eyes the color of bluebonnets.

"I'm fine." He must have known taking off his sunglasses would help. Seeing the concern in his gaze, she didn't feel quite so alone. "Thank you for chasing them. That was brave of you."

He shrugged. "Not really. Anyone could see they were yellow-bellied cowards if they'd attack a woman. Speaking of that, they knocked you down. Are you sure you didn't get scraped up?"

"Just a little." She showed him her hands.

"Let's take a look." Tucking his sunglasses inside his jacket, he grasped her wrists and examined the heels of her hands. "Damn it. You should put something on that."

His touch felt nice. His big hands were gentle, and she found that sexy. Although it would be totally inappropriate, she wished he'd kiss her scrapes and make them all better. "I have Neosporin in my suitcase back at the hotel." At least she'd have a place to stay. She'd given them her credit card number. That card was gone, but she hoped to get a replacement before she checked out.

"Are you traveling with someone? I can call them." He reached inside his jacket and pulled out a phone.

She shook her head. "I came by myself."

"Then let's start with the police. Did you get a look at those old boys?"

"Not really."

"Never mind. I did." He punched in a number and spoke in French.

Melanie listened with great admiration. He no longer sounded like a Texan as he carried on a conversation without stumbling. Prior to this trip she'd enrolled in an online course and had learned enough to find a bathroom and order a meal. But this guy was fluent, which was her good luck.

If she was super lucky, he had an international plan and she'd be able to borrow his phone to call Val, who could help her straighten things out with the credit card companies. Maybe it was cheeky to ask, but she was in desperate circumstances.

Although he was dressed casually, his jacket looked expensive and his watch might even be a real Rolex. Judging from his ease with the language, he could be a businessman who traveled to Paris regularly. If so, he wouldn't mind loaning her his phone for two minutes.

He disconnected the call and tucked the phone inside his jacket. "They're sending someone over, so we need to stay put." He gestured toward a stone bench a few feet away. "Let's sit a spell." He was once again her guy from Texas.

"Sounds good." She wouldn't mind sitting down. She

felt a little shaky. "I'm afraid I've ruined your plans for this morning."

"No, ma'am, you certainly haven't." He waited until she sat down before joining her on the bench. "You're the one with ruined plans. When did you get here?"

"This morning."

He swore softly under his breath. "I figured that might be the situation when I saw you eyeballing Notre Dame as if you'd never seen it before."

"I hadn't, except in pictures." Then she realized the significance of his statement. He'd noticed her before the mugging. "Did I stick out that much?"

He smiled. "Let's just say I pegged you as an American."

"How?" She liked the way he'd managed to smile without appearing to patronize her. And he had a great smile, one that made the corners of his eyes crinkle just enough to add character. As the shock of being mugged wore off, she registered the fact that her rescuer was drop-dead gorgeous.

"White gym shoes, for one thing. French women don't usually wear gym shoes unless they're working up a sweat. But the whole getup—the jeans, the hoodie, the backpack—told me you were from the States, probably a new arrival."

She grimaced. "I'll bet the muggers figured that out, too."

"They might have." He held out his hand. "I'm Drew Eldridge, by the way."

Eldridge. She'd heard that name, and she thought it might have been from Astrid, whose family was rich. Did that mean her Texan was wearing a real Rolex? His handshake was warm, firm, and gave her goose bumps. She was really sorry when the handshake was over. "I'm Melanie Shaw."

"Pleased to meet you, Miss Melanie. I wish it had been under different circumstances."

"Me, too." If he was related to the Eldridge family Astrid knew, Melanie wouldn't have been likely to meet him under any circumstances, unless she was with Astrid, who moved in those circles. "Are you from Dallas?"

"Yes, ma'am."

"Then you might know a friend of mine, Astrid Lindberg."

"Astrid Lindberg?" He chuckled. "I haven't seen her in a coon's age. We were at the same equestrian camp one summer, although she was with the younger kids. Some old horse tried to run off with her and I was handy. I was worried she'd swear off riding, but she didn't."

"She sure didn't." Melanie noticed that although Drew had come to Astrid's rescue, he downplayed his role by saying he was *handy*. "She's a large-animal vet now."

"Is she? That's great."

"So are you here on business?" Melanie imagined multinational deals involving millions. From what she could recall, the Eldridge family was loaded.

"Some business. Some pleasure."

"Ah." So the multinational deal-making was followed by glittering parties and sophisticated French women who never wore gym shoes with their regular clothes. Yet he'd interrupted all that to help a stranger from home. "Listen, I really appreciate all you've done. I'm sure I've screwed up your morning, and you're too polite to say so."

"Nope. It's a sunny day and I'd decided to—" A soft chime interrupted whatever he'd been about to say. "Excuse me." Taking out his phone, he glanced at the readout. "I should take this." He stood and walked a few feet away.

Hanging out with such a good-looking guy was a heady experience that kept her adrenaline pumping, so she was relieved for a few moments alone to gather her thoughts. If not for her friendship with Astrid, she might have been intimidated by someone like Drew Eldridge. As it was, she was simply grateful. And a little turned on, which served as a great antidote to worrying about losing her stuff.

Having Drew show up was a stroke of luck. Someone with his wealth would have an international calling plan. If she didn't pay him back until she got home, he probably wouldn't care. Once he was off the phone, she would ask to make a call. Val had a key to her apartment and could retrieve her credit card information.

The police arrived right after Drew ended his call, so she didn't have a chance to borrow the phone. Thank God Drew was there to guide her through the process, though. After the officers left, she glanced up at him. "Do you think they'll recover my backpack?"

"There's always a chance."

"But not a very good one, right?"

"I won't lie to you, Melanie. They may find your backpack, although I figure it's in a Dumpster by now. But the contents . . ." He shrugged. "Not likely."

"Speaking of those contents, could I please borrow your phone to call my friend Valerie back home? She can access my credit card info so I can cancel my cards."

"Yes, ma'am, you sure can. Tell you what. I'll give you a lift to your hotel so you can doctor those hands. You can call your friend on the way there."

"You have a car?"

"I do."

Silly of her to think he'd be on foot, like she was. "You know, that's a lovely offer, but my hotel isn't very far away." That wasn't quite true. She'd walked at least ten blocks to get here. "I'll just borrow your phone for a minute. I've taken up too much of your valuable time already."

"Sorry. But my mama raised me better than that. You've suffered a shock, and I intend to see you safely back to your hotel."

Oh, wow. He not only looked like a god, he knew the right things to say that would make a girl melt into a puddle. She'd be a fool to resist a display of gentlemanly manners by a heroic figure like Drew, especially when she'd just been mugged by two guys from the shallow end of the gene pool. "Thank you. That would be wonderful. Where are you parked?"

"In a garage." He pulled out his phone, punched a speed dial number, and said something in French. Then he tucked the phone away again. "Henri's on his way."

"Henri?"

"My driver."

"Oh." Of course he'd have a driver on call. She'd have to remember all the details of this adventure to tell Astrid and Val over drinks next week. "Are you here for long?"

"Two weeks. How about you?"

"Five days."

"That's all? Five days will go by like lightning."

"I know, but this was supposed to be a girls' trip with my two friends, and that's all the time we felt we could manage for now."

"And they didn't come, after all."

"No."

He studied her. "I admire your gumption, Melanie Shaw."

She basked in the warmth of that gaze. She even imagined that she saw interest there, but she didn't know him well enough to tell for sure. He might give everyone that same warm glance.

In truth, she did feel proud of herself, even if she had managed to get her backpack stolen within two hours of landing. "Thank you."

"And there's Henri." Drew gestured toward a black Mercedes sedan that had pulled up to the curb. Immediately a uniformed driver hopped out and opened the back door.

"Where was he, around the corner?"

"More or less. Hop in."

She slid onto the soft leather and wondered if Henri had ever chauffeured a woman wearing white gym shoes. Probably not. She buckled her seat belt.

Drew climbed in beside her and Henri closed the door. Inside the car, Melanie became more aware of the scent of Drew's aftershave. She didn't recognize the spicy aroma, but then again, she didn't hang out with rich guys. Plus he might have bought it here.

Drew glanced at her. "Where to?"

She gave him the name of the hotel.

"Never heard of it, but Henri probably knows." He

leaned forward and spoke to his driver in French. The chauffeur nodded, and Drew settled back against the seat. "He'll get us there." Reaching inside his jacket, he took out his phone and handed it to her before buckling his seat belt.

"Thank you." She dialed Val's cell and got her voice mail. Damn it. She didn't want to leave a message that would worry Val. So she left a cheery greeting saying that she'd arrived and was having a great time. Then she disconnected and sighed.

"Not available?"

"Unfortunately not."

"I'll be happy to go online and look up the number for the credit card company if you want to go that route. They should be able to wire you some money to tide you over, too."

"Oh." She blinked. "Right. I'll need money until the new card gets here. I must be jet-lagged, because I didn't think of going online for the number. If you'll look it up, that would be awesome."

The Mercedes drew alongside the curb in front of her hotel and Drew peered out the window. "Is this the place?"

"Yes. If you wouldn't mind getting that number for me, I'll make the call and then you can be on your way."

He glanced over at her. "Melanie, you can't stay here."

"It'll be fine. I gave them my credit card number earlier, and although that card will be canceled, I can probably get a new one by the time I check out."

"I wasn't thinking about that. I don't like the looks of this place." He studied the hotel again before turning his blue gaze on her. "You need to stay somewhere else."

Her chin lifted. "This is what I can afford. Besides, I don't have a new credit card yet, so I can't book a different hotel. I have to stay here."

"Have you inspected the room?"

"No, but it doesn't matter. I can deal with whatever. It won't be the first lumpy mattress I've slept on."

"What about bedbugs?"

"You think they have bedbugs?" Those grossed her out. For some reason she hadn't anticipated bedbugs in the City of Light.

"I wouldn't be surprised."

"If they do, I'll demand a different room. As I said, this place fits my budget."

"I understand that, but there's a better solution."

"Like what?"

"My town house."

She stared at him, blindsided by the suggestion. "But . . . I thought you were in a hotel."

"Nope. I have a house here with several bedrooms, and you're welcome to one of them."

Her pulse kicked up. "My goodness, that's way too much of a favor." And she wondered if he wanted something in return. Thinking of what that might be made her pulse race even faster.

"Not the way I see it. You need a room and I have one available." He met her gaze. "And to clarify, this is not an indecent proposal."

Dear God, could he read her mind? Heat rose in her cheeks. "I know it's not."

"Do you? Because you were looking sort of wary."

"I didn't mean to." She had to get a grip. This was a guy who didn't have to drag women in off the street. She flattered herself if she thought he was interested in her. "I just don't think it's right for me to accept your generous hospitality."

"It's not all that generous. The rooms are sitting there empty. Maybe you'll use a little water and electricity, but that's it. No big deal."

She glanced over at the hotel with its peeling paint and dirty windows. She shouldn't accept his offer, but damn, she wanted to. He might be a stranger, but he didn't feel like one. First chance she got, though, she'd call Astrid and confirm what Melanie felt in her gut, that Drew could be trusted.

Growing up on a ranch with salt-of-the-earth parents, Melanie had been taught not to take advantage of people, but she'd also been told never to look a gift horse in the mouth. This was a gift horse if she'd ever seen one.

She took a deep breath. "All right. And thank you."

Two

"You're more than welcome." The tension eased from Drew's shoulders. He couldn't leave her here, but he couldn't exactly kidnap her to keep her out of that flea-bag hotel, either.

She had no idea how vulnerable she looked with her big gray eyes and freckle-faced innocence. In her red sweatshirt, with any makeup worn off during the flight, she seemed like a teenager, even though he guessed her age to be mid-twenties. No wonder the bastards had targeted her. He had the urge to wrap her in his arms, stroke her glossy brown hair, and protect her from every danger, both real and imagined.

But any woman who'd climbed on a plane by herself for her first trip to Paris wouldn't appreciate an overprotective attitude. He'd keep that in mind. Somehow he had to watch out for her in a way that wouldn't get her back up.

"I'll fetch my suitcase." She reached for the door handle.

"Might as well let Henri get it." He deliberately made it sound like a casual suggestion.

"But I can do it. Oh, wait." She looked over her shoulder at him. "My claim check was in my backpack."

"Then why not let Henri handle it? He's good at these things."

She opened her mouth to argue, and then closed it again. "Okay."

Drew leaned forward and spoke to his chauffeur in French. He hoped Melanie didn't understand the language well enough to know that he'd told Henri to bribe the desk clerk if there was any question about the missing claim check. Because Melanie had yet to utter a word in French, Drew thought he was safe on that score.

The chauffeur exited the car and headed toward the hotel lobby with the brisk stride of a man who would not be denied. Drew smiled. Henri lived for this kind of drama.

"He probably will have better luck than I would." Melanie watched Henri walk into the hotel. "He looks very official."

"Don't think he doesn't realize that. He plays it to the hilt." He pulled out his cell. "What's your credit card company?" When she gave him the name, he looked up the international contact number and keyed it in before handing her the phone.

"Thank you." She settled back in her seat and put the phone to her ear. Moments into the conversation, her body visibly relaxed and her tone was no longer anxious.

He enjoyed watching the transformation and was glad he could be part of putting her dream vacation back on track. From that first glimpse of her in front of Notre Dame, he'd instinctively known how much this trip meant to her. Unlike most of the women in his circle, she'd had to scrimp and save to get over here. He'd never had to scrimp in his life, and he was fascinated by how much that raised the stakes for her.

Her resilience in the face of potential disaster impressed him, too. She had character, and he responded to that almost as much as he responded to her curvy figure and full pink mouth. He wanted her, but he'd meant what he'd said. Inviting her to his town house wasn't a proposition.

Still holding the phone, she glanced over at him. "I don't know the address," she said to the representative, "but I have someone here who can give it to you." She gave Drew the phone. "They need an address for shipping the new credit card."

"You bet." He provided the necessary information and handed the phone back so she could complete the call, which didn't take long.

After disconnecting, she returned the phone. "Thank you. They're wiring money to a Western Union office near your town house." She sighed happily. "I feel so much better."

"Good."

"So where is your town house? I don't recognize street names yet."

"It's on the Île de la Cité, about three blocks from Notre Dame."

Her eyes widened. "Wow. Prime real estate."

"I like being in the heart of the city." He'd paid a ridiculous amount of money for the place, but he was buying a piece of history, and that usually cost more.

"So you weren't far from home when you saw me this morning."

"No. I had tickets for the Louvre, so I'd decided to walk down there for the exercise and get my fine art fix."

"The Louvre." Her expression grew dreamy. "I can hardly wait to see it."

"Maybe we could go later. I—" His phone chimed again. "Excuse me." He checked the readout. Not critical. They could leave a voice mail.

"I'm sure you're busy."

"Everyone's busy these days." Especially him. As the only son of Stephen Eldridge, he'd felt obligated to succeed, and in a big way, too. He hadn't wanted to ride on his father's coattails. At thirty-two, he was a billionaire in his own right. He'd gotten there by taking risks, and for the most part, they'd paid off handsomely. But wealth without social responsibility was, in his estimation, immoral. So he'd devoted himself to several causes.

The one currently in the works was especially dear to his heart—aid to orphans in war-torn areas of the world. Although he'd been born with a silver spoon in his mouth, he well knew many children hadn't been so lucky. So he was working on organizing a dinner featuring many A-list performers, which would bring in a hefty amount if all the stars arrived.

But Drew had learned that working with famous people meant dealing with a few flakes. His staff could put the event together, but only his personal attention would get the famous faces he needed to actually show up.

Yet he was glad to do it . . . most of the time. This morning, though, he longed to give his attention to a certain tourist from Dallas. He hadn't been a superhero and successfully recovered her backpack, but he had the resources to make up for her crummy introduction to the city and he intended to use them.

After listening to his voice mail, he texted a reply. By that time, Henri was back with Melanie's plain black rolling bag. Her presence in his town house was closer to becoming a reality, and that stirred his blood.

He liked the fact that she'd resisted his invitation to stay there. Despite knowing that he was a member of the wealthy Eldridge family and that he'd met her friend Astrid, she hadn't leaped at the opportunity to stay under his roof. He'd known several women who, given similar circumstances, would have moved heaven and earth for such an invitation.

A man in his position couldn't afford to be naïve. Gold diggers were real and they circled him constantly. Melanie, however, didn't seem to give a damn. She might even consider it a point of honor not to care whether he was King Midas.

With a loud thump that jiggled the car, Henri loaded the suitcase in the trunk.

Drew looked over at Melanie. "What do you have in there, rocks?"

She laughed. "Almost as bad. Books. I've been collecting books on Paris ever since my friends and I booked the trip. I brought them all. When I packed, I had to sacrifice clothes for books, so I don't have a lot with me." She stuck out her foot. "These are my only shoes."

"They're practical."

"Yes, but as you pointed out, they label me. I don't look French."

"Do you want to?" He thought she looked perfectly fine as she was.

She seemed to consider that. "I guess not."

He liked that answer. In his mind, people should be who they were instead of pretending to be someone they weren't.

Henri climbed into the driver's seat. *"C'est bien?"*

Belatedly Drew remembered her scraped hands. "Do you want the Neosporin out of your suitcase before we take off?"

"That's okay. My hands don't sting anymore. I can get it later."

"Then we're off." Drew nodded to his driver. As the car pulled away from the curb, he blew out a breath. Mission accomplished. He'd succeeded in scooping up his lady fair and carrying her out of harm's way. Of course, part of him realized that Melanie would have probably spent her nights at that hotel without encountering a problem. But Drew wasn't dealing in logic right now.

His need to get her away from that depressing hotel with its peeling paint and cracked cement steps had been a visceral thing not to be explained. She was alone in the city, and he'd appointed himself as her watchdog. He had the urge to surround her with a fence labeled KEEP OFF. An electrified fence would be even better.

"What's your town house like?"

He turned toward her. "Old."

Her forehead wrinkled. "How old?"

"Old enough that the first residents used chamber pots. I have a collection of them."

"Oh! Is that what you use?"

How refreshing that she'd come right out and asked. "No. The place has all the modern conveniences now.

The last owner even installed an elevator, but I like taking the stairs."

"And walking to the Louvre. That's why you almost caught those muggers."

"I would have, too, except for a busload of kids. They piled out right in front of me and I had to put on the brakes or I'd have run them down. By the time I worked my way through them, the muggers had disappeared."

"I wouldn't have wanted you to run over any little children to get my backpack." She'd leaned her head against the seat.

"I wouldn't have."

"No." She covered a yawn with her hand. "You're a nice guy." Her eyelids drifted down.

"Mm." Some of his business associates might not agree with her. If he'd caught the muggers, they wouldn't have thought so, either.

The steady sound of her breathing told him she was asleep. He could hardly blame her. She'd been on a plane all night long, and then she'd been assaulted. The good news was that she must feel safe with him or she never would have dropped off so easily. Apparently she trusted him.

And she had every reason to. He had no intention of taking advantage of this situation. But he had to admit she was damned appealing. And sexy in a subtle way that really got to him. He'd felt a connection from the moment he'd seen her standing in front of Notre Dame. And it wasn't just because she was Texan. What he really noticed was that her face had reflected the same awe that had struck him when he'd first seen the cathedral twenty-five years ago.

From a distance, he'd sensed a kindred spirit. When he'd drawn closer, he'd been captured by a primitive tug of sexuality. Her snug jeans and red sweatshirt outlined the body of a flesh-and-blood Venus de Milo. Just as he decided to strike up a conversation, she'd been attacked.

He hated that, but considering how much closer it had brought the two of them, he couldn't hate it too much. He would have spared her the trauma if he could have, but now . . . well, he'd have to see how things turned out.

Henri drove more sedately than usual, as if he didn't want to jostle his sleeping passenger. Consequently she was still sleeping when the Mercedes stopped in front of Drew's town house.

Speaking in a low voice, Drew instructed Henri to open Melanie's door before getting the suitcase out of the trunk. The click of the door opening didn't rouse her. When Drew walked around the car and crouched down to shake her awake, she murmured something he couldn't understand and sleepily wrapped her arms around his neck. Apparently he'd be carrying her inside.

If he hadn't felt like the great protector before, this maneuver would have done the trick. As he lifted her into his arms, he breathed in peppermint and wondered if she had a roll of them in her sweatshirt pocket. But under that scent he detected a sweet, womanly aroma that sent an urgent signal to his groin.

Cradling her soft body with one arm under her shoulders and the other behind her knees, he started up the walkway. She sighed and snuggled closer. Dear God, he was getting an erection. Not cool. Fortunately her cute little fanny covered his crotch, but that was part of the problem. Every step caused more friction between her bottom and his cock.

Henri had beaten him to the door with the suitcase. He opened it and stood back so Drew could turn sideways and ease through the doorway without bumping either Melanie's head or her feet. Once inside, he glanced at the staircase. Not happening. Not three flights.

Smiling, Henri walked over to the elevator and pushed the button. Drew stepped inside and vowed he wouldn't make fun of the contraption ever again. Initially he'd scoffed at the idea of an elevator for a three-story building, but then he'd never imagined hauling a sleeping woman up those stairs, either.

Moving with the silent grace of a cat burglar, Henri entered the elevator behind him and brought the suitcase along, too. Drew decided that Henri needed a raise. The driver had the rare quality of anticipating correctly what his employer needed.

The gilded elevator was beautiful but slow. Considering the circumstances, Drew appreciated the easy ascent. Now that they'd made it this far, he'd like to deposit Melanie on a bed without waking her. She'd probably be embarrassed as hell to find herself in his arms. Besides that, if she insisted on getting down, his arousal wouldn't be a secret anymore.

When they left the elevator, Henri turned to Drew. *"Bleu?"* he said softly.

"Oui." Drew had decided on the way up to put Melanie in the Blue Room. Other than his own bedroom, he liked the Blue Room the best. The other two on this floor were nice—one in shades of gold and the other decorated in green—but the blue was prettier.

In the five years he'd owned this place, he'd mostly entertained business associates here. Whenever he'd given them a choice, they picked the Blue Room. He'd brought one girlfriend here, thinking she'd enjoy Paris. He'd been wrong and she'd been miserable.

He couldn't understand why anybody wouldn't love this ancient city with its centuries-old buildings and the Seine winding past all that historic architecture. Sure, the native language wasn't English, but he liked the sound of French in his ears. Of course, it helped that he'd learnd to speak it so easily at school. Maybe he'd been Parisian in another life.

Henri opened the door to the Blue Room and stepped back.

Drew glanced down to check whether Melanie was still asleep. Yep, out like a light. He edged through the doorway with the same care he'd used getting into the house and the elevator. Bonking her head at this stage would be criminal.

The Blue Room was at the front of the house with a view to the street, whereas his was at the back with a view of a small formal garden and courtyard below. That put Melanie all the way down the hall from him. The bulge in his jeans told him that was a very good idea.

The canopy bed held center stage and was draped with blue brocade trimmed with gold fringe and tassels. Matching curtains hung at the window. The antique furniture— an armoire, a writing desk, and an upholstered chair—could have come straight from Versailles. It hadn't, but it had been purchased from an estate nearby.

Drew leaned over and laid Melanie on the brocade

bedspread. Her eyelids didn't even flicker. She was down for the count.

He stayed by her bedside, his back to Henri, and willed his erection to subside. He didn't dare look at her lush mouth or he'd be tempted to kiss her, like some prince in a fairy tale. Except the kiss he had in mind didn't belong in a kid's storybook.

When he imagined kissing Melanie, it wasn't some chaste brush of lips. Tongues would be involved, and heavy breathing, and unfastening of clothing, and . . . this wasn't helping his condition at all. Taking a deep breath, he glanced across the room at a painting of fruit and flowers.

Technically, a still life created by some artist he couldn't remember should have calmed him. Instead he pictured Melanie opening her petals to him and himself as the banana in the fruit bowl.

Behind him, Henri unzipped Melanie's suitcase and began quietly putting her clothes in the armoire. The slide of drawers was the loudest sound in the room, but it wasn't enough to wake the sleeping beauty. Drew couldn't stand beside the bed too much longer without looking like an idiot. He decided to take off her shoes. Nobody should sleep in their shoes.

She'd double-knotted them, and he struggled with the laces. That was good, though, because concentrating on her shoelaces took his mind off sex, and he was in much better shape by the time he eased one shoe from her foot. As he fiddled with the second shoe, she woke up.

She wasn't slow about it, either. She sat straight up and glared at him. "What are you doing?"

He almost laughed, because her angry question was in

sharp contrast to the gentle cuddle she'd given him while she was asleep. He stepped away from the bed. "I was taking off your shoes so you could be more comfortable."

She frowned and surveyed her surroundings. "Oh. Now I remember." Her gaze softened. "I didn't mean to be rude. I forgot where I was."

"You fell asleep in the car, so I carried you up here."

"You did?" Her cheeks turned pink. "That's embarrassing."

"You were exhausted."

"Yeah. Guess so. Still, I feel bad for conking out on you. I must have been heavy."

"No."

"Did you climb the stairs?"

He smiled. "Elevator."

"That's good."

Henri cleared his throat. *"C'est tout?"*

Drew glanced over his shoulder. "Yes, that's all for now, Henri. *Merci.*"

Henri nodded and left.

"This is nice." Melanie glanced around the room. "Very nice. Thank you."

"There's a bathroom through that door." Drew gestured toward it. "I'll leave you alone so you can get some rest." He hesitated. "Or are you hungry? I could have some food sent up."

"No, I'm not hungry. They fed us constantly on the plane."

"Then all you really need is sleep." He backed toward the door.

Her gaze found his, and she looked uncertain. "Where will you be?"

His heart squeezed. In her dazed condition, he'd become her lifeline and she didn't want him to leave. "Just downstairs. I have an office on the first floor. It's not hard to find."

"Okay."

"If you need anything, come and find me."

"I will."

He forced himself to walk out of the room and close the door behind him. But he felt as if he should be in there, holding her while she fell asleep again. How crazy was that?

Three

After Drew left, Melanie eased off the bed and prowled around the room. What a room it was, too. She fingered the thick fabric draping the bed. Marie Antoinette would have been thrilled with something like this.

The floor was hardwood and the blue-patterned carpets looked like vintage Aubusson. Once again, if she hadn't known Astrid, such things would have been lost on her. She should take a picture of this room to show her friends.

Then she remembered. She couldn't take a picture of anything because she didn't have a phone. She also hadn't called Astrid to get the lowdown on Drew. Besides that, she should notify someone back home that she was not at the hotel she'd booked. If she called Astrid, that would accomplish everything at once. Astrid could attest to Drew's character and also spread the word that Melanie's plans had changed.

Much as she longed to climb under the covers in that beautiful canopy bed, she couldn't do it until she'd borrowed Drew's phone and made that call. She smiled as she imagined Astrid's reaction to the news that she was in a historic town house within walking distance of Notre Dame, and the house belonged to none other than Drew Eldridge, who'd rescued her from a runaway horse.

But no matter how lovely the accommodations were, Melanie didn't intend to sponge off Drew for the next five days. Once she had a credit card, she'd move out of Drew's town house and then treat him to a nice meal as a gesture of gratitude.

Then she remembered her clothing situation. Drew's idea of a nice meal would undoubtedly involve dressing up, and she hadn't planned for that. She'd expected to explore Paris on her own, and elegant restaurants hadn't figured into her wardrobe choices.

Well, she'd figure out something else, then. But first she had to head back downstairs and borrow Drew's phone. He'd gone to the trouble of taking off one of her shoes, but she put it back on again and retied the laces of the other one.

Before leaving, she used her bathroom, which sparkled with gold-plated faucets, an enormous tub, and a sleek shower with a spotless glass door. The white towels looked like pure luxury. The designer had made room for both a toilet and a bidet.

Melanie had never seen a bidet, but she'd read about them. She knew the word was pronounced *buh-day* and just saying it made her feel European and sort of sexy. After all, a bidet was designed for a quick wash of one's private parts, so it would come in very handy if one were having lots of sex. Not that she would be.

Nope. This girl had no use for a bidet. But she could sure use a shower. After she'd made her call she'd come back up here, take a hot shower, and crawl into that big canopy bed. All the guide books suggested staying up until nighttime to readjust a person's body clock, but she wasn't doing that. She'd had a rough morning.

The hallway was empty and silent. Maybe later she'd inspect the paintings hanging on the walls, but she was on a mission, so she started downstairs. The runner cushioning her steps glowed with red and gold threads, and the dark wood of the banister gleamed.

She slid her hand along it as she descended, and she wondered if kids had ever polished it with the seat of their pants. The house seemed too formal for children to play in, but if it had been here for centuries, they must have at some time.

Three flights down she finally heard noise, but most of it was coming up from a simple stairway that led to a basement level. She'd seen enough foreign movies to know that the servants probably stayed on the bottom floor, and they were the ones she could hear talking and laughing.

She paused in the foyer. Above her head a crystal chandelier glittered. To her left, double doors opened to what she would call a living room, but it might be known by a different name over here. She registered the contents as expensive, with vivid upholstery, polished wood, more art on the walls, no doubt originals, and a marble fireplace. But the room was empty, and Drew had said he'd be in his office, so she needed to find that.

The door was open to the next room down the hallway, and when she glanced in, she found Drew. He sat facing her, but all his attention was on the computer screen sitting on a dark wood desk. He'd taken off his jacket, and the top two buttons of his snowy long-sleeved shirt were undone, revealing the strong column of his throat. His dark hair was rumpled, as if he'd run his fingers through it several times.

His expression was intense as his fingers flew over the keys, and he wore a pair of dark-rimmed reading glasses. Seeing that small vulnerability, a lack of perfect eyesight, touched her heart. He was concentrating so hard that she hated to interrupt him.

But if she didn't, no telling how long he'd continue to work. He looked completely engrossed. As she stood in the doorway, she spoke his name softly, not wanting to startle him.

His head came up immediately and he blinked. "Oh, Melanie. Sorry. I didn't hear you."

"I was being quiet."

"Is something wrong?"

"Not at all. The room's beautiful and the bathroom's to die for. But I'd like to call home before I take a shower and conk out. Someone needs to know I'm not staying at the place I gave them the number for." She decided not to mention that she planned to call Astrid, because he thought she was checking up on him, which she was. "Could I please borrow your phone again?"

"You bet. Come on in." Standing, he picked the phone up from where it lay next to his computer, but it chimed before he could hand it to her. "Hang on." He checked the readout. "That can wait. That old boy can leave a message."

"But I don't want to interfere with your—"

"You're not." He smiled and gave her the phone. "Sometimes it's better to leave 'em hangin' for a while."

The warmth of his smile took her breath away. It also took care of any weariness she'd been feeling. Earlier he'd mentioned plans to go to the Louvre, but she'd interrupted that. She wanted to go *now*, with him. He probably knew the place inside and out.

Then again, he might not be free to traipse off with her. Come to think of it, she'd bought tickets in advance for the Louvre, and they were gone, along with everything else in her backpack. She didn't have money for a new ticket, even if she could get one.

But she was in *Paris*. Who took a nap when they could be exploring a city they'd wanted to visit forever? And how fabulous if they could have a guide who looked like Drew Eldridge?

He gazed at her. "You must really be looking forward to calling home."

"Why?"

"Your eyes got all sparkly just now."

"I wasn't thinking about that."

"Oh?"

She couldn't very well admit that he'd been responsible for a good part of that sparkle. "It just hit me. I'm in Paris. To heck with sleep. If my money's arrived at Western Union, I'd love to go to the Louvre, although I'm not sure if I could get a ticket this late in the day. Even if the money's not there yet, I could walk along the Seine, and through the Tuileries Garden, and . . ." Then she remembered that she'd interrupted his work. "But I don't expect you to go. You helped me this morning instead, so you probably have work to do this afternoon. I'll be fine on my own."

"I'm sure you would be fine and dandy."

And that statement was the biggest gift he could have given her. A lesser man would have reminded her that on her own she'd managed to get mugged. But the thing was, and this almost made her laugh, she had nothing left to lose. She wouldn't be a target because she wouldn't be carrying anything of value, except maybe a little bit of money if Western Union came through for her.

"Are you sure you wouldn't rather take a nice long nap?"

"I thought I would, but now I'm excited again. Sleeping in the car was probably like a power nap. Now I want to get out there and make the most of my time here. Besides, all the guide books tell you to stay up until bedtime to get over jet lag."

He nodded. "That's a fact. It helps if you can, but not everybody's built that way. How about lettin' me come along? I didn't get my art fix today."

"You can spare the time?"

"I won't promise not to take any phone calls, but if you can put up with that, I can spare the time."

"Then I'd love to have you come." She was secretly relieved that he'd invited himself along. Although she'd sounded brave and self-sufficient, her recent experience had made her a little nervous about setting off on her own. "But please know that I intend to pay my own way. If the money hasn't arrived, I'll gratefully accept a temporary loan, and I'll be reimbursing you the minute I get some money."

He started to say something, but stopped and cleared his throat. "All right."

She'd bet anything he'd wanted to tell her to forget paying him back. But he'd recognized that she had her pride and needed to stand on her own feet financially. Swallowing his argument was the second-biggest gift he could give her.

"Take the phone up to your room so y'all can have a private conversation. You can bring it back down after you've showered and changed."

She hesitated, torn between making off with his phone when he probably needed to have it, and thinking of the info she could share with Astrid if he was out of earshot. "All right. I won't be long." Turning, she hurried down the hall.

"Take the elevator," he called after her.

"I like the stairs," she hollered back. Then she wondered if hollering was appropriate in a house with museum-quality furnishings and live-in servants. Oh, well. She was a gym-shoe-wearing Texas girl, not a sophisticated French woman. So far, Drew hadn't seemed to mind.

The minute she got to her bedroom, she closed the door. Then she dialed Astrid's number and walked over to the window that looked out on a quaint residential street lined with buildings much like this one. Window boxes filled with flowers brightened the view, and a man wearing a beret rode past on a bicycle. Yes, she had to get out there. Paris was waiting.

Astrid answered on the third ring, but she sounded suspicious. That's when Melanie remembered that the readout would seem really strange to Astrid, like a voice from the past, maybe, because this was Drew's phone, not hers.

"Valerie, it's me! I'm in Paris, but I lost my phone, so I'm borrowing Drew Eldridge's."

Astrid was silent for a beat. "Are we talking about Drew Eldridge, of the Dallas Eldridge family?"

"I hope so, because that's what he told me. He said you two were at camp together and he stopped your runaway horse. Did he?"

"Oh, my God. Yes, he did, but how in hell did you hook up with him in Paris, of all places?"

"It's a long story, but I'm fine. Everything's fine."

"Why wouldn't it be?" Panic edged her voice. "Why are you reassuring me? Did something happen?"

"I was mugged."

"Oh, my God! Oh, Melanie, no."

"But Drew came to my rescue." Melanie explained what had happened. "So I'm staying in his town house, at least until I get my new credit card, but if you have any reservations about me doing that, then—"

"Absolutely not. He's terrific. At least he was when I knew him, and from what I hear from my parents, he continues to do good deeds. He's big into charity events."

"I'm not surprised after the way he's insisted on helping me out." She didn't like to think of herself as a charity, though, so she'd have to move on when she had the means to do so.

"He's a good guy. I hate that this happened, but it sounds like you came out in pretty good shape."

"I did. His town house is amazing. I wish I had my phone so I could send you pictures."

"What about him? He was pretty cute as a teenager, but I haven't seen him since then. Is he handsome? So-so? The Hunchback of Notre Dame?"

Melanie laughed. "He's gorgeous. Tall, dark hair, and the bluest eyes. When he's on his computer, he wears these dark-framed glasses that make him look all serious and scholarly."

"Well, now. Sounds as if you have a crush going on."

"Nah. It's like drooling over movie stars. We're from different worlds."

"I'm not so sure about that. You and I are friends, and I'm from that world."

"That's different. We were sorority pledges together. We went through Hell Week. I've seen you at your worst."

Astrid laughed. "That's the truth."

"Drew's just being nice. He saw a fellow Texan in need."

"Maybe, but you still don't know that he's not interested in you. Why are you writing him off as a lost cause?"

"Astrid, you haven't seen him or this place. My daddy is a cowboy, and my mama is a cowgirl, and my two brothers are both cowboys. We all know I'll end up with a cowboy eventually. You might end up with a billionaire because you move in those circles, but I'll be perfectly happy with some broad-shouldered rancher."

"You haven't been happy with one so far."

"Jeff's a bad example."

"Before Jeff was Pete, and before that, Jeremy. I know you think a cowboy's in your future, but I question that."

"I just haven't found the right one."

"If you say so, toots. Like you said, you're there and I'm not. But it sounds like a great setup for a romantic interlude."

"Uh, no. But you're welcome to your fantasies." She glanced at an ornate clock on the bedside table. "I need to get going. He's offered to take me to see the sights this afternoon."

"Uh-huh. Like I said, don't discount the possibility that he likes you."

"Okay, I won't." The thought that Drew might think of her as something more than a goodwill project sent squiggles of excitement through her stomach.

"Have fun."

"I will. I'm in Paris!" She disconnected, set the phone on the nightstand, and started stripping down for her shower. But as she stepped into the elegant bathroom, reality intruded.

She might have stumbled into this fantasy world where Drew lived, but it was only a tiny blip in her life. When it came to men, Astrid might feel comfortable with guys like Drew. But Melanie had more in common with a cowboy of modest means, someone like her father.

Drew was kind, as evidenced by his interest in charitable causes. He might even want to think of her as a charitable cause, but she wouldn't allow him to. Maybe she couldn't pay him for the water and electricity she used while she was here because she had no way of tracking what she owed. But whenever a receipt was involved, she would grab it and keep a running total. He'd never miss the amount if she didn't reimburse him, but she'd never taken advantage of a generous person and she didn't intend to start now.

Four

Drew usually had an exceptional ability to focus. That ability had been recognized early by his tutors and had played a huge part in his financial success. But knowing that Melanie would be coming downstairs shortly so they could spend the afternoon together had blown his fabled concentration all to hell.

He could explain his fascination with her, but that didn't mean he could eliminate it. She was so unusual to him because she clearly had no interest in cashing in on his wealth. She didn't view him as a human ATM ready to spew cash and grant her every wish.

Instead she had the habit, both endearing and maddening, of wanting to balance the scales. He didn't want to balance them. She was adorable, and he longed to shower her with anything she desired. Ironically, she didn't desire a single thing from him.

If she'd had the resources, she would have left by now. Once her new credit card arrived, she would be able to leave. He didn't want that, either.

It was a frustrating scenario. Any hotel in her price

range would be inferior to having her stay here for the rest of her visit to Paris. She'd have to sacrifice location to get a reasonable rate, which would make it impossible for her to see the sights she'd come to Paris to enjoy. If she insisted on moving into a hotel, he'd want to check it out and see if it was decent. She might not let him. He was used to being in the power position, and with her he wasn't.

But his lack of control over her living quarters wasn't the only thing that had him pacing the floor of his office. As he'd told her, he admired her gumption. And that admiration was firing up his already hot physical reaction to her.

But he didn't know what to do about that, either. God knows he didn't want her to think that because he'd offered her a place to stay he expected sex in return. Some men in his position might work that angle and feel justified in doing it, but he recoiled at the idea.

So what was he supposed to do about his attraction to her? Any move on his part might be misinterpreted. He didn't think she'd humor him out of gratitude, but the possibility was there and it made him wince.

This was why his friends had always told him to stick with women who had money, either because they'd made it or inherited it. That would even the playing field, they'd said. But he'd reached a financial pinnacle that few women had gained, and many of those who had were old enough to be his mother or his grandmother.

And frankly, the women he'd dated who were "acceptable" lacked the very quality he cherished in Melanie—a sense of wonder. When you had the resources to see and do whatever you wanted, keeping that sense of awe was a challenge many people failed to meet. Personally he worked at it, which was one of the reasons he'd bought a place in Paris.

The city had a host of awe-inspiring aspects, beginning with Notre Dame. The Louvre gave him regular doses of awe. A sculpture by Michelangelo could do it in a few seconds. Then there was the view from the top of the Eiffel Tower and a lazy boat ride down the Seine at night. The wonders of this city didn't work for everyone, but they worked for him.

In Melanie he saw a woman who might understand his yearning to be awed, someone who wouldn't think his love of Paris was corny or clichéd. But he didn't know how to get close to her without scaring her away. For the first time in a long while, he feared that he might be rejected.

So he did the caretaking things that wouldn't be suspect. First he contacted the museum. Although he already had a ticket, no more were left for that day, but a sizable pledge from him produced one for Melanie.

Next he ordered some sandwiches to take with them, because whether she'd admit it or not, she had to be hungry. His cook tucked a couple of bottles of Perrier in the wicker hamper. Drew had considered wine and decided against it. If anything, she needed caffeine to keep her from falling asleep before ten tonight.

The wicker basket was delivered to his office, and when she came downstairs wearing a fresh pair of jeans, a yellow T-shirt, and a navy hoodie, he stared at her as if she'd arrived in satin and pearls. He took off his glasses, which he only used for reading, so he could get a better look.

She'd pulled her hair back into a ponytail and put on

makeup, but her freckles still showed. He was used to porcelain-skinned women, and he was entranced by those freckles. He wanted to count them and then kiss each one.

God, she was so refreshingly *real.* He could look at her for hours. But if he didn't come up with something to say pretty soon, she'd conclude he was dim-witted. "I called ahead to the museum and reserved a ticket for you. Didn't want to take a chance they'd be out when we got there."

"Thanks. Good thinking. Would you mind if we stopped by Western Union first?"

"We can do that." He understood her preoccupation with getting cash. In her shoes, he would have felt the same.

"No rush, though. Keep working if you need to. I can wait."

"No need. I'm done." He used the chore of shutting down his computer to get his bearings. More than anything he desperately wanted to kiss her, and he had no idea how she'd react to that. Before he kissed a woman, he liked to have some guesstimate of how that would be received. With Melanie he hadn't a clue.

"Is that a picnic basket for us?"

"Yep. We'll eat it in the car. You said you weren't hungry, but you will be."

"I'm hungry now. But why will we eat it in the car instead of on a bench somewhere? Aren't we going to walk to the Louvre?" She looked as if she'd be fine with that.

"We could, but then you might not have as much energy for the museum. You'll want to see as much as you can before you get tuckered out. It's a big place."

"Good point. And we can eat on the way. It's hard to eat and walk, at least for me."

"For me, too." He smiled at her because she made him want to. That was worth a lot all by itself.

Henri picked them up and took them to Western Union, where cash was indeed waiting for Melanie. Her elation touched him. Being penniless had obviously been eating at her more than he'd realized.

The trip to the Louvre was an adventure in which Melanie tried to eat and keep track of everything they passed at the same time. He repeated *we'll come back* more times than he could count, but Melanie was an in-the-moment kind of girl who wanted to absorb everything that was in her field of vision. Drew couldn't help thinking of all he'd have missed if she hadn't been mugged.

If the thieves hadn't come along, he would have exchanged a few words with her in front of Notre Dame. He might have given her his card. But she wouldn't have contacted him. She would have been off to see the city without him because she wouldn't have wanted to impose. Those bastards, scum that they were, had done him a favor.

Henri dropped them off, and Drew glanced at his watch. Melanie was a trouper, but he'd be surprised if she made it much longer than three hours, all things considered. Whatever time they spent here would be special for him, though, because he'd be seeing the wonders within these walls with someone who had never been here. Her enthusiasm would carry them along on a wave of discovery . . . and awe.

She didn't start to droop until well past the four-hour mark. He was impressed. Despite all the walking they'd done, she remained cheerful, even as she reluctantly admitted being tired. As they left the museum, she raved about what she'd seen.

He drank in her excitement and wondered how in hell he was going to show her Paris the way he longed to, by pulling out all the stops. He wanted to arrange a special tour of the Louvre so she could stand in front of the Mona Lisa all by herself instead of having to peer over the heads of other visitors. He wanted to stage a private tour of the Eiffel Tower followed by an after-hours dinner in their restaurant. He wanted to take her on a moonlit boat ride along the Seine in a luxury yacht and walk with her through the soaring arches of Notre Dame before the cathedral opened to the public.

He'd drop a bundle doing that, but he didn't care. Showing his favorite places to someone who would see them the same way he did would be worth it. Maybe he could make her understand that and she'd stop using her mental calculator every blessed second. It was worth a try.

As they walked away from the Louvre, he suggested they stop at a sidewalk café for some wine and cheese before calling Henri to pick them up. As he'd expected, she was enchanted by the idea of doing something so Parisian. So far, so good.

He chose a place right out of a postcard, with round metal tables and the distinctive tan wicker chairs that were so common in the cafés around town. There was a slight nip in the air, but her hoodie should keep her warm enough for them to stay outside. That was, after all, the way to best enjoy the experience.

After they were seated he picked up the wine menu.

Because it was hard to get bad wine in Paris, he suggested a medium-priced bottle, and she seemed relieved.

They talked some more about the Louvre and the thrill of gazing at original sculptures and paintings by world-famous artists. He asked how she spent her time back in Dallas and found out she worked on her daddy's ranch. She was a cowgirl. That made him smile, because a job like that fit her so perfectly. He'd never met a real cowgirl before, and he certainly never thought he'd fall for one, but now he realized that it explained a lot about what he liked about Melanie.

The wine arrived with a plate of assorted cheeses, and once the waiter had filled their glasses, he raised his in her direction. "To your first trip to Paris."

"I'll drink to that. And to you, for turning a bad beginning into something amazing." Smiling, she touched her glass to his. Then she leaned back in her chair and took a sip. "Wow, this is fabulous!"

"You'd better believe it. You're drinking French wine in Paris. It always tastes better here."

"I pictured doing this, having some wine and cheese at a sidewalk café while I watched the people go by."

"And here you are." Her pleasure was contagious. He'd sat in similar cafés many times, but he couldn't remember ever feeling this much gratitude for the experience.

"Yes, thanks to you. No telling what my situation would be right now if you hadn't shown up."

"But I did." He'd always believed in making his own luck, but coming upon her this morning right when she needed him almost felt preordained. He took a swallow of wine and put down his glass. "Going to the Louvre with you today reminded me of the first time I went."

"So tell me, does it ever get old?"

"No, but . . . today had a special shine because you were so excited, like a puppy at the beach."

She laughed at that. "I suppose I was."

"And that's a good thing." He leaned forward, needing to make her understand. "I've always loved the place, but I loved it even more today. You gave the experience added value."

Her cheeks turned rosy. "I'm glad. Now I feel better about imposing on you."

"You're not imposing." This could be an uphill slog. "Have you ever seen a movie, and then somebody comes along who's dying to see that same movie, so you see it again with them and it seems twice as good the second time around?"

"Sure! Their reaction makes it even better."

He sank back in his chair. "That's what I'm tryin' to tell you."

"That you liked the Louvre even more this afternoon? Yeah, I got that."

"But it would also be that way for all the special places in Paris."

"If you're asking to tag along while I play tourist for the next five days—well, four, really—then I'd be happy to have you do that, Drew. You're good company."

"Thank you, ma'am." He drank his wine while he considered that alternative. He tried to imagine standing in line for hours in front of the Eiffel Tower. He'd be with her, enjoying the sunny disposition that seemed to be hard-wired into her psyche. It wouldn't be the worst thing in the world.

On the other hand, he'd earned the right to bypass long lines, and he was spoiled in that regard. Besides, she'd waste precious time doing that. If she agreed to his idea, she'd see more of Paris.

But after he'd proposed his plan, she would no longer be comfortable making him stand in line with her at any attraction. Tagging along while she played tourist would be permanently off the table once she understood how he preferred to see the sights. He ran the risk of widening the gulf between them.

Aw, hell. He'd made it to where he was by taking risks, so why stop now? "Melanie, I don't want to just tag along." He set down his empty wineglass and looked at her. "I want to drive the bus."

She gazed at him. "This is a metaphorical bus, right?"

"Exactly. Showing you Paris would be a real kick in the head, but I want to do it my way."

"And what would that be?"

At least she'd asked the question instead of giving him a flat no. He outlined some of his plans and watched her eyes. He saw eagerness and yearning there, but in the end, resignation eclipsed everything else.

"All that sounds lovely, and I won't pretend that I wouldn't enjoy being treated like a princess. Any woman would. I also understand why you wouldn't want to see Paris on a budget. You're beyond that. But I can't have you spending that kind of money to entertain me, and even if I could deal with that issue, I don't have the wardrobe for most of what you have in mind."

"The wardrobe problem can be fixed, Cinderella." He'd hoped that she'd laugh at that.

She did. "What, you have a fairy godmother living in your town house, Prince Charming?"

"No, I have a personal shopper. Give her your sizes, style preference, and color choices, and she can fetch whatever you need right over to the town house. She does it for me all the time."

"I guarantee I can't afford the clothes, let alone the personal shopper."

"I know that. Because I'm asking a favor of you, I would cover the cost."

She blinked. "*You're* asking a favor of *me*? How do you figure that?"

"Let's go back to the movie analogy. Say this friend who was hankering to see the movie didn't have the money to go. Would you want to treat her?"

"Of course."

"What if she was too proud to let you buy the ticket?"

She gazed at him over the rim of her wineglass. "Nicely done. But your example involves me laying out what's basically lunch money. Whereas you—"

"Would be laying out lunch money."

She regarded him silently for several seconds. "I can't even get my mind around that."

"Then don't try. Let me show you Paris. Do me that favor."

"I need time to consider this. My brain isn't functioning very well right now. Lack of sleep is catching up with me."

"I'll bet." He signaled for the waiter and pulled out

his phone. "I'll have Henri come get us." He quickly texted their location to his chauffeur.

"And please don't think I'm not grateful for your fabulous offer. But if I accept it, I'll be spoiled. Every visit to Paris, maybe every trip I take from now on, will seem lame in comparison."

"Maybe." If she agreed to his plan, he ran the risk of creating an experience for himself that also might never be equaled. And he was willing to take that risk.

"But if I don't do it, I'll always wonder what it would have been like."

He smiled. Her natural curiosity meant that his chances had just improved. "Tell you what. On the way home, give me some basic info for Josette so she can pick out a few things and bring them over in the morning. If your answer is no, then she can return it all and nobody loses money."

"Won't she charge you for the service?"

"I have her on retainer."

"Oh." She shook her head. "We live in completely different worlds."

He tossed some money on the table. "Not at the moment."

Five

Dictating her clothing sizes, including her bra size in case a dress needed a unique undergarment, was a more intimate discussion than Melanie had expected.

Drew recorded everything in a text message and sent it off to Josette. "That way she can start shopping tonight."

"I guess stores are open in the evenings here like they are back home, then."

"Some are, but she goes after they close."

"Of course she does. I should have known." Melanie felt the giggles coming on. They were partly due to exhaustion and partly due to wine, but mostly she found herself laughing at her unbelievable situation. This sort of thing didn't happen in real life, especially to a girl like her.

She'd grown up in a loving family, but her father's ranch had never provided them with more than the basics. She was raised doing chores and cleaning hay out of her hair, not learning to charm people at cocktail parties. She'd attended college on a scholarship and had come out with a liberal arts degree and the realization that working on her daddy's ranch pleased her more than any job she could imagine. She expected to marry a cowboy and maybe they'd buy their own spread someday.

Drew Eldridge was about as far from that vision of her future as a person could get. But he was a very real part of her present as he sat beside her in the backseat of the Mercedes. He smelled good, too. Maybe it was the smell of money. That thought made her want to giggle all the more.

"What's so funny?"

"Everything. I go from losing all my possessions to the prospect of wearing designer outfits while I do up the city in style. At least I assume they'll be designer outfits?"

"Yes, ma'am. That's Josette's specialty."

"Knowing that a personal shopper named Josette is out there choosing Parisian fashions for little ol' me, a rootin', tootin' cowgirl, makes me laugh. Don't you think it's funny?" She turned to him, expecting a smile, a twinkle in those blue eyes as he shared the joke with her.

Instead he looked at her with such warmth that her heart started pounding. She'd assured Val that he wasn't interested, but he sure seemed interested now. She'd been around him enough to realize he didn't wear that expression all the time.

"I think you'll look great in those designer clothes," he said.

Or out of them? Maybe before she said yes or no to this new plan of his, she should clarify the details. But she couldn't do that now with Henri all ears in the driver's seat. She faced forward, but she could feel Drew's gaze on her. Oh, yes, he was sexually attracted to her, and apparently he didn't mind that she'd figured that out.

Her pulse was still out of control when they reached the town house. She'd been carrying on an inner debate the whole way. Neither of them had spoken again, which was fine with her because she had to think, but she could feel the tension in the car.

Was she horrified by the thought that Drew would like to get cozy with her in addition to escorting her around town? No. He could be between girlfriends and she was handy. That wasn't so terrible. She was between boyfriends and he was handy.

She'd never been one for brief affairs, but then she'd never been to Paris, either. Or been rescued by a billionaire who wanted to temporarily spoil her rotten. He'd said that her fresh take on the city energized him, or words to that effect. It might have energized his sex drive, too.

Ever since meeting Drew, she'd thought of him the same way she thought of the marble statues in the Louvre—beautiful to look at, but not a part of her world. Sure, she'd realized that he was sexy. Any woman would realize that. So what? His sex appeal had nothing to do with her. But perhaps it did, at least during the next four days.

Henri dropped them off and drove away to park the car. When they came to the door, Drew reached around her and opened it for her.

"You don't need a key?" She walked into the foyer. Now that it was dusk, the crystal chandelier sparkled with light and turned the foyer into a magical space.

"Henri calls ahead and tells the housekeeper to open the door for me." He closed it behind him. "I have a key, though, in case I happen to be coming in late. No reason to get someone out of bed."

Bed. The word hung in the air, and she swallowed. "Could I talk to you for a minute?"

"Sure." He took off his jacket. "Let's go into the sittin' room. Are you hungry? I could have the cook fix us some food."

"Don't be silly. We just came from eating." She realized he must be nervous too ... or have his mind on something else. She unzipped her hoodie but kept it on. "I'll be going off to bed soon." Yikes, there was that word again. She was jumpier than some virginal bride, and yet she'd had lovers—three, to be exact. They'd all been cowboys who could ride and rope as well as she could. Drew might be a billionaire, but once his clothes were off, he'd be no different from any other man.

Or so she tried to tell herself. Yet in her heart she suspected it wasn't true. Her other lovers had been strong and straightforward, making love like they did their cowboying. What would a billionaire like Drew be like in bed? He was used to being masterful and in control in the boardroom. Is that what he'd be like in the bedroom?

They went into the front parlor, a magnificent room with marble floors and a floor-to-ceiling fireplace with a coat of arms carved into the wall. She sat in a green silk wingback, and Drew took the sofa opposite her. He laid his jacket over the arm. Now that she was here in this formal setting and not tucked into the backseat of a car with him, she wondered if she'd imagined his sexual interest. If so, she was about to make a fool of herself.

Taking a deep breath, she gripped the upholstered

arms of the chair. When she noticed that she was holding on for dear life, she relaxed her fingers. "I think we can agree that I'm not as worldly as you."

"I'm not so sure about that." He leaned forward and clasped his hands loosely between his knees. His blue gaze sought hers. "You knew plenty about the art in the Louvre."

"I'm educated, especially in the arts, but that's not the same as worldly."

"You're splittin' hairs."

"Drew, I'm talking about . . ." She glanced at the open double doors and lowered her voice. "Sex."

He made a sound deep in his throat that could have been a groan or a laugh. He coughed into his fist and cleared his throat before looking at her. "You are?"

"Yes, and if I got the wrong impression from that moment in the car, I'll die of embarrassment."

"You didn't get the wrong impression, darlin'."

Her heartbeat thundered in her ears. She'd asked for this conversation, but she had no idea what to say next.

He focused those amazing blue eyes on her. "I think you're wonderful, in every way. Your zest for life is like a shot in the arm. That's why I want to give you the grand tour of Paris, because I know we'd have ourselves a terrific time. But I also find you tempting as all get-out, and I've struggled with that."

"You have? For how long?"

"Pretty much since I first saw you. Your expression when you were looking at Notre Dame was . . . I don't know if I can explain it, but I had an instant gut reaction. There was a sensual look about you that I couldn't resist. I was determined to say hi."

"Is that attraction . . . is that why you invited me to stay with you?"

"No. At least I hope I'm not that much of a schemer. But from the moment those bastards grabbed your backpack and knocked you down, I've felt in charge of your welfare. The easiest way to make sure that you'll be safe is to keep you here."

"I do feel safe."

"You are." He paused. "And you're safe from me, too."

That was disappointing news. She was just getting used to the idea of having a wild and crazy affair with him. "Why?"

He laughed and shook his head. "You're something else. Only you would ask that." He cleared his throat again. "It's simple. I've offered you a place to stay and a top-drawer introduction to Paris. I'm doing it as much for me as for you, but you'll still feel indebted. After the few hours we've spent together, I'm positive about that."

"You're right. I do feel indebted."

He spread his hands, palms up. "There you go. What kind of man would make a woman feel beholden to him and then hit on her? I don't tolerate that kind of manipulation from others, and I sure as hell won't tolerate it in myself."

So he was claiming the moral high ground. She wasn't sure where that left her. Probably sleeping alone for the rest of her visit. She could protest that she wouldn't feel manipulated, but that was more forward than she was prepared to be at this point.

Plus she had her own issues. Throwing herself at a billionaire was tacky, even if the billionaire had admitted that she turned him on. She didn't want to put herself anywhere near the gold-digger category. Her daddy had raised her to be hardworking and honest, so it just wasn't her way.

"I'm glad we had this talk." She stood.

"So am I." He got up, too. "Because I have to tell you, I weakened when we were in the car. When you started getting giggly, I had a tough time not kissing you."

Zing. That comment certainly put a match to her fuse. "But you controlled yourself."

"Only because you wouldn't look at me. If you'd turned your head the slightest little bit, that would have been all she wrote."

She noticed that his drawl became more pronounced when his emotions were involved. Sometimes he didn't sound like a guy from Dallas, but other times, like now, he could have been the boy next door. She wondered if he'd deliberately tried to iron out the Texas from his speech.

He shoved his hands in the pockets of his jeans, and now he really looked like a Texan. "Now that we've talked about this, we'll both be aware of it. I swear that I can take you on all those excursions without forgettin' myself, so don't let that be a factor in your decision."

She debated saying what she was thinking, and finally decided that she might regret going upstairs and leaving it unsaid. "You haven't asked how I feel regarding this subject."

He sucked in a breath. "No, I haven't. That's not good." He hesitated. "How do you feel about this subject?"

"I'm not sure yet. Until I saw the way you looked at me in the car, I thought I was sort of like a homeless pet you'd adopted to keep me from roaming the streets alone and getting hurt."

"Melanie, I never—"

"Don't worry. You didn't give me that impression. That was all in my head. I tried to figure out why you were being so nice, and then I found out that you're into charity work, so everything made sense. You look out for those who can't look out for themselves."

"I do, but I don't put you in that category. I respect your resourcefulness and your optimism."

She smiled. "Drew, you've already told me that from the moment I was mugged you've felt in charge of my welfare. Which is it? Do you want to protect me or send me out to slay my own dragons?"

"Both!" He groaned and shoved his fingers through his hair. "Both," he said more quietly. "I never want to undermine your confidence. But if you need me . . ."

The note of yearning in his voice touched her. Closing the gap between them, she stood on tiptoe and brushed her mouth against his.

"Thank you," she murmured.

Then she hurried out of the room, because the wine-rich taste of his mouth lingered on her lips, and she wanted more. Much more. She just didn't know what she'd be getting into if she took it.

Drew balled his hands into fists to keep from reaching for her. Then she ran out of the room, which was a good thing. He could control himself as long as she kept her distance, but he needed to warn her that light fairy kisses from a woman in a T-shirt and jeans could be more tempting than a blatant display of cleavage, at least for him.

He was a veteran of what he called the Titty Wars. There was a certain kind of woman, and thank God Melanie wasn't of that tribe, who thought a man could be enslaved by generous breasts, temptingly showcased in tight shirts or plunging necklines and pressed against his arm as often as possible.

Not one of those women would have honestly told him what they thought about anything, much less how they felt about having sex with him. He couldn't really blame them. They'd bought the cultural stereotype, which had been perpetuated mostly by men, if you got right down to it. Powerful men had often molded the behavior of women. Maybe that was another thing about Melanie that attracted him. She wouldn't be easily molded by anyone, least of all a guy like him.

His phone chimed and he glanced at the number. Josette. He took the call.

"Andre, *mon ami*, how are you on this lovely evening?" She had the husky voice of a lifelong smoker. And no matter how many times he'd coached her, she just couldn't—or wouldn't—pronounce his name the American way, so she just pretended he used the French version when he was in Paris.

"Great, Josette. Were you able to find anything for my friend?"

"Many things. Many lovely things. I could bring them over now, but if you're having a little *tête-à-tête* with your lady, I can wait until tomorrow."

"She's not really my lady, and she landed in Paris this morning. I'm sure by now she's fast asleep, so if you'd like to come by, that would be just fine."

"Then I'll do it. I'm so excited with the clothes. I want to show you."

"Good. I want to see them, too. *Merci,* Josette." He disconnected and closed down his computer. Then he clicked the intercom on his desk, which was connected to the servants' quarters downstairs. "Raoul, bring up a bottle of that pinot noir I had last night. Madame Theroux is due any minute and she'll want some. And a sliced baguette and warm brie, too."

"Right away, *monsieur.*"

Drew enjoyed the French way of doing business, which was often over a glass of wine. Some of his oldest friends gave him a hard time for preferring wine to whiskey or beer. He came from cowboy country, and cowboys didn't drink wine.

Josette must not have been far away when she'd called, because the doorbell rang before Raoul had brought up the wine. Drew left his office to greet Josette, a brunette in her sixties who'd probably worn five-inch heels every day of her life since she'd turned eighteen. Even if he hadn't needed a personal shopper, he would have pretended to so that he could have regular dealings with this feisty woman.

She was loaded down with garment bags and boxes from the best shops along the Champs Élysées. "Andre!" She handed everything to the maid who'd opened the door, and then came toward him, arms outstretched. Grabbing his head, she kissed him on both cheeks.

Laughing, he returned the favor and breathed in her signature Chanel Number Five, something she'd probably also been wearing since she'd turned eighteen.

"I have so many beautiful things for your lady friend, Andre." She beamed at him. "Is she from Dallas?"

"Yes, as a matter of fact, but she's not my—"

"How nice for you." Josette's brown eyes twinkled. "And you're going to show her the city, yes?"

"I hope so." He gestured toward the sitting room.

"Why wouldn't you?" Josette walked briskly into the room and sat on one end of the sofa. "Too busy?" She glanced at the maid who'd come in with all the packages. "*Merci*, Isabella." She patted the sofa. "*Ici.*"

"I can make the time," Drew said. "But she feels uncomfortable accepting such extravagance."

Josette's eyebrows lifted. "*C'est unique.*"

"Yeah. And I like that she's hesitant about spending my money. But it's frustrating, too, because I want her to experience the best the city has to offer."

"And Les Folies Bergère?"

"Yes! I hadn't thought of that, but what a brilliant idea. She should see that, too."

Raoul showed up with a tray and set it on the low table in front of the sofa. After pouring the wine, he left.

Josette smiled as she spread a piece of bread with the melted cheese. "Andre, you are turning into a Frenchman."

"I need to search my family tree." He picked up his wineglass. "I'll bet there's a French branch stuck on there somewhere."

"*Mais, oui.*" Josette savored her bread and cheese and sipped her wine. Then she set down the glass and gazed at him. "This lady, she is special, *non*?"

Drew nodded. "She impresses me."

"Then I hope she likes what I found for her." Dusting

off her hands, Josette reached for a long box and opened it. *"Voilà!"* She shook out a red-and-black silk dress that shimmered in the lamplight.

Drew swallowed. If the sleeveless confection looked sexy lying there against the sofa cushions, he could imagine the dynamite effect once Melanie put it on. "Nice."

"And because the evenings are cool, I added this." She plunged her hand into a glossy black shopping bag and came out with an elegant cape in black satin.

"How about shoes?"

"Certainment, mon ami." She flipped open a shoe box to reveal black satin pumps.

Following that, Josette laid out her other purchases, but Drew couldn't stop staring at the red-and-black dress. He was determined to see Melanie wearing it, along with the do-me shoes and the short black cape. Her reluctance was merely a challenge, and he thrived on overcoming obstacles.

"C'est bon?"

"Yes. *Très bon.* Thank you, Josette."

She stood. "Treat this one well, *chéri.*"

"Excuse me?" Josette was always free with wardrobe advice, but she'd never said a word about his personal life.

"If she's worried about spending your money, I like her already."

"So do I." He escorted Josette to the door and they exchanged good-bye kisses. After he closed the door, he stood there thinking about Melanie tucked into the Blue Room upstairs. "So do I," he murmured.

Six

Melanie slept like a rock until three in the morning. Then she was awake. So very awake. And starving to death. Perhaps she shouldn't have gone to bed without eating something besides the two pieces of cheese she'd nibbled at the sidewalk café.

This international travel was more complicated than she'd expected. On the plane over she'd been pestered with food every five minutes. Now that she was here, she hadn't figured out when to eat.

She couldn't blame it on being secluded in Drew's townhouse. Even if she'd been staying in the hotel she'd chosen, she'd hesitate to venture out into a strange city at three in the morning in search of a meal. And that hotel certainly hadn't been set up for room service.

The house was totally silent, unless she counted the growling of her stomach. Although that seemed loud to her, she doubted it would wake Drew or the servants. She sat up in bed and turned on a bedside lamp.

Her Paris travel books were stacked neatly on the delicate writing desk. She'd never had anyone unpack for her, and she'd had to rearrange things in the drawers a little. But the idea that someone had taken care of that menial chore was a heady one. She could get used to that.

She'd better not, though, because in four days she'd be on a plane back to reality. In the meantime, she might as well admit that she'd decided to stay here instead of moving to a hotel. First of all, she'd have to take time to choose one, and nothing would feel as secure or be located so perfectly.

And there was the possibility that she'd insult Drew if she rejected his hospitality. He'd also worry about her. Causing him any kind of distress would be a poor way to repay his generosity. She was touched that he was concerned about her.

The rest of his proposed program, though—creating the Paris trip of her wildest dreams—was still under consideration. Now that she'd had some sleep, she could think more clearly about it. His analogy about treating a friend to a movie made a good point, but she still couldn't equate that with four days of an all-expense-paid luxury tour of Paris.

Maybe they could negotiate a compromise. She didn't need a private tour of the Louvre, and she'd see the Eiffel Tower on her own. But she'd accept his generous offer of a moonlit cruise of the Seine, because that was an experience to be shared with a friend. If they were on a private yacht it wouldn't matter what she wore, so her wardrobe wouldn't be an issue.

Good. She'd solved that thorny problem. And she was

still starving. Sliding out of bed, she padded over and picked up several of her books. Maybe reading in bed would take her mind off her stomach.

It didn't. It seemed that travel books about Paris couldn't resist talking about the food every other paragraph. Fifteen minutes later, she couldn't concentrate on the page as hunger gnawed at her. She had at least three hours to go before she could reasonably expect the servants to be in the kitchen preparing breakfast.

But there was a kitchen somewhere on that basement level. Back in her college days, she'd lived in the sorority house with Val and Astrid, and they'd staged many raids on the kitchen in the middle of the night. They'd developed it into an art form. This was a French kitchen, but it couldn't be all that different.

Taking food without asking wasn't polite, but she had a stomachache from not eating. She couldn't imagine three more hours of torture while she waited for the sun to rise and the kitchen to open. Neither could she imagine waking someone and asking them to fix her a snack.

How ironic that she was in Paris, the gourmet capital of the world, and she'd never been hungrier. A careful trip to the kitchen seemed like the sensible course of action and the most considerate of the household. If Drew was prepared to spend hundreds of euros on her, he wouldn't begrudge her a little bread and cheese.

Putting down her book, she climbed out of bed. The nightwear she'd packed to wear on this trip was practical, cotton lounge pants and a roomy T-shirt. She hadn't bothered with slippers or a robe because they'd only have taken up room in her suitcase.

But if she planned to roam around Drew's house in

the middle of the night, she should probably put on a sweatshirt for modesty's sake. After doing that, she slowly opened her bedroom door and crept into the hallway. A few stairs creaked on her way down, but this was an old house. It must creak and groan all the time. No one would notice.

Motion-sensitive lights along the baseboards helped her find her way downstairs. In minutes she'd navigated her way to the servants' floor and located the kitchen. The hum of a refrigerator and the lingering fragrance of cooked food led her through an open door into a space dimly lit by a fluorescent light over the stove.

Once inside, she opened the refrigerator door. Finding a small wedge of cheese and a bottle of Perrier was easy. Searching out where the bread was stored posed more of a challenge, but at last she opened a metal box on the granite counter and hit pay dirt—one full loaf and half of a baguette. Taking the baguette, cheese, and Perrier, she left the kitchen.

Thoughts of Melanie had made Drew restless. Knowing she was right down the hall, he tossed and turned. Then a sound penetrated the thin veil of sleep. The stairs creaked.

At first he wondered if Melanie might be going down, but a second later he realized someone was coming up. Was it her? Had she gone down without him hearing and was now returning? Or was it an intruder?

He got out of bed, pulled on his briefs, and grabbed a robe out of the armoire. His security system was top-notch, but that didn't mean it couldn't be breached by a clever thief hoping to steal the Monet hanging in the hallway. An intruder was a threat to more than his art collection. Melanie was sleeping in a bedroom nearby.

Stepping silently into the hall, poised for action, he waited for whoever was climbing the stairs. They were breathing hard from the exertion. It could be Melanie, but why would she go downstairs in the middle of the night?

Belatedly he realized that if this was an intruder, he had no weapon but his fists. No baseball bat or tire iron. A vase, two centuries old and valued in the high six figures, sat on a table in the hall. He picked it up.

As a shadowy figure rose from the stairwell, he started forward, vase raised. Melanie screamed a split second after he recognized her. Something sailed past his head and thudded against the wall as she yelled again, this time sounding like a samurai warrior. She cocked her arm as if to throw something else at him.

"Melanie! It's me!" He set down the vase and backed up, palms facing her, heart racing. Jesus. She'd scared the hell out of him, and obviously he'd returned the favor.

"Drew?" Her voice shook and she lowered her arm.

"Yeah." He sucked in a breath.

"Oh, God." She clutched the banister. "I was hungry, but I didn't want to wake anybody."

Three floors below, footsteps pounded up the servants' stairway. It sounded like a minor stampede.

"Guess that didn't work out," she said.

"*Monsieur* Eldridge?" A man called from below. "*Qu'est-ce que c'est? Désirez-vous la police?*"

"No, Henri, no police." Drew walked to the head of the stairs and peered over the banister at Henri, who stood below in his nightshirt. Henri also served as his houseman. "*Mademoiselle* had a scare. All's well."

"Ah. *Bonne nuit.*" After some murmured conversations, Henri and the other servants retreated down the stairs and closed their bedroom doors.

"I feel terrible." Melanie climbed the remaining steps to stand before him. "Some guest I am, raiding the refrigerator and rousing the entire household."

"I should have guessed it was you, but all I could think was that someone had broken in, so I—"

"Rushed to defend the castle. That's so you."

It was true he seemed to go into protector mode whenever she was concerned. "Are you still hungry, or did I scare that idea straight out of your head?"

She hesitated, as if taking inventory. "Still hungry. My heart rate is almost back to normal, which means I can now hear my tummy growling. But I threw the wedge of cheese when I saw you coming, so no telling what shape it's in. Thank God you said something before I hit you with the Perrier."

"Or I bashed you with a priceless vase." Now that the crisis was over and nobody was hurt, he could see the funny side of it. "Let's get a little light on the situation." Stepping over to the wall, he hit a switch and glass sconces flickered to life. He loved those crazy things, which he'd found in Venice.

"Pretty!"

And so was she. No, not just pretty. Beautiful. His glance swept over glossy curls tousled from sleep, a freckled face still pink from embarrassment, and gray eyes that reflected the dancing light of the sconces. "Glad you like them." He couldn't stop gazing at her.

His attention drifted to her rosy mouth. Last time they'd been alone, she'd kissed him. He could still feel the softness of her lips as they'd brushed his, and he wanted that again.

Her loose pants, T-shirt, and hoodie shouldn't have looked sexy on her, but they did. Maybe it was her bare feet and pink toenails that aroused him so much, or his suspicion that she wore nothing under her shirt. That would explain why she'd added the hoodie, because the house wasn't cold enough to justify it.

But she'd left the sweatshirt unzipped. It hung open now, allowing him to see the slight tightening of the T-shirt where it stretched over what appeared to be her unbound breasts. The house wasn't cold enough to make her nipples pucker, either, but it looked like they had.

He looked into her eyes, and what he saw there sent heat surging through his veins. Lust settled heavily between his legs, and the knit briefs stretched as he grew hard. "Melanie, I . . ."

"The first kiss was mine to give." She took a shaky breath. "The second one is up to you."

Stepping forward, he cupped her face in both hands. Her dark lashes fluttered down as he lowered his head. *Easy, Eldridge. Easy.* Reining in his passion, he slowly mapped the contours of her mouth with the tip of his tongue. His heartbeat thudded in his ears as he tasted, touched down, and molded his mouth to hers.

Her tiny whimper loosened the bindings on his control. He delved deeper, thrusting with his tongue and sliding his fingers through her silken hair to grip the back of her head. The baguette and Perrier she'd been holding slipped to the floor and she wound her arms around his neck.

The more he invaded, the more she surrendered. This could only end one way. But she deserved a warning. Reluctantly ending the kiss, he looked into her passion-glazed eyes. "I'm taking you to bed."

"Oh, thank God."

That was all he needed. With a hoarse chuckle, he swept her up in his arms and carried her down the hall. She wanted him. In this erotic, predawn darkness, all arguments against making love had vanished in the heat of their kiss. Holding her in his arms felt so right, as if he'd known her forever.

He laid her in the middle of his bed and climbed in beside her without turning on a light. The pale glow of the moon through the sheer curtains at his window seemed fitting to this magical moment. He didn't speak, and neither did she.

They didn't need words as they discarded clothing and greeted each new discovery with lips and tongue. He was used to taking the dominant role, but she'd have none of that. She was clearly the kind of cowgirl who wasn't hesitant to go after what she wanted. Once he was naked, she pushed him onto his back and explored him with such thoroughness that he clenched his jaw against the urge to come.

As if she sensed that he was losing control, she gave him one last intimate kiss on the head of his cock before turning onto her back and stretching out in silent invitation. That simple gesture drove him wild. The urge to ravage her was strong, but he curbed it.

Instead he mimicked her technique and took his time. With slow kisses and gentle laps of his tongue, he roamed at will until she began to pant and writhe beneath him. But when he nuzzled the dark curls between her thighs, eager to make her come, she finally spoke.

"No."

He lifted his head, surprised. "Why not? Don't you like—"

"Oh, yes." She gulped for air. "But I want . . . all of you."

All of him. She wasn't in his bed purely for her own pleasure. She was here because she wanted that ultimate connection . . . with him. She wanted to be as close as humanly possible. That told him something important about her, something he was very glad to know.

His cock seemed glad to hear it, too. By the time he'd slipped out of bed and located the box of condoms in his armoire, he was as rigid as a battering ram. That didn't mean he had to act like one, though.

When he returned to her, he leaned down and gave her a gentle kiss. "I'm mighty grateful for tonight."

Her smile was barely visible in the faint light from the moon, but that smile shimmered in her reply. "Me, too."

"I'm glad." He moved over her, his heart beating fast. He'd bedded many women, but he'd never had the feeling that this one act could change his life. The feeling scared him a little, but not enough to make him stop. Nothing short of an earthquake could stop him now.

Her entrance was slick and hot. He'd meant to ease in so she could gradually get used to him, but she lifted her hips and instinct took over. He shoved deep, locking them together. And there it was again—the sense that he'd remember this moment forever.

She sighed and wrapped her arms around him, as if welcoming him home after a long journey. He wanted to believe that this connection felt significant to her, too. But he wouldn't ask. Not now.

Bracing himself on his forearms, he leaned down and brushed his mouth over hers. "This is good."

Her warm breath tickled his mouth. "Extremely good."

"I could stay right here for a long time."

"So could I." She clenched her muscles, squeezing his cock.

"But not if you do that."

"You don't like it?"

"Oh, I like it just fine. But you're going to—" He gasped as she squeezed again. "You'll make me come."

"Don't you want to?"

"Eventually." He withdrew and pushed forward again. "But you're first on the agenda."

"Mm." She executed a little rotating motion with her hips. "Let's come together."

"The first time? I don't know if we can."

"Let's try."

"Okay." He began to pump slowly. God, that felt amazing, and he was seconds away. He fought the urge. "Talk to me. Tell me when you're close."

"Pretty close." She rose to meet his next thrust. *"Oh."* She quivered.

And then he didn't need her to tell him anything. He knew. They were in perfect sync. He bore down, stroking faster, finding the right angle that made her gasp and tighten around his cock. His orgasm hovered, ready to pounce. There. Right . . . *there.*

She exploded. Her cries blended with his as he pounded into her quivering body and came . . . and came . . . in a rush of pleasure so intense he lost himself in the tumbling glory of it. Joyfully he abandoned his fate to the woman in his arms. To Melanie.

He'd been right. After this moment, his life would never be the same.

Seven

Melanie woke to the sound of bells. Disoriented, she sat up in a canopy bed draped in burgundy with gold trim. Drew's bed. A blush covered every inch of her naked body as she remembered . . . all of it.

Maybe jet lag was affecting her perception, but she was pretty sure Drew was the best lover she'd ever had. Thinking about the pleasure they'd shared made her hot all over again. But she was glad he wasn't there to see her in the unforgiving glare of morning light, because she must look like a mess.

The bells of Notre Dame finished their majestic musical number and began counting the hour with a resonance that sent chills down her spine. She counted along with the bells, because there was no clock in sight. *Eleven?* She was wasting valuable time!

The rest of the household was awake, naturally. The aroma of cooked food drifted up from downstairs, and her stomach cramped. She'd been starving at three in the morning. She'd moved past that stage to unbearable hunger pangs.

No doubt Drew had instructed his staff to stay off the third floor so she could sleep. She appreciated that, for modesty's sake. She wouldn't have wanted anyone bringing up a tray and finding her naked in Drew's bed.

A polite guest would shower and dress before heading downstairs, but she wasn't sure she could wait that long to eat. Maybe that hunk of cheese she'd thrown at Drew was still lying in the hall and she could gnaw on that before taking a shower.

When she climbed out of bed to look for her clothes, she found them neatly folded on an upholstered chair, along with a quickly scrawled note. *Pull the cord by your bed in your room and someone will bring you food. Drew*

She glanced beside Drew's bed and discovered a tasseled cord hanging there. How Old World. She'd seen such things in movies set in the early part of the twentieth century, but she would have expected Drew to install an intercom. Then again, he was the guy who preferred taking the stairs.

Apparently her room came equipped with the same old-fashioned way of summoning the help, and he was sensitive enough to know that she'd want food brought to her room instead of his. She slipped into her lounge pants and T-shirt.

Glancing at the bed, the scene of their mutual seduction, she smoothed the covers so it wouldn't look quite so much like hot sex had taken place there a few hours before. She would have made the bed, but Drew probably didn't do that and a made bed would look strange to whoever cleaned his room. Last of all she grabbed her hoodie and the note, which was another piece of incriminating evidence.

She opened the door warily and peered out. The hall-way was empty. Scurrying down to her room, she dashed inside and closed the door. Safe.

Too bad she wasn't sophisticated enough to sashay out of Drew's bedroom without worrying about being seen. But she was a simple country girl who wasn't used to having sex with a man she'd known less than twenty-four hours. The concept still boggled her mind, but the reality had been *wonderful.* She wasn't the least bit sorry, but she'd still rather not have the servants know.

Walking over to the tasseled cord she'd missed seeing earlier, she gave it a pull. Now, that was decadence. She wondered what sort of breakfast they'd bring her, but in her current state, she didn't care. She headed for the shower.

She'd wrapped a towel around her wet hair and was drying off with a second one from the heated rack when she heard footsteps and smelled coffee. Hallelujah, her food had arrived! Wrapping herself in the white towel, she walked out of the bathroom and came face-to-face with Drew. "Oh! I didn't expect you to deliver it!"

"Hope you don't mind." He wore an open-necked dress shirt and jeans, the same yummy combination he'd had on the day before, complemented by the sexy aroma of his cologne.

"Of course not." Just like that, food lost its number one ranking. Melanie looked into his blue eyes and basked in the warmth of his smile. She couldn't help smiling back. He had that kind of effect on her. "Thank you."

"Actually, I came up to thank you . . . for last night."

Her heart pounded faster. "The feeling's mutual."

"No regrets?"

"None."

He let out a breath. "Good. I was afraid . . . well, never mind." His glance swept over her. "I'm gettin' out of here before I forget myself." His Texas drawl was more pronounced. "You look way too good to me, darlin'."

"I could say the same." She trembled as she imagined herself pressed against his lean body.

He groaned and backed toward the door. "I mean it. I'm gone. Eat some breakfast and get dressed. I have something downstairs in the sitting room that I want to show you." He went out the door and closed it.

As she listened to his footsteps retreating down the hall, she battled the urge to call him back. Her body throbbed in anticipation of something that wouldn't happen anytime soon. She wished he'd kissed her, at the very least. But that would have been a mistake if he hadn't wanted to start something, considering that she was one dropped towel away from being conveniently naked.

She reminded herself that the servants were up and about. In that charged moment when he'd stood close enough to touch, she'd forgotten anyone else was in the house, or in the world, for that matter. Whenever she looked into his eyes, her surroundings disappeared. He was one potent dude.

With an effort, she pushed away all thoughts of getting hot and sweaty with Drew Eldridge. She dressed quickly in a clean T-shirt and jeans, finger-combed her damp hair, and sat at the desk to eat. The meal was incredible—a gourmet version of eggs Benedict, a bowl of sliced fruit, warm croissants with butter and jam, and the best coffee she'd ever been privileged to drink.

She forced herself to slow down and savor it, even though she was extremely hungry and also curious about what Drew wanted to show her downstairs. Then she remembered that he'd asked for her clothing sizes while they'd ridden home in the car yesterday. Maybe the outfits had arrived.

Damned if she didn't feel like Cinderella. Her life on the ranch didn't require fancy clothes. She'd kept a couple of dresses she'd worn to parties in college, and now they gathered dust in her closet.

But Prince Charming had asked her to the ball, or the equivalent of that. And she would be transformed, just like Cinderella, so she could attend in style. This fairy tale didn't feel wrong or bad, but it did seem weird. She couldn't equate anything that had happened to her in the past twenty-four hours with previous experience. Even the sex had been more dazzling than any she'd known.

Before the amazing sex, she'd planned to suggest a compromise that involved accepting some of Drew's plan without abandoning herself to the entire program. But as it always did, sex had changed everything. She didn't want to trundle off by herself and waste hours standing in line at the Eiffel Tower. She wanted to spend every available minute of her visit with Drew, either by his side as they enjoyed Paris or in his bed as they enjoyed each other.

She'd never in a million years expect this interlude to transfer to their lives in Dallas, but he was offering her paradise for the rest of her stay in Paris. Only a fool would say no to that. She wasn't worried anymore that he'd spoil her for normal life, either. She was living a dream, and when she flew home, she'd wake up.

After eating every last morsel on her tray, she found a blow dryer in the bathroom and styled her hair. She suspected that the clothes she was about to try on would require more than a casual ponytail. She was both curious and eager to see what a Paris shopping guru had picked out for her.

Finally, she put on her running shoes because she had nothing else. Then she made her bed, replaced her towels on the rack, and picked up the breakfast tray. Servants were probably supposed to do all that, but she hadn't been raised to leave chaos in her wake.

A middle-aged woman dressed in black slacks and a white blouse was polishing the banister on the second floor. She spoke only French, but she made it clear that she would take the tray from *mademoiselle* or know the reason why. Melanie relinquished the tray and followed the woman down the stairs.

The double doors to the formal parlor stood open, and sure enough, the elegant furniture was draped with a rainbow of colorful garments. Drew paced the room, his phone to his ear, but he turned when she came in and quickly ended the call.

His eyes were lit with excitement. "So? What do you think?"

She gazed at the beautiful clothes in colors she loved—red, purple, turquoise, and jade—outfits that would have been right at home in a Neiman Marcus trunk show. "It's overwhelming, Drew. I couldn't even wear all of these in the days I have left."

"I know." He didn't sound worried about it. "Just pick what you want for now. You can take the rest ho–"

"No." She cleared her throat. "I mean, no, thank you, I won't be taking anything home with me. I don't mean to sound ungracious, but I can't accept clothes I won't be wearing here. That's . . ." She hesitated, not sure what she wanted to say.

"Opportunistic?"

She pointed a finger at him. "Exactly! I get that you want to show me the city your way. I understand you'll have fun in the process and I'll need the right outfits. But scooping up this entire wardrobe and making off with it feels like I just won the jackpot in some televised game show. *Melanie Shaw! Come on down!* I can't do it."

He studied her, a smile tugging at the corners of his sculpted mouth. "Does that mean you're ready to go along with my plan?"

"Yes." She wondered if he'd offered her the extra clothes on purpose, so that she'd reject that idea but accept the initial concept.

"Excellent." His expression was triumphant. "Take whatever you want, but I do hope you'll choose the red-and-black dress and the cape that goes with it."

She'd been drawn to it from the moment she'd walked into the room. The abstract swirls of red against the black made her think of passion, and passion made her think of Drew. "Where would I wear it?"

"At Les Folies Bergère," he said. "I have tickets for tonight."

Her gaze met his. She was intensely curious about the

show, but she'd crossed it off her list once her friends had canceled. Going alone hadn't sounded like much fun. Seeing it with Drew, however, would be a total turn-on. "I'd love that," she said. "And I'll wear the dress."

They spent most of the afternoon at the Musée d'Orsay because Melanie wanted a destination that allowed them to walk along the Seine both there and back. Once again, she was transfixed by the artwork and admitted that she'd done a little painting herself in college. Drew wasn't surprised to hear it. Her enthusiasm for her surroundings told him she had the soul of an artist.

While they toured the museum, he'd deliberately put a leash on his libido. Other than an occasional brush of hands or touch on the shoulder, he hadn't made physical contact with Melanie all afternoon. He ached to do that, but he wanted to give her space to appreciate the experience.

Still, memories of making love to her taunted him constantly. When she paused before a Renoir nude, he had to look away. Otherwise he might have given in to the urge to drag her somewhere private and kiss her until they were both senseless with lust.

The worst part was that he thought she'd be okay with the idea of his doing that. More than once he'd caught her looking at him with a sexy gleam in those big gray eyes of hers. But then the moment would pass, and her face would light up at the sight of a painting by Monet or van Gogh.

That's why they were here, so she could see those works, and he was determined she would get the most out of the visit. Her enthusiasm fueled his, and he found himself looking at the paintings more intently. Consequently he saw things that he'd missed before.

After they left the museum, they strolled past the colorful shops and cafés of the Left Bank. Drew offered his sunglasses to Melanie, and typical of her, she refused them. He'd tried to buy her a pair earlier, but she'd insisted she could do without them for a few days.

A cloud drifted over the sun and Drew tucked his glasses inside his jacket. He couldn't help taking her arm as they crossed the street and headed toward Notre Dame. That kind of thing was bred into him. But he released her once they were safely across.

"And this is where we first met." She paused in front of the cathedral.

"Yes, ma'am. I hope the spot didn't get ruined for you because of what happened to you here."

She gazed up at him. "Meeting you more than made up for it, so no, nothing's ruined."

"Good." He was also glad she wasn't wearing his sunglasses, because then he would have missed that soft glow in her eyes.

"By the way, why haven't you held my hand at all this afternoon?"

His breath caught. "What?"

"I've been sending out signals, and you seem to be picking them up, but you still haven't touched me. I understand that you don't want to be affectionate in front of your household help. I don't want that, either, but we're among strangers now."

"Melanie, I—"

"If you don't like PDA under any circumstances, I'm

cool with that. I just need to know for future reference, so I don't accidentally embarrass you."

He was stunned. "I didn't want to interfere."

"Interfere?" She looked puzzled.

"With all of this." He gestured toward the cathedral, the river, and the vivid bustle that was Paris. "You've never experienced it, and I didn't want to distract you from—"

"Oh." She smiled, and her gaze grew even warmer. "That's incredibly sweet." She held out her hand. "Could we hold hands the rest of the way back, though?"

"We sure as hell can." He laced his fingers through hers and tugged her closer. "And while we're on the subject, how do you feel about kissing in public?"

"We're in Paris. I thought it was expected."

"So it is." Drawing her into his arms with a sigh of relief, he leaned down and finally, *finally* did what he'd longed to do for hours. Ah. Her mouth was as lush as he remembered, and he groaned when she opened to him.

So generous. So giving. Blood pumped through his veins and settled in a predictable spot. He didn't want to stop kissing her. He liked it too much. But that was the problem—he liked it *way* too much.

When he realized that he'd cupped her bottom, he forced himself to end the kiss and back away, but he held on to her hand. "Sorry." He gulped in air. "I got carried away."

"Don't apologize." She was breathing fast, too. "I've wanted you to kiss me since this morning."

"And God knows I've wanted to, but you see what happens."

Her gaze lowered to the crotch of his jeans, and her

smile was filled with feminine satisfaction. "It's nice to be wanted."

"Darlin', you have no idea how wanted you are."

She looked into his eyes. "Likewise."

His cock strained at the denim of his jeans, and he wondered how he would ever make it through an evening at Les Folies Bergère with this woman. They might have to leave at intermission.

Eight

Melanie had never felt more desirable than she did while sitting at a cozy table drinking champagne with Drew at the famed Les Folies Bergère. The look in his eyes when she'd come downstairs in the red-and-black dress would stroke her ego for months. She'd carried the cape specifically so that he could help her with it.

Having him settle that silken cape around her shoulders had been like foreplay. And now, as they watched nearly nude dancers on stage, he held her hand and stroked his thumb over her palm so erotically that she wondered if she could have a climax simply from that single caress.

The show itself was a sensual delight that celebrated the elegance of the human body. Costumes were often scanty but vibrantly colored. Les Folies Bergère was historic and spoke of the Paris that had captured Melanie's imagination long ago—an exuberant blend of art and sexuality.

She loved the show, but it wasn't the only reason she was getting more turned on by the second. She thought maybe Drew had planned it that way. If so, she was ready to fall in with that plan.

Leaning toward him, she put her mouth close to his ear and breathed in his signature fragrance. "I want you," she murmured.

"Same here," he whispered back. "It's almost intermission."

She wasn't sure what that meant, exactly, but she was more than willing to find out when the show took a break and everyone rose from their seats. As they joined the rest of the audience in the extravagantly decorated lobby, Drew put his arm around her and leaned down. "We can stay or leave. Up to you."

She glanced into blue eyes hot with desire. "You'll call Henri?"

"No. I told him we'd catch a taxi."

She felt a sense of freedom at hearing that. "Let's go." The words were no sooner out of her mouth than Drew propelled her through the crowd and out the door.

Once on the sidewalk, he whistled for a cab. She climbed in and a thrill shot through her. No Henri to chaperone. She wondered if Drew had set that up on purpose, too.

He slid onto the seat beside her and gave the driver the name of a hotel.

"We're not going to your place?"

"No." He pulled her into his arms. "I can't wait that long." Then he kissed her with such urgency that he left no doubt that he was on fire for her.

The cab ride was short, but he made good use of it. His kiss was thorough as he used his tongue to suggest what he had in mind the minute they were alone. Meanwhile, he fondled every bit of her he could reach. He cupped her breast through the silken material of the dress and slid his other hand under her skirt.

She hadn't ridden in many cabs in her life, and she'd certainly never made out in one, but the anonymity of it excited her. She stroked the fly of his slacks where the material strained over his erection. He groaned against her mouth.

Lights flashed past as the cabdriver veered left and right, and the wild motion added to the feeling of reckless abandon. The sound of traffic outside disguised the soft whimpers of desire that escaped from her lips as Drew breached the barrier of her panties and caressed her with deliberate intent.

By the time they left the cab, she was as desperate for him as he was for her. Her wet panties bore testament to that. But she straightened her clothes and did her best to look cool and collected.

The lobby was small yet tasteful. The desk clerk seemed to be expecting them, which told Melanie that Drew had arranged this part in advance. That was a thrilling thought.

He gave his name and was issued a key without any questions about luggage. Taking Melanie's hand, he led her up one flight of stairs, opened a polished wooden door, and pulled her inside a softly lit bedroom.

They'd barely closed the door before they were on each other, tugging at clothes and moaning in frustration. Fumbling with the zipper at the back of her dress, Drew walked her toward the bed and tumbled her backward. He'd made no progress on her zipper.

Abandoning that project, he stood, chest heaving, and unzipped his slacks. Without taking them off, he freed his rigid penis. She lay there, gasping for breath as he fished a condom from his pocket and put it on. All the while he kept his gaze on her.

She was equally entranced with her view. Last night had been much darker and more mysterious. He was an awesome specimen and he seemed ready to take some decisive action with that top-of-the-line bad boy.

But she was still wearing the expensive dress he'd bought. She sat up and reached behind her back to work on the zipper.

His reply was hoarse with desperation. "Never mind that." Cupping the back of her head, he covered her mouth with his and guided her down to the mattress while shoving her skirt to her waist.

Her pulse rate skyrocketed. She was being taken, and she loved it. When he encountered the barrier of her drenched panties, he ripped the delicate lace in two. All her life she'd dreamed of a man wanting her so much that he'd tear the clothes from her body. Drew was that man.

And he was there, braced above her, his jaw clenched, as he found her slick entrance and pushed deep. He squeezed his eyes shut and cursed softly. "I'm ready to come."

Her heart pounded frantically. "Do it."

"No." His forehead creased in a frown as he concentrated.

She felt his penis twitch deep inside her, and her body responded. She gasped. "I might."

"Wait."

She took several quick breaths. "Okay."

Slowly he opened his eyes and looked down at her with a sigh. "Better."

"Want to take off my dress now?"

"No. I'm not that much better."

"It will wrinkle."

"We'll have it steamed. I'm not leaving this spot just yet." He leaned down and kissed her gently before lifting his head to gaze into her eyes. "But I won't let you walk out of here later on looking as if you've been ravished."

"Thank you." She wanted him so much she could hear the hum of her blood in her ears. "Will I be ravished?"

"I hope so. I just . . . had to get inside you."

She cupped his face in both hands. "I want you there."

"Good, because I don't think you could have stopped me. Not tonight." He eased back and rocked forward again. "I like being able to see your eyes. I like watching them get darker." He began to pump slowly.

She trembled as the friction wound the tension deep inside her, tightening it with each thrust. "Yours are darker, too, almost navy."

"No wonder." His breathing grew rough. "This is intense."

"I know." She lifted her hips to meet him and matched his rhythm.

"That's good. That's real good, darlin'." He increased the pace, and the room filled with the liquid sound of their bodies sliding together. "Now I want you to come for me."

"No problem." She focused on the blue flame in his eyes. "Especially if you keep doing that."

He grinned. "That's what I like to hear." He began to piston back and forth even faster. "I can feel you gettin' ready."

"Uh-huh." She gulped for air as her climax bore down on her, demanding release. "Oh, yeah . . . there . . .

there!" With a cry she arched upward, wanting everything he had to give her. He surged forward, and she dove into a whirlpool of sensation. She cried out again as he plunged deeper, touching her core.

"Yes! God, Melanie, yes!" With a deep bellow, he drove home one last time. His eyes closed while he pulsed within her and shuddered in reaction.

Gradually his forehead came to rest on hers, and his warm breath tickled her face. Yet somehow he managed to keep himself braced on his forearms instead of collapsing on her. She couldn't imagine the strength of will that would take.

After several long seconds, he lifted his head and opened his eyes. After drawing in a long, shaky breath, he looked down at her and smiled. "That . . . is what sex should be like."

"Agreed." But she was smart enough to realize that sex wouldn't be like this with anyone else. And she had to be okay with that.

Although Drew had never rushed a woman to a hotel room before, in Paris or anywhere else, he'd had sense enough to preplan this episode, thank God. He'd intended their night at Les Folies to ramp up the sexual tension, and it had certainly accomplished that. They'd been wild for each other, as he'd hoped they would be.

But he'd decided in advance he didn't want Henri driving them back home in that condition. Either Henri would have been embarrassed or Drew would have been frustrated. The taxi had been a much better option.

So far the night was everything he'd hoped for and more. Sending Melanie's dress out to be steamed was a bonus. It meant she was conveniently naked for a while. Because he was a gentleman, he offered her one of the two robes in the closet, in case she felt modest.

Fortunately for him, she hadn't. Instead she coaxed him out of his clothes, which didn't take much coaxing. They romped on the bed like kids, which led to romping on the bed like adults. He'd brought several condoms to take care of that possibility.

The pillows they'd used to whack each other during the pillow fight became a support system for some interesting sexual maneuvers. He'd concluded that she had some acquaintance with the Kama Sutra, and he was more than happy to try anything she had in mind. Variety was good. Variety was excellent, in fact.

Eventually, climaxed out, they lay facing each other, sweaty and smiling.

"We'll need showers," she said.

"We're in luck. There's a shower through that door." He pointed toward the attached bath. "I'll be glad to wash your back for you."

"How gallant."

"No, how devious. I'll take any old excuse to get my hands on that gorgeous body."

"Where?" Gray eyes sparkling, she glanced around. "What gorgeous body?"

"This one." He cupped her full breast and brushed his thumb over her dusky nipple until it stiffened. "This amazing, beautiful body." He looked into her eyes. "Want to come again?"

"I don't think I can, not after that last time when you kept going and I kept coming. I didn't know I could do that three times in a row."

"But now you know." He shouldn't already be thinking about the next time they'd be naked together and how many orgasms he might give her then. She had plenty to see and do tomorrow before he managed to get her undressed and back in his arms.

But he couldn't help anticipating that moment. He longed to whisk her away to a tropical island where they wore few clothes and had no responsibilities. He began to dream of traveling with her and making love in every corner of the world.

He teased her other breast so it matched the first. "Your nipples seem interested in having another round."

She captured his hand and held it between both of hers. "You're becoming greedy."

"That's a fact. I am. But I'll let you rest."

"Good." She released his hand. "We should just talk until my dress arrives. What's taking so long, anyway?"

"They won't bring it until I call."

She laughed. "I see how this works."

"You wouldn't want them knocking on the door in the middle of a rip-roarin' orgasm, would you, darlin'?"

"No, guess not. Did you have the dress steaming in mind, too?"

"No, but this is a full-service hotel. They'll bring food if we want it. Do you?"

"No, believe it or not."

"I felt sort of guilty for robbing you of your snack last night. I don't want to starve you."

She shook her head. "I won't let that happen. But thank you for choosing a hotel that delivers food. I'm impressed that you planned everything in advance. I had no idea."

"Like it?"

"Very much. I feel way less inhibited in this hotel than in your town house. Your town house is elegant and I'm honored to stay there, but I worry about the servants discovering what's going on between us."

"Then we'll come here again tomorrow night." He made a mental note to set it up. "After the Eiffel Tower."

"But if we come back here again, then you're spending—"

"Shh." He laid a finger over her mouth. "It's worth every euro if you can relax while you're with me."

"Mm." Her tongue darted out and licked his finger.

He waited to see what she'd do next. Sure enough, she pulled his finger into her mouth and began to suck. He'd thought he was all played out, but seeing the action of her full lips curved around his finger proved that he had life in him, after all.

He couldn't help teasing her, though. "Now who's greedy?"

She slid her mouth free of his finger. "I am." Then she glanced down and laughed. "And you're glad about that."

"'Fraid so."

"Then lie back and enjoy." She slid down on the mattress and transferred her attention to his cock.

"I'd rather watch." He propped himself on his elbows.

"In that case, I'll give you the superdeluxe version."

And, boy howdy, did she ever. Apparently she was telling the truth about losing her inhibitions, because she put on a show—cradling his pride and joy between her creamy breasts and giving him a tongue bath such as he'd never had.

He'd intended to stop her before it was too late, but she had some amazing moves. She took him over the edge before he saw the edge looming, and then she drank every last drop. When she lifted her head and met his gaze, she winked at him. "Gotcha."

Oh, yes, she had him, all right. He was falling fast and hard. But she wasn't. No matter how uninhibited she might be when they were naked, she was keeping a part of herself separate, walled off. He could guess why, too. She thought this was a temporary deal they had going on.

He'd thought so at first, too. But with every minute they shared, he became more convinced that he'd found something extraordinary, some*one* extraordinary. He'd made a fortune trusting his instincts, and he was ready to trust them now.

If he told her all that, though, she wouldn't believe him, not after less than two days together. She didn't know him well enough yet. But she would. Oh, yes, she definitely would.

Nine

Time was so fickle. It slowed down when Melanie least wanted it to, like whenever she was sitting in the dentist's chair, or she had to wait in line to renew her driver's license. But the next two days with Drew shot past with blinding speed.

The hours were packed with a blur of images—their private tour of the Louvre, a candlelit dinner at the Eiffel Tower, an early-morning visit to Notre Dame, café au lait sipped at a sidewalk café, an afternoon stroll past brilliant flower stalls and fruit markets, and an evening boat ride on the Seine.

The new credit card was delivered to Drew's town house, and Melanie was able to pick up souvenirs for her mother and her friends. She also bought a cheap camera and took pictures of everything she saw. No doubt her friends would like pictures of Drew, but she was shy about taking any. She didn't want to make assumptions, or cross any invisible barriers by mistake.

Way before she was ready for the end of her fairy tale, she found herself lying with Drew in their cozy hotel room for the last time. They'd come together with a different kind of desperation tonight, one tinged with sadness that their time together in Paris was nearly over.

She faced him and looked into those incredibly blue eyes. She hated talking about the details of leaving, but she needed to. "I should get to the airport early in the morning," she said.

He stroked her hair back from her face. "Not too early, darlin'. You're going home in my plane."

She sighed. She should have anticipated that he wouldn't let her suffer through any potential airport drama. "That's very generous, but I have a ticket. I may have to navigate a little red tape because I physically am not in possession of it, but—"

"I'm going back, too, so you might as well catch a ride with me." He smiled, and when he did that, he was irresistible. "There will be empty seats."

"Are you fibbing to me for the first time? You said when we met that you planned to stay two weeks. I distinctly recall you saying that." She remembered their meeting in vivid detail and probably always would.

"I did plan to stay two weeks, but some unexpected business came up, and I have to head on home."

She narrowed her eyes, still suspicious of his motives. "Are you sure about that?"

"You bet." His expression was relaxed, as if he had truth on his side. "I really have to go back."

"I still say it's very convenient that you suddenly have to leave when I have to leave."

He shrugged. "Suit yourself. If you insist, you can be crammed into a center seat of the middle row with crying babies on one side of you and partying college kids on the other side. Or, you can fly back in a quiet cabin with me."

She couldn't help laughing. The trip over had been a real rodeo very much like he'd just described. "Well, when you put it that way . . ."

"I knew you'd come to your senses." He grabbed her and rolled her onto her back. "And we can leave on our schedule, so you don't have to get up at dawn."

She gazed at him and fluttered her eyelashes. "Meaning what, kind sir?"

"We have more time for this, dear lady." He lowered his head and gave her a kiss that was both gentle and sweet.

But she wanted more than gentle and sweet. Thrusting her hands through his hair, she gripped the back of his head and pulled him into an open-mouthed kiss filled with all the passionate longing churning in her heart.

Catching fire, he gave it right back to her. He continued to ravage her mouth as he reached for a condom. Lifting his head, he brushed the condom packet against her cheek. "Put it on for me?"

"Gladly." She took the packed, ripped it open, and tossed the packaging aside. Then she reached down and grasped his thick, warm penis.

He groaned. "Damn, that feels good."

"It gets better."

"I know, darlin'. That's why I gave you the condom."

She rolled it on with practiced ease, caressing him as she went along. In their nights together, he'd become quite fond of having her take care of this chore. She finished by cupping his heavy balls and squeezing gently. How she ached for him!

His breathing grew ragged as his lips hovered over hers. "Tell me what you want, Melanie." Easing down, he settled between her thighs. "You can have anything—anything in the world."

"Just you."

"That's too easy."

"That's all I want."

"Then I'm yours." Looking into her eyes, he probed once and slid home. "All yours."

She drank in the fierce heat of his blue gaze as he began to move within her. How easily he said those words. Too easily. But he was hers for the rest of the night. She would treasure every minute in his arms.

The following morning was a busy one for Drew as he talked with his staff about the maintenance projects he wanted them to handle while he was gone. He hoped to be back in less than a month, which would give them time for a thorough cleaning of all drapes, rugs, and bed hangings. They could also deal with the plumbing problems he'd noticed. The town house was old, and something was always going wrong with it. Drew didn't care, but he wanted to stay on top of things.

He hadn't lied to Melanie about having urgent business in Dallas, either. He'd put off important phone calls concerning the charity event while he'd concentrated all his attention on her. To use an old-fashioned term, he'd been courting her, although she was charmingly oblivious to the fact.

When he'd finally returned some of those calls yesterday, he'd realized that he could handle the issues more efficiently in person. But that wasn't the most important reason to go back. Now that he'd found Melanie, he wasn't about to let her out of his sight, at least not until they'd had a serious discussion about the future.

Over the years he'd learned the value of timing, and he knew that picking the right moment to tell Melanie how he felt about her was critical. He'd considered talking to her during their last night together. He had confessed his feelings, in fact, but she obviously hadn't realized that he'd meant exactly what he'd said.

No doubt she'd thought that his *I'm all yours* statement had been made in the heat of the moment. Other men might throw those words around when they had sex with a woman, but he never had. She couldn't know that, though.

Thank God she'd taken his suggestion of flying home with him. Had she insisted on going commercial, he would have had to do that, too. It would have been ugly, but he would have done it.

She was such an independent little critter, and he loved that about her, but damn, he would have liked her to take home all the clothes Josette had picked out. She'd refused. Maybe it didn't matter, because she'd get them eventually, unless everything went horribly wrong between them.

She boarded his corporate jet wearing the same outfit she'd had on the morning he'd first seen her, although it had been freshly washed by his staff. It reminded him of what had attracted him in the first place—a woman who'd grabbed the chance to experience awe. From now on, if he had anything to say about it, she would have someone there to share the awesome moments.

Because they'd been awake most of the night, they

both slept for the first few hours. Drew encouraged that. He wanted her to be rested when he broached the all-important topic of where they went from here.

He woke before she did and lay in the reclining seat gazing at her. She'd won his heart without even trying. She'd won it by being herself, a person who wasn't dazzled by his wealth and didn't expect him to shower her with material things. He'd never in a million years thought he'd fall for a cowgirl, but there it was. He had.

She made him laugh, and even better, he made her laugh, too. They'd connected in a way he never had with the socialites he'd dated his entire adult life. Had finding the right woman been simply a matter of moving out of his social circle?

No, he didn't believe that. Materialistic women existed in all parts of society. Those who shared his values existed at all levels, too. He'd met a few, but they'd been friends, not lovers. A combination of shared values and unbelievable chemistry didn't come along every day. It had never happened to him. Until Melanie.

She opened sleepy eyes and caught him staring at her. For one precious moment, warmth that mirrored his shone from those gray depths. Then, as if she was censoring the emotion, her gaze gentled to friendliness.

"Good dreams?" he asked.

"Yes."

"About me?"

"Egotist! I'm not telling." She grinned at him.

He had his answer. She'd been dreaming about him, and the glow of happiness in her eyes when she'd first opened them gave him hope. "Ready to eat?"

"You know it."

He'd looked forward to offering her the gourmet food on board his plane, and she was gratifyingly appreciative of the cheese soufflé, glazed fruit, and steamed veggies. The chocolate lava cake, though, sent her over the moon.

She leaned close. "It's almost better than sex," she murmured with a furtive glance at Suzanne, the cabin attendant.

"Almost." He winked at her. "But not quite."

"No, not quite." Her smile flashed, but she looked away quickly, as if not wanting to meet his gaze.

Hm. He hadn't considered this trip from her point of view, but now he realized it could seem like slow torture, a long, excruciating good-bye. That wasn't fair, when he had a totally different scenario in mind. He put down his spoon. "It's not over, Melanie."

"You mean lunch? There's more?" But then she met his gaze, and saw how serious he was. All merriment left her expression. "Yes, it is. We both know that, so you don't have to pretend. I was happy to accept your offer of a ride home, but when we get there, we'll each move back into our respective worlds. It's okay. I completely understand."

"No, you don't. I—"

"I'm grateful for all we've shared. You're a wonderful host. You showed me Paris as no one else could have, and I'll never forget it."

"You're talking as if we'll never see each other again!"

"I doubt that we will." Her expression seemed absolutely blank. Was she protecting her feelings? Or was she actually as okay with that idea as she sounded?

He'd expected an argument, but not this solid wall of

resistance. And his timing sucked. He'd started this discussion while they both sat, seat belts fastened, so they could eat a messy chocolate lava cake. Worse yet, Suzanne hovered within earshot.

He called over to the flight attendant. "Suzanne, would you please take our trays? Keep the desserts warm. We'll finish them later. And please give us some privacy."

Melanie glanced at him in alarm. "What's wrong?"

"Everything." Once the trays were gone he unbuckled his seat belt and got up. Then he crouched down in front of Melanie's chair. "I've been waiting for the right moment to talk to you, but I didn't stop to think that you'd spend the whole blessed flight anticipating the end of our relationship."

She lifted her chin. "I'm not, either. I had a nice nap, and a wonderful meal. I promise you I'm not brooding about what happens after we land."

"No, you wouldn't do that." He took both her hands in his. "You're not a brooder. It's one of the many things that I love about you."

Her eyes grew wide and she began to tremble. "Drew . . ."

He forged on. Might as well lay all his cards on the table. "I love other things, too, like the way you really look at the world around you with wonder in your eyes, and your fierce independence, and your spirit of adventure, and your lack of concern about luxury, and the way you react to me in bed."

She stared at him as her whole body quivered.

He gripped her hands more tightly. "I love *you*, Melanie Shaw. I never thought I'd fall in love with a cowgirl, but it looks like I have. I began to love you that first morning, and that love has grown stronger every hour of every day we've spent together. But I knew you wouldn't believe me if I said that too soon, so I've been hoping to find a moment when this speech would make sense to you." He searched her expression for some sign, some flicker of understanding. "I'm powerfully afraid this isn't that moment."

She blinked. "You *love* me?"

"Yes. I know it's fast, darlin', but I'm a fast mover. I don't expect you to love me back, at least not yet. All I ask is a chance. Just . . ." His throat closed with fear as he realized how much was at stake. "Just give me a chance."

She continued to gaze at him without speaking.

He waited, massaging her cold hands, letting her see the caring in his expression, and praying that she would accept that he was not a raving lunatic, just a man in love.

The light in her gray eyes was faint at first, and he almost missed it. Then it grew brighter, and he felt the pressure of her hands clutching his. Heart pounding, he watched her expression change from disbelief to tentative hope.

"I love you," he murmured again.

Her smile began slowly, and as it widened, her eyes glistened with unshed tears.

"Do you believe me?"

Still not speaking, she swallowed and nodded.

"Will you give me a chance?"

"Oh, Drew." Her voice was hoarse with emotion. "You don't need any more chances. You had me the minute you ran after those muggers."

"I did?"

"Of course! Didn't anyone ever tell you a woman loves a knight in shining armor?"

"I wasn't trying to be—"

"I know." She pulled her hands from his and cupped his face. "And that's why I love *you*."

She loved him. He felt the tightness in his chest give way as warmth flowed in. She hadn't known about his money, and she hadn't been looking to cash in on her relationship with him. She'd been taken by his effort to protect her not with his money but with his strength. *She loved him.*

She leaned closer. "Do you believe me?"

"Yes." He was grinning like an idiot and couldn't stop doing it. "You know this means we're getting married, right?" Then he winced. What a bonehead proposal. He was not bringing his A game.

"My mama and daddy will like that."

"What about you? Will you like that?"

"You mean will I like sleeping in your bed every night and making love whenever we feel like it?"

He chuckled. "Among other things. Listen, I can give you a much better proposal than this. You don't have to say yes, yet. Let me get the ring and do it up right."

"Good grief. Never mind all that drama. My answer is yes, I will like being married to you. I will like it very much."

"Good. I'll slip the ring under your pillow some night after we've had lots of good sex. How about that?"

"Sure. Whatever."

"You don't care about the ring?" He should have known that, too.

"I only care about you." She met his gaze.

"And that's why I'm the luckiest man on Earth."

"And I'm the luckiest woman. I guess that takes care of everything, huh?"

"Almost." He reached for her seat belt and unbuckled it. "Except for the kissing part. Please stand up. My knees are killing me."

Laughing, she let him pull her up and into his arms. Their kiss was long and heartfelt, punctuated by more murmured words of love. It lasted until the plane lurched and Suzanne came back to advise them of turbulence.

Drew held Melanie close for one second more and gazed into her eyes. "There's so much to talk about— whether we want kids, where we'll live, the size of the wedding, where we should go on our honeymoon . . ."

"We have a long plane ride. We'll figure it out. But I know where I want to go on our honeymoon."

"Bali? Tahiti?"

She shook her head. "Paris. There's a small hotel there, and—"

"I can't think of anything better." He supposed at some point in his life he'd been this happy, but if so, he couldn't remember when.

Epilogue

It was a three-margarita night when Melanie met her friends Astrid Lindberg and Valerie Wolitzky at Golden Spurs & Stetson, their favorite watering hole in downtown Dallas. Two weeks earlier, Drew had joined them so Val could meet the paragon Melanie planned to marry and Astrid could get reacquainted with the childhood friend she hadn't seen in years. But tonight was just for the girls. Melanie wanted to show them the antique ring Drew had given her, which was perfect and so much better than a huge rock. And meanwhile, Astrid said she needed some advice on her own love life.

The three friends went back a long way. They'd met and bonded their freshman year at a small college in East Texas. They'd joined the same sorority, and because they were all only children, they'd cherished the sense of sisterhood more than most. After graduation they'd stayed close. Val, the only one who wasn't from the Dallas area, had deliberately taken a job with a Dallas law firm so she wouldn't lose touch with her buddies.

Melanie's wedding plans took up most of the first

round of drinks. They discussed dress designs, venues, and the bachelorette party. Because Melanie was the first to get engaged, they spent part of the time on their phones doing Internet research on current wedding fashions.

By the second round of margaritas, Astrid began to open up about her problems. Blond and petite, she didn't look like anyone's idea of a large-animal vet, but she loved the work. She also came from money and was expected to marry a wealthy man. She was currently dating Edward, who had all the right credentials.

"My mother *loves* him," Astrid said. "So does my father. Edward fits into my family beautifully. And he's a nice guy. I just . . ."

"What?" Val, a redhead with an eccentric sense of style, leaned forward. "Is he terrible in bed?"

Astrid shrugged. "I don't know."

"You don't know?" Melanie stared at her. "You're practically engaged to the guy. You haven't kicked the tires?"

"He hasn't pushed for that, and neither have I. I don't . . . like how he kisses."

Val threw up her hands. "Don't you dare marry him. Mark my words, a bad kisser is going to be a nightmare between the sheets. Somebody needs to educate this guy, but not you. And some men are tone deaf when it comes to these things. Edward could be one of those."

"But my parents are wild to have him as their son-in-law."

Melanie laughed. "Yeah, but they don't have to go to bed with him. Val's right. Back in the Dark Ages, women had to make a bad match for the good of the family. Those days are gone."

"Maybe it's me." Astrid polished off her drink. "Maybe I'm a cold fish."

"You are not." Val smirked. "We remember what you were like in college. You have the soul of a seductress, chica. You just need the right Zorro to light your fire."

"Like Fletch." Astrid gazed dreamily into her empty glass.

"Who?" Melanie leaned forward. "Who's Fletch?"

Astrid glanced up, startled. "Oh, nobody. Just a client. He's the one with the mare who's having a rough time."

"A client." Val nodded wisely. "Methinks he's a sexy client. Tell us more."

"He's a rancher. Like all ranchers, his money is tied up in land and livestock."

Melanie studied her friend. Astrid moved in the same circles as Drew, so Melanie understood the issues more than she might have otherwise. "A cash-strapped rancher wouldn't make your parents very happy, right?"

"No." Astrid looked at Melanie. "He wouldn't. My mother has warned me for years to marry someone with money so I'd never have to worry about his motives. But Fletch is not like that. I know he's not."

Their third round arrived, and they all drank a toast to true love.

Val was the one who asked the critical question. "How does this Fletch guy feel about you?"

"Ah, there's the big question." Astrid sipped her drink. "Sometimes I think he's interested, but other times he acts as if I'm simply a vet he's hired to take care of his pregnant mare. And he *is* a client, so I can't very well make a move."

Val cradled her goblet in both hands. "Sticky situation. But promise me you won't go to bed with Edward until you've had a chance to find out if Fletch is in the market."

"I agree." Melanie raised her glass. "To talented lovers, which we all deserve."

"Yeah." Astrid touched her glass to Melanie's. "May we all find a guy who floats our boat the way Drew does Melanie's." Then she glanced at Val. "Gonna toast with us?"

"I'll toast the two of you. As for me, I'm on hiatus. No boat floating going on over here."

Melanie met Astrid's gaze. Now was not the time to confront Val about her issues. Melanie amended the toast. "To each of us finding what we need."

Val looked relieved. "I'll drink to that."

The three women clicked their glasses together. As Melanie drank her margarita, she counted her blessings. She never would have expected a down-home cowgirl would end up with a Prince Charming like Drew. But she'd learned that love could come along when a person least expected it. She hoped her friends would find that out soon, too.

Tempted by a Cowboy

ASTRID

One

"I can't lose her." Fletcher Grayson crouched beside the bay mare and stroked her sweat-dampened neck as she lay on her side in the foaling stall, her breath labored.

"We're not going to lose her." Astrid Lindberg was determined that both mare and foal would survive this night. Fletch had called her emergency line at ten p.m. It was a testimony to her lack of a social life that she'd been home on a Saturday night.

She'd rushed out to the Rocking G, driving through a summer downpour. It was what locals called a trash mover of a rain, falling in endless sheets of water. Four hours later, the rain continued to pound the roof of the barn, and Janis still hadn't foaled.

Astrid had monitored the pregnant mare for weeks, ever since the first signs of edema. Because of the swelling, Janis's abdomen was far more distended than it would have been in a normal pregnancy. The condition was worrisome, and recently Fletch had kept her confined to the barn and a small paddock to restrict her movements.

Some vets might have performed a C-section by now.

Astrid preferred to see if Janis could deliver naturally, which would mean a better start for both mother and baby. Luckily Fletch agreed with her.

Fletch tended to agree with her on most things, which made her job as his vet much easier. It also made her life as a woman frustrating as hell. From her first glimpse of the broad-shouldered rancher, she'd been in trouble. Fletch Grayson was hot. And single. And a client. He was definitely off-limits.

"I think she wants to get up." Fletch stood and backed away. Concern shone in his brown eyes. "I wish she'd just have that foal and be done with it."

"Me, too." Astrid rose and edged back as Janis lumbered to her feet. "Let's move out of the stall and give her room to pace if she needs to."

"Sure." He followed her out and they leaned side by side against the front of the stall so they could observe the mare as she walked the perimeter of her enclosure.

Standing close together in this cozy barn watching Janis as the rain came down outside was the most natural thing in the world for them to be doing. Yet stormy nights always made Astrid long to be held, and it drove her crazy to be within touching distance of the yummy Mr. Grayson. She imagined the feel of all those muscles under his blue denim shirt and barely controlled a shiver.

He'd named his ranch the Rocking G because he had a fondness for classic rock and roll. This horse honored Janis Joplin, and the stable was filled with namesakes of other famous rockers. In Astrid's opinion, Fletch was the one who rocked.

He'd hung his Stetson on a peg outside the stall. When he was nervous, he had a habit of running his fingers through his chocolate brown hair, which only made that wavy hair sexier. No one should look this good at two in the morning. Or smell this good. Fletch's woodsy after-shave was one of the many things about him that made her pulse race.

He possessed a killer combo of square-jawed masculinity and a heart of gold. The same passionate love of animals that had propelled her into the field of veterinary medicine had caused him to sink all his savings into a horse-breeding operation. Although he was finally turning a profit, he did so only by carefully managing his budget.

They'd become so comfortable with each other during the six months she'd tended his horses that he'd shared major decisions, such as when he'd postponed the purchase of a new truck so he could install more efficient heating in the horse barn. She treasured those long conversations, even though they stirred up inappropriate thoughts. Would he be even better at pillow talk?

But she also treasured her professional standing in the Dallas area, so she wouldn't be sharing a pillow with gorgeous Fletch Grayson. It was hard enough for a girl to be taken seriously as a vet in Texas, even harder for someone like Astrid, the daughter of a rich family. Besides, she didn't know if he would welcome that idea. Sometimes she imagined him looking at her with interest, but that might have been wishful thinking on her part.

"One thing's for sure," he said. "I won't breed her again. She deserves a rest."

"Yes, she does." Although he didn't know it, Astrid could offer to invest in his ranch and eliminate most of his money problems. She constantly battled the urge to do exactly that. But giving him money would change their relationship forever, and she selfishly wanted to keep that relationship as it was, even if friendship was all she'd ever have.

None of her clients realized she came from a wealthy family, and she preferred it that way. She'd learned from sad experience that being worth millions usually affected how people viewed her. She wanted to be seen as a competent professional who took her vocation seriously.

She might not need the money she earned, but she considered it validation that she was good at her job. Her parents wished she'd spend less time at work and more time at social events looking for eligible billionaires to marry. She didn't care to take the time right now. Eventually she'd want a home and kids, and she'd probably end up with a wealthy man. Her mother thought that was the only way to avoid hooking up with a fortune hunter, and there was some truth in that.

"Good, she's lying down again." Fletch went back into the stall. "Maybe this is it."

"Fingers crossed." Astrid picked up her bag and followed him.

He walked around behind the horse and glanced over at Astrid. "I hate that you have to be up so late, but I really need—"

"Don't give it another thought. I want to be here." Janis, and Fletch's concern for his favorite brood mare, had been her priority for some time. She'd reluctantly canceled a trip to Paris with her girlfriends because Janis's condition had been unstable. Now they were down to the wire, and she couldn't imagine being anywhere but here in this stall with the mare . . . and Fletch.

He hadn't owned the ranch long, only about three years, but he'd been a cowhand all his adult life, and the Rocking G was evidence of his ability to work hard toward a goal. She admired his grit more than she could say. Compared to him, she'd encountered no real obstacles in her quest to become a vet, unless she counted the expectations of her parents. They weren't pleased that she'd chosen a profession that included getting covered in blood and occasionally horse manure.

Although their snooty attitudes bothered her, she loved them deeply and couldn't deny how much they'd done for her, in spite of their disapproval of her choices. They'd paid for her extensive schooling, and her trust fund had financed her clinic. To completely ignore their wishes and advice on marriage would be ungrateful.

But sometimes she wished that she could be what Fletch assumed her to be—a self-made woman in the same way he was a self-made man. She wondered if he'd respect her as much if he knew her career had been handed to her on a silver platter. Maybe he wouldn't care. He seemed open-minded about most things. Still, she wasn't ready to test it.

For now, they had a birth to attend. And finally, Janis appeared ready to get the job done. Astrid knelt behind her and said a little prayer. This was the moment of truth. If the mare couldn't manage this on her own, Astrid was prepared to intervene, but that would require methods that would stress both mother and baby.

Fletch stroked Janis's neck as he'd done before and crooned encouraging words.

"That's good," Astrid said. "Keep talking to her." She had a sudden flash of what he'd be like in the delivery room waiting for his own child. He'd be solid as a rock, but empathetic, too.

"I'd sing her 'The Rose,' except my singing has been known to stampede cattle."

Astrid smiled. "I love that song." She wasn't surprised that he did, too. They connected on so many levels.

"You wouldn't after I finished singing it. You'd beg for mercy."

"Talking works just fine. I'm sure she senses your confidence in her." So did Astrid. Knowing he trusted her with an animal he loved did wonders for her self-esteem.

"I hope so. But I have to tell you, I'm sweating bullets."

"Join the club."

And then Janis groaned, heaved, and just like that, the process started. No matter how many times Astrid witnessed the birth of a foal, she was awed by the first thrust of tiny forelegs, followed by a nose, a neck, and finally, the entire baby horse, all wrapped in a glistening, semitransparent membrane.

Eleven months of effort culminated in one glorious miracle. She and Fletch had worried about this event for weeks, but the foaling, as with most equine births, took less than twenty minutes.

"Beautiful," Astrid murmured.

"Are we good down there?"

"We're good. We're so good." Astrid's chest tightened with gratitude. "Janis has a beautiful baby."

"Thank God." Fletch's voice was thick with emotion.

Astrid glanced up and caught a moment he might not have meant her to see. He buried his face against the mare's neck and murmured something she couldn't hear. Not wanting to embarrass him, she returned her focus to the foal, which seemed perfectly formed and healthy.

Janis had been Fletch's first brood mare, and the horse had obviously won his heart with her gentle disposition. He cared about the foal, too, but his biggest concern had been for Janis. Convinced that neither mare nor foal was in distress, Astrid scooted away to let Janis attend to her baby.

Fletch also sat back on his heels as the horse maneuvered so that she could lick her newborn clean. He gazed at the foal. "It's a colt."

"Yep. The ultrasound was right. You never can know for sure with those."

A grin lit his face. "And four white socks, like his mother's."

"He'll look a lot like her."

"I'd hoped for that. And now it's official. Buddy Holly is in residence at the Rocking G."

Astrid laughed. "Yes, he certainly is. They both seem to be doing great."

"I can order the nameplate for his stall now. I was too superstitious to do it before." Fletch's glance sought hers. "Thank you."

"You're welcome. But after all, it's my job."

"I know, but you don't treat it like a job. My previous vet did, which was why I stopped using him. I've watched you work with these animals. You put your heart and soul into it."

She couldn't imagine higher praise than that. "I love my work. That makes me a lucky lady."

"And I'm lucky to have found you."

Dear God, there *was* something more than friendship in those warm brown eyes. She swallowed. "Fletch . . ."

"I know." His jaw firmed. "You're my vet. I'm a client. I understand the parameters, but damn it, Astrid, does that mean we can't . . ."

Her heart beat as if she were a wild creature suddenly trapped in a net. "I think it does mean that."

"I could fire you."

"You could." That wouldn't remove all the barriers. She'd still be a very rich woman and he would be a financially strapped rancher. But he didn't know about that issue.

"I don't want to fire you." He got to his feet. "You're a fantastic vet, a thousand times better than the guy I had before. I can't imagine having anyone else now that I've seen how you work."

She took a deep breath and stood, too. "I don't want you to fire me, either." She looked into his eyes, which mirrored the frustration she felt. "I love having you as a client."

"Can't I be a client and something more, too? Who has to know? I'm certainly not going to make a big deal about it."

"Okay, let's say we're discreet." She picked up her bag and walked out of the stall. "What if we discover somewhere down the line that we're not right for each other? What happens to our client-vet relationship then?" She put down the bag and turned to face him as he stepped into the aisle.

His stance was wide, his expression calm, the epitome of confident male. "We wouldn't discover that. You and I get along great."

"In this setting, we do, but . . ."

"But what?"

She pictured dragging him to some charity ball hosted by her wealthy friends, or coaxing him to attend the opening of a show by some new darling of the Dallas art community. She'd been inside Fletch's home. He liked Western artists like Remington and Shoofly. He also didn't seem like the tux-wearing type, but now wasn't the time to reveal the difference in their lifestyles.

"Are you worried that we might not get along in bed?"

Oh, boy. Her hesitation had led him to the wrong conclusion. She wasn't worried about that at *all*. "I—"

"Lady, we would burn up the sheets." He smiled as he took a step closer. "And you damned well know we would."

"Maybe." The nearer he came, the faster her heart beat. It seemed to keep time with the rapid tattoo of the rain on the roof.

He chuckled. "I guarantee you do. I can see it in those baby blues. I wasn't sure until this minute, when I finally got the courage to broach the subject, but we're on the same page, you and I."

"Okay, so I'm attracted to you, but acting on that attraction would be a really bad idea."

He nodded. "You could be right. But that doesn't keep me from wanting to kiss you."

Oh. She should protest, should move back, out of the magic circle he'd created with his considerable charm. But she couldn't seem to do that.

"I know you have reservations about getting involved with me." He reached for her and cupped her face in his big hands.

She closed her eyes. That touch . . . so gentle, yet sure. She'd imagined his touch for so long, and now she allowed herself to savor it.

"I respect that," he murmured. "So for now, all I ask is one kiss, to celebrate the arrival of a new foal."

One kiss. One little kiss. Surely she could indulge herself a wee bit without compromising her principles. And they *had* successfully navigated Janis's problem pregnancy. They both deserved a reward for that.

"One kiss." His warm breath caressed her mouth, and his thumb brushed across her lower lip, urging her to open to him.

She didn't need much urging. Here in the privacy of his barn, shrouded by rain and darkness, she could act out a fantasy months in the making. *Yes*. She'd kiss Fletcher Grayson.

And if this was the only liberty she ever allowed herself with this man, she would give it all she had.

Two

When Astrid parted her lips and issued a silent invitation for Fletch to invade that sweet mouth, a hot stab of lust nearly swamped his noble intentions. He beat back the red haze short-circuiting his brain. If he came on too strong now, he could ruin his chances in the future.

The effort of holding back made him tremble, but he managed to touch down gently. He couldn't stop the groan that rumbled deep in his chest, though. His mouth fit hers with a kind of perfection he'd never known before.

As he settled in, the contact was so right that he became a little dizzy with the pleasure of it. The hitch in her breathing told him she wasn't immune, either. That ate at his control, but he wouldn't grab her and haul her into an empty stall mounded with fresh hay.

If he did that, they'd both be guilty of neglecting Janis and her foal. And he'd have broken his promise to give her one kiss, and one kiss only. He prided himself on being a man of his word.

Slowly, keeping himself in check, he began to explore

her mouth with his tongue. She tasted like the coffee they'd had earlier, and the raspberry Life Savers he'd taken from his pocket to share with her. When he thrust his tongue deeper, she moaned.

That moan nearly undid him. Any woman who made that kind of sound would not object if he turned one kiss into two, or twenty. He sensed her surrender and fought not to take advantage of it. It was late. She was tired. Her defenses were down. Most important of all, Janis still needed them.

But her lips were so ripe, so ready. Before he realized what he was doing, he'd slid both hands from her cheeks to her collarbone. Unless he put those hands to work somewhere else, he'd go lower. He'd cup her breasts, and then he'd unbutton her blouse. After that, all bets would be off.

Until he lifted his mouth, though, he was still involved in that one kiss he'd asked for. So he deepened that kiss and went to work on the clip she'd used to fasten her hair. Taking down her golden, silky hair wasn't the same as stripping away her clothes.

Or so he told himself. Yet his blood heated as his fingers encountered those soft strands and released them from the clasp. He let it drop and delved into those tresses with greedy hands. He'd wanted to release her hair and feel its softness ever since they'd met.

She'd always imprisoned it in some way, either with a clip, a bandanna, or a tie. He understood the practicality of that while she worked, but he'd longed for this—to stroke her unbound hair and let it sift through his fingers. Her hair made him think of sunbeams, and the tactile pleasure of touching it caused him to imagine caressing her bare skin and kissing those tender, moist places that would inspire more moaning.

They would be good together. He knew it with an unshakable certainty. But willing as she might be now, if she lost track of her duty to her patient, she'd hate herself and him. That was no way to begin a love affair.

With thoughts of their shared responsibility to the mare and her foal, he lifted his head and stepped back, releasing her. His breathing was unsteady, but thank God, so was hers. He wasn't in this alone.

She opened her eyes slowly, and the heat in her gaze told him all he needed to know. Her passion matched his. Now all he had to do was convince her that surrendering to it, in a more appropriate time and place, wouldn't brand her as unprofessional.

He understood the stakes, but he was willing to risk losing an excellent vet in order to gain . . . He wasn't ready to put a name to it. Not yet. He and Astrid needed more time, more intimacy, before he could think in those terms. But he saw the possibilities, and they were breathtaking.

His parents were a couple who had known the kind of devotion he yearned for in a partner. Now that he was older and could handle his grief, he could view the car accident as a blessing for them, in some ways. If either had survived alone, the pain of losing the other would have been crippling.

Astrid smiled, which was a beautiful thing to see when paired with her sparkling eyes. "That was lovely."

"Told you so."

"But you're still a client."

"And a man."

"Oh, I'm well aware of that."

"Good. The word *client* is so impersonal. I'd like to progress to *friend*."

"I already think of you that way, Fletch."

"You do? Hey, that's great. Then maybe we can move right past that designation. I'd like to suggest —"

"I'm sure you would." The sparkle remained in her incredible eyes. "But right now, I need to return to being your vet and make sure Janis continues to do as well as she can."

"You bet." He stepped aside immediately. By his calculation, the kiss had only lasted a few minutes. He'd packed a lot of sensory delights into those few minutes, but he couldn't imagine they'd been involved with each other long enough to cause a problem with the mare and her foal.

Astrid started into the stall and paused to comb her hands through her hair. "My hair's down." She seemed bemused by the fact.

"My fault." He scanned the wooden floor of the barn aisle and found the clasp lying there. He picked it up. "Here."

"Thanks." She scooped her hair back and fastened the clasp. "I didn't even realize that you'd done that."

"That's because I'm such a smooth operator."

She laughed. "I'll keep that in mind."

"For next time?"

"Nice try, cowboy. There won't be a next time. That was a delicious kiss, but we won't be — oh, Fletch! Janis is getting up!"

"I see that." He watched his brave girl struggle to her feet, and his heart swelled with pride. Despite her outstanding bloodlines, she'd been offered at a bargain price three years ago because she was past her prime. He'd feared if he didn't take her, she might end up in a bad situation or sold to a meat packer.

He hadn't bought her simply out of charity, though. He'd believed she could produce at least one more quality foal, and he'd gambled on that by paying an outrageous stud fee. The first attempt hadn't worked, but the second had resulted in this pregnancy.

When she'd run into problems, he'd questioned his judgment, but thanks to Astrid's excellent care, Janis had come through for him and delivered a healthy colt. Now she'd get her well-deserved rest.

Once Janis was upright, she began nudging her foal, Buddy Holly. Fletch had picked out the name after an ultrasound seemed to indicate Janis would have a colt. Sure, these rocker names were corny, but his mom had loved rock music. He was a sentimental sap and proud of it.

"Oh, my God. This is it." Astrid rushed back to her bag and pulled out a point-and-shoot camera. "This is the money shot. Buddy Holly is about to get to his feet for the first time."

Fletch hadn't even thought to bring a camera. Maybe he'd been a little superstitious about that, too. If he'd brought a camera and the worst had happened . . . But it hadn't, and Astrid was ready to record the moment.

He'd experienced this event several times with his other vet, and the contrast in that guy's response and Astrid's was dramatic. Where the other vet obviously had been eager to get the process over so that he could go home, Astrid behaved as if being here was a privilege.

No wonder he was so drawn to her. She understood the importance of honoring new life. He wanted her here every time a foal was born on the Rocking G. She had the kind of energy he craved.

The colt was shaky, and he took several tries to get up on those impossibly slender legs. But he kept at it with a determination that made Fletch's heart squeeze. Janis coaxed him to try again, and this time, he got all four legs under him and stood. His damp body quivered with the effort, but he was up.

Astrid let out a muted whoop of joy, enough to show she was thrilled, but not enough to scare the wobbly colt. She snapped picture after picture, and Fletch reminded himself to ask for copies. Something told him Buddy would be a remarkable colt, and an even more remarkable stallion. This birth could be the beginning of a legacy for the Rocking G. A shiver of anticipation raced up Fletch's spine at the thought.

He didn't think it was coincidence that Astrid was here to share this moment, either. He'd had a feeling about her ever since she'd climbed out of her truck that first day six months ago. She was a bitty thing, probably only about five-two, but her size didn't stop her from doing a bang-up job as a large-animal vet.

Although he didn't know a lot about her background, he figured she'd grown up on a ranch somewhere. He'd meant to ask her, but the timing had never seemed right. She knew far more about him, he realized now, than he knew about her. Time to fix that.

After Buddy began to nurse, Astrid left the stall and came to stand beside him. "Was that exciting or what?"

"Yep." He smiled at her. "Thanks for remembering a camera. You'll send me the pictures, right?"

"Absolutely. Part of the service." She tucked the camera back in her bag and stood. "Wow. Adrenaline rush." She blew out a breath and glanced at him. "The process will be pretty boring for the next couple of hours or so. I have to make sure Janis passes the entire placenta, and that can take a while. If you want to go to bed . . ." Her voice trailed off and she blushed a becoming shade of pink. "I mean, if you—"

"I know what you meant, although a proposition would be welcome right now."

Her cheeks still pink, she shook her head. "No can do. I'm already worried that we'll be uncomfortable working with each other after that kiss."

"We won't," he said quickly. That was the last thing he wanted. "I'll cut the loaded comments. I don't want you to think about dropping me as a client. That would be bad for my animals." And worse for him. He looked forward to her visits more than he'd been willing to admit.

"I would hate that, too. The Rocking G is my favorite call."

He longed to ask her if that was the ranch itself, or if the rancher had something to do with it. But he wouldn't say another word. He'd just hope that over time he'd win her over.

"Anyway, you don't have to stick around," she said. "I can finish up here alone and lock up the barn when I leave."

"I wouldn't dream of letting you do that. The rain's been constant, which means that usually dry gulch is full of water. I'm going to follow you as far as the bridge to make sure you get across okay."

"Fletch, that's not necessary. The bridge is sturdy and I'll be fine. Besides, I'm not a risk-taker. If I'm worried, I'll come back here and wait until the water goes down."

He folded his arms. "That's all good to hear, but I'm going with you as far as the bridge. Then, if you have to come back, I can give you breakfast while you wait."

"Okay." She sounded hesitant.

"Or were you trying to get rid of me because I make you nervous?"

"Maybe a little bit."

He sighed and let his arms drop to his sides. "I regret that. I can't make myself regret kissing you, but I'd hate to think I've messed up the dynamic between us."

"Let's just say it's not quite as relaxed as it was before."

"Then I'll work on that, which is a good reason for me to hang around. I'll prove to you that we can get along the way we always have."

"All right. Any more coffee left?"

"There is." He'd brought the biggest thermos he had for that very reason. "I'll get us some." Moments later he handed her a full mug. "Astrid, no matter what happens or doesn't happen between us, I want you to continue to care for my animals. That's a top priority for me."

She accepted the mug and wrapped both hands around it. "I could help you find someone. I realize your last vet wasn't very good, but I could recommend—"

"I want you."

Her eyes widened.

"Hell. I want you as my *vet*." Then honesty prodded

him. "I also want *you*, in the larger sense, but that is the last time you'll hear me bring up the subject. So, let's talk about something else."

She still seemed extremely wary. "Like what?"

"How about you? Your family? I realized tonight that I've rattled on about my parents and my dreams for the ranch, but I don't know much about your background."

Surprisingly, her wariness seemed to increase. "It's not very interesting."

She was hiding something. He couldn't imagine what, but for some reason she didn't want to talk about her family. For all he knew, her dad was in jail and her mother was a drunk. That would explain not wanting to discuss them.

"Sorry," he said. "I didn't mean to pry." He settled on an easier question. "But I would like to know how you ended up wanting to be a vet, if that's not too personal."

"Not at all." She brightened immediately. "I can tell you exactly what got me started. I read *Black Beauty* when I was eight years old."

"Yeah, me, too. But I didn't end up in veterinary school."

"No, but you work with horses. I was determined to do that, too. I was struck by the fact that they can't talk and tell us what's wrong, so it seemed like a wonderful challenge to learn how to diagnose their problems and see if I could fix them."

"I'll bet you were good in science."

"I loved my science classes, especially biology. I had this one teacher, Mr. Dudley. He was great. Let me tell you about this experiment he had us do. It was so cool."

And she was off and running, describing her journey

through the various stages of education that had resulted in becoming a licensed vet. Relieved to have found a safe topic, Fletch leaned against the stall and soaked up her enthusiasm. She'd loved every challenge, even the difficult college courses that required her to memorize every bone, tendon, and muscle in the body of a horse.

He was full of questions, some he'd never thought of until she explained important things she'd learned. As a horse owner, he needed to know more about the animals under his care, and now was a great time to get a minicourse in horse physiology.

She took breaks to check on Janis, and fortunately the mare was progressing exactly as she was supposed to. Even better, Fletch and Astrid had returned to the ease they'd enjoyed with each other before he'd kissed her. If he wanted her, and he absolutely did, then he'd have to be patient. Considering the potential reward, having the woman of his dreams, he could be very patient, indeed.

Three

Astrid was impressed with how well they passed the time without veering into dangerous territory again. She credited it to all the time they'd spent together before that lollapalooza of a kiss. They'd established their friendship firmly enough that they could settle back into it and put forbidden pleasures aside.

Sort of. During those couple of hours she'd had flashbacks to that electric moment when his mouth had claimed hers. She'd banished the thoughts immediately, but not before they'd kick-started her hormones. A low-grade sexual fever hummed beneath the surface, ready to spike at the slightest touch.

He was very careful, though. His hands never strayed close, and neither did hers. She didn't trust herself enough to allow even a slight brush of her hand against his.

Thank goodness he'd backed off when he'd figured out she didn't want to talk about her family. She wasn't being nearly as open as he'd been about his. Weeks ago he'd told her that he'd been orphaned as a teenager and the small inheritance he'd received had allowed him to make a down payment on this ranch.

Someday she might tell him about her privileged background, but not now, especially right after he'd kissed the daylights out of her. Sure, she could just say that her mom and dad lived in Dallas and she had no siblings, but simplistic answers like that inevitably led to more questions.

Frankly, she didn't know how they'd navigate from here on out. Until he'd kissed her, she'd yearned for him, but that yearning had been more in the order of a crush. Now that the object of her crush had stated his desire, her passion was a live thing, pacing the cage, searching for an escape.

Sharing the emotional high of a successful foaling hadn't helped matters any. She'd grabbed the camera because photographic evidence was important, but also because she needed to hold on to something and direct her energy elsewhere. Without the camera and an opportunity to take pictures, she might have been right back in his arms.

Once she drove away from here, she'd be able to put some psychic distance between them, too. Sleep would help. Her judgment was never good when she was sleep-deprived.

When she'd finally determined that Janis had passed all of the placenta and was successful nursing Buddy, she packed her bag and glanced over at Fletch. He had an endearing shadow of a beard, and his clothes were rumpled. He'd spattered coffee on himself at one point, and he'd plowed his fingers through his hair so often that strands of it stuck straight up.

She'd never been so taken with a man in her entire life. His disheveled appearance came from devotion to an animal, and she understood and admired that quality in him. Besides, he looked good all mussed. It gave him a rakish air.

He met her gaze. "Ready to head out?"

"I think it's safe. Janis shows no signs of infection or undue stress. I predict she'll be fine. You can certainly call me if you notice anything unusual, but I don't expect to hear from you until it's time for me to come back and give them both a check-up."

An emotion flickered briefly in his brown eyes. "That's good news." But his words were at war with the tone of his voice. "I'll get my keys and follow you to the bridge."

"You really don't have to. The rain's stopped."

His jaw firmed. "I'll get my keys." Taking his hat from the peg beside the stall, he settled it on his head and tugged the brim down. "Wait for me."

Whoa. She'd never been privy to this side of Fletch, an unbending commander of the troops. Then she remembered that his parents had died in an automobile accident. He hadn't said what kind of an accident, and she doubted they'd drowned in their car, but still . . . he would be extra cautious when it came to people taking chances in vehicles.

She'd honor that and wait for him. Making sure the stall door was securely latched, she walked out of the barn, closed the double door, and fastened the padlock in place. By the time she'd climbed into her pickup, he was on his way, his truck's headlights swerving as he navigated around puddles in the dirt road from the main house to the barn.

She was glad for his company, even though she'd wanted to save him the trouble. He had to be at least as exhausted as she was. But the road to the bridge was unpaved, and after the rain it would be thick with mud. Her four-wheel-drive should handle it, but in case it didn't, she'd be grateful to have him there to help pull her out.

Starting the engine, she put the truck in gear and began the slippery journey to the bridge. Her truck fish-tailed a couple of times, and she slowed down. Technically, she was in no hurry.

She'd planned for a relaxing Sunday—catching up on her sleep, doing some laundry, picking up takeout for dinner. She wasn't seeing her family or friends today, so she could spend the day in bed if she wanted to. When she got home wasn't particularly important.

Leaving the Rocking G, however, was extremely important. The sooner she did that, the sooner she could assess her situation in the privacy of her own space. In Fletch's magnetic presence, she couldn't think straight, and she worried that she'd do something unwise. Like kiss him again.

The memory of that kiss hadn't faded one iota in the time since he'd released her and stepped away. The velvet imprint of his lips remained on hers, and the thought of how he'd used his tongue got her juices flowing every time. That cowboy certainly knew how to kiss.

If he made love the same way, then the lucky recipient would be in for a real treat. Her imagination conjured up an image of Fletch stripping off his cowboy duds and climbing into bed with her. Mmm. Was she a complete fool to deny herself that kind of pleasure?

The blare of a horn snapped her back to reality. She'd meant to brake before crossing the bridge and assess the potential threat of high water. Lost in thought about a naked and sexy Mr. Grayson, she'd driven onto the bridge without pausing. Oh, well. She was committed now.

The span was about seventy-five feet, and the wooden structure quivered as water surged beneath it. And over it. Too late she saw what she'd missed earlier. The bridge was partly under water.

Perhaps only an inch or two covered the wooden planks, but the water was moving fast, and her truck's tires began to lose traction. She gripped the wheel and forged on. Had she stopped to look, she wouldn't have continued onto the bridge at all, but now she was nearly halfway across. Might as well keep going.

The groan of timbers was her only warning before the bridge collapsed under her. A frantic shout from the bank—Fletch telling her to jump—penetrated her terror for a split second. Then, as if in slow motion, her truck teetered for a moment before beginning its slide into the swirling stream.

Fletch's command rang in her ears. Unbuckling her seat belt, she reached for the door. Her truck might be lost, but she'd be damned if she'd go down with it. She leapt free right as the truck plummeted into the water.

She hit the surface and it hurt like hell, the same smacking pain as a belly flop into the pool. And God, it was cold. The momentum of her impact took her breath and dragged her under, but she immediately began fighting to get to the surface.

Fletch was out there, and if he knew where she was, if

he even caught a glimpse, he'd find a way to pull her out. She knew that more surely than her own name. Holding on to the thought of Fletch was like reaching for a lifeline.

Thrashing her way upward, she broke through the surface of the water. She wanted to yell, but she didn't have enough air left. Instead she turned upstream and clawed her way through the eddies to get back to the bank where she'd last seen Fletch. The pale dawn would help him see her. In total darkness she would have been lost.

"Astrid! Catch the rope!"

Through blurred vision, she saw him running along the bank. A rope sailed out, a loop at the end. She tried to grab it. She really tried, but the rope sank uselessly into the water just out of reach. She struggled toward it, but the water kept pushing it away.

"Hang on! I'm coming in!"

"No!" Her protest sounded weak, but she feared for him. The current was wicked. If he came in, they might both be lost. He should haul in the rope and try again.

But when she looked toward the bank, he wasn't there, which meant he was in the steam with her, that damned stupid man! He would never find her in this wild torrent. They would both drown, and then—

"Gotcha!" Breathless but triumphant, he hooked one strong arm under her breasts. "Now be still."

Unquestioning trust seeped through her, and she became pliant as a kitten caught by the nape of her neck. She'd heard of drowning victims who'd doomed their rescuers by flailing around. She'd already screwed up by driving onto a dangerous bridge. She wouldn't compound that by sabotaging his rescue efforts.

His labored breathing was punctuated by colorful swearwords as he swam with one arm and pulled her along with the other. She hated being a deadweight. Her clothes had to make her even heavier. He was swimming in his clothes, too, and that couldn't be easy.

The urge to help him was nearly irresistible. But he'd told her to be still. She forced herself to stay limp and let him do all the work. After what seemed like hours, but must have been mere minutes, her heels scraped bottom. She scrambled to stand.

"Be still." He gulped for air. "I'll navigate."

She slumped against him once more, and he hauled her up the bank like a sack of potatoes. At last they lay side by side on their backs in the mud at the top of the gulch. Their gasps mingled with the distant rumble of his truck's still-running motor and the gurgle of the water that had almost killed them both.

When she could finally speak, she knew what had to come first. "Fletch, I'm so sor—"

Her apology was cut off as he rolled on top of her and took her mouth in a kiss that was part desperation, part conquering hero, and one hundred percent sexual male.

All her repressed desire erupted in a flow of hot lust for this man, and she knew it would never be contained again. Grabbing his head, she kissed him back with a groan of surrender.

His tongue plundered her mouth as his hands eagerly roamed her body. He seemed determined to make sure she was all there, that the water had not swallowed her forever. She wiggled against him, aroused beyond belief by his questing hands and the sensual squish of mud beneath her. Even the scratch of his beard excited her.

They'd cheated death. They were alive. *Alive!* The jubilation of that filled her with an undeniable need to taste all that life had to offer. Right now, it offered Fletch, the man who'd saved her from drowning, and he deserved any reward he chose to claim. She wanted that magic connection as much as or more than he seemed to. If he chose to take her right here in the mud, it would be fine with her.

At first she thought he would. His hands were everywhere—stroking and squeezing with a frenzy that convinced her he had no intention of stopping until he was deep inside her. He fumbled with the snap of her jeans . . . and abruptly paused.

Lifting his head, he stared down at her, and gradually the wildness in his dark eyes gave way to tenderness. His ragged breathing slowed.

"Not like this," he murmured.

She gazed up at him, hiding nothing.

"You were going to let me, weren't you?"

She nodded.

"Ah, my sweet Astrid." He dipped his head again and kissed her softly. His breath was warm against her face. "I've already scratched your chin with my beard. We're going home so we can do this right." Rolling away from her, he got to his feet.

She sat up, but before she could stand, he was there, scooping her muddy body into his arms. "I can walk!" she squeaked out.

"I like carrying you."

And it turned out she liked being carried. No man had ever done that before, but then, no man had ever saved her from drowning, either. She nestled against him and felt the rapid beat of his heart keeping time with hers.

She had no doubt of his immediate plans, and the thought of those plans made her heart beat even faster. When they reached his truck, he braced her against the crew cab so he could open the passenger door.

"You should toss me in the back. I'm a mess."

"No more than me. This truck's seen mud before." And he set her gently in the seat. "Buckle up."

She did, although it hardly seemed necessary. He wouldn't be driving in traffic and he sure wouldn't be speeding along the muddy road. But he was a safety-conscious guy for a reason, so she buckled up.

While doing that, she gave a passing thought to her truck and the medical bag inside. Her phone was gone, too. The reality of losing all that hadn't penetrated yet.

In fact, nothing about this experience felt quite real. Driving across a semi-submerged bridge wasn't like her at all. A cautious person, she'd never before been in a life-threatening situation. She used to wonder how she'd react to imminent danger, and now she knew. She'd un-fastened the seat belt and jumped. That knowledge filled her with pride and confidence.

But she might not be sitting here in Fletch's truck, hale and hearty, if he hadn't come in after her. She looked over at him as he climbed behind the wheel and closed the door. "Thank you for saving my life." It sounded lame, but she couldn't think of a better way to put it.

He'd started to fasten his seat belt, and he glanced up in midmotion and frowned. "I sure hope your response to me wasn't all about gratitude."

She laughed. Maybe that was inappropriate, but she couldn't help it. He was so far off base.

Abandoning his seat belt, he reached for her. "You're

not getting hysterical on me, are you? Because I can take you to a clinic. We'll have to go the long way, but . . . or maybe I should call for a helicopter. You've had a shock. I should get you to some—"

"Dear God, Fletch. Please don't have me airlifted out of here." She cupped his bristly morning face in both hands. "Especially when you've just promised to take me to bed."

"So you really want to?" He massaged her shoulders. "You're not just going along with the idea because I saved you and you feel obligated?"

Obligated? That made her giggle some more. "I don't feel obligated, but you have to admit saving a girl's life is bound to affect how she feels about a guy."

His eyes darkened. "I don't want that to be the reason."

"It's not the reason." She stroked his prickly cheeks. "But it might be the excuse."

His frown disappeared and the rakish smile he gave her made him look like a swashbuckling pirate. "Okay, pretty lady. I can live with that. Let's go home."

Four

On the way back to the ranch, Fletch took his phone from its holder on the dash and called the sheriff's office. He wouldn't want someone to find Astrid's swamped truck and assume the worst. He said the truck's owner was safe with him and gave his number as a contact if the truck was spotted.

Then he called his foreman, Herman, and told him about the foal and the bridge being out. "We'll contact the insurance adjuster about the bridge tomorrow, after the water's gone down," he said to Herman. "Meanwhile, it's been a long night and I plan to get some shut-eye. Please check on Janis and Buddy, but don't call me unless there's an emergency." After he disconnected he looked at Astrid. "That takes care of my situation. What about yours?"

"No one expects to hear from me today. I usually hibernate on Sundays."

Now, that surprised him. "I didn't know that about you. I thought you might be a type A workaholic."

"I sort of am, but only six days a week."

He nodded. "Good to hear. Taking breaks is important."

"You, on the other hand, probably work seven days a week."

Having her mention his work schedule was a promising sign. Maybe this wouldn't be a one-morning stand. He hoped to hell not, but he wasn't making any assumptions. "Sometimes I work seven days straight," he said, "but I've been meaning to do something about that." He wasn't the type to lie in a hammock all day, though. He needed a compelling reason to clear his schedule once a week. Could be he'd found one.

"I notice you didn't say anything about me when you talked to Herman."

"Nope. You are none of Herman's business."

"What about Edna, your cook?"

"She takes Sunday off, so if you're hungry, you'll have to make do with me."

For some reason she found that funny. Then he thought about what he'd said and realized how she might have taken it. Damned if that didn't get a rise out of him, in a good but semi-uncomfortable way. Wet denim and a hard cock weren't an optimal combination.

But he intended to take care of both circumstances real quick. Pulling to the back of the ranch house, he turned off the motor and unfastened his seat belt. "I came around back so we can go straight into the laundry room."

"And that way we don't advertise that I rode back here with you. I appreciate that."

He gazed at her. "I'm not too worried about the folks who work on my ranch gossiping. If I ask them to keep their mouths shut, they will."

"I'd rather not have to ask them."

That made life a little more complicated, but he could deal. "Okay, then here's the plan. We go into the laundry room, shuck our clothes, throw them in the washer, and turn it on. Then—"

"What if we get turned on before the washer does?" Laughter danced in her blue eyes.

"I suppose we will, smart-aleck." He was glad she'd recovered enough from her harrowing experience to tease him. "But if we don't start the washer first, I guarantee we'll forget all about the damned thing and you won't have any clothes to wear home."

"Good point."

"Just trying to protect your reputation, ma'am."

Her gaze softened. "You're a sweet man, Fletch."

"Ouch. You really know how to hurt a guy."

"It was a compliment!"

"Maybe to you, but sweet men usually lose out to the reckless and the dashing kind. I'd rather you thought of me that way."

"I can't go with reckless. And you might have to deal with hero, since you did just save my life. But as for dashing, well, your beard gives you a real shot at that."

"Yeah?" He rubbed a hand over his chin and winced. "Too bad. It's history." He pocketed his keys and opened his door. "Stay put. I'll come around and get you."

"That's silly. I'm not some china doll who needs to be handled with care." She unsnapped her seat belt. "I can get out on my own."

He paused and turned back to her. "Obviously you don't understand that I look for every excuse to touch you. Stay put."

Her eyes widened. "Oh."

"Yeah, *oh*. Lifting you in and out of the truck makes me feel very macho, and you feel really good, so indulge me." She also might not be as steady on her pins as she thought.

"All right." Her voice had a cute little quiver to it, like maybe that idea was exciting to her.

When he came around to her side of the truck and opened the door, she held out her arms. "Please help me down, you big strong man, you."

"You try my patience, woman." But he lifted her out of the truck, and to his delight, she wrapped her arms around his neck and her legs around his hips. "That's more like it." He held her close and climbed the steps to the back door.

"Sorry. I didn't know the drill."

"You're kidding. Nobody's ever carried you before?" He fished out his keys and unlocked the door.

"Not since I was five."

"Then some guy's missing the boat." He got her inside just as the rain started up again. "A little thing like you is perfect for this." He had to wonder what kind of wimpy men she'd dated, but he didn't want to spend a whole lot of time on that subject. Thinking of her with other men could be crazy-making.

The laundry room was neat and smelled of soap and clean towels. Edna did light housekeeping for him, too, although he was a fair hand with a vacuum cleaner when necessary. Kicking the door shut, he set Astrid on the nearest available surface, which happened to be the dryer.

Then he stood back and just looked at her, astounded

that she was here, and she wanted to have sex with him. "Take off your clothes."

"Wow, that's romantic."

He cursed softly. "If I take them off, we'll never accomplish getting the washing machine started." He leaned against the wall and pulled off his boot. "I won't even watch you do it." After taking off the second boot, he turned away and began unbuttoning his shirt.

"Yes, but I can watch you."

"Don't." He pulled off the wet shirt and tossed it to the floor. "Focus."

Her soft laughter surrounded him like soap bubbles. "I've fantasized for months about seeing you naked. I'm not going to miss watching you strip."

He turned, his hands at the waistband of his jeans, and sure enough, she was staring at him. She hadn't removed a stitch of clothing. No, wait. She'd taken off her boots, which lay where she'd dropped them on the floor.

Blowing out a breath, he walked over to stand in front of her. "Guess this is up to me, after all." He reached for the top button on her blouse.

"Just don't forget to start the washer."

He looked into her eyes, and they burned with the same fire that licked through his veins. "You're a devil woman, you know that?" He kept unbuttoning.

Her smile taunted him. "You bring it out in me with all that macho he-man stuff."

His cock stiffened so forcefully that he sucked in a breath. "Careful, lady." He finished with the buttons but avoided looking at her breasts as he slid the shirt over her arms. "You're taunting the beast."

"Am I? I kind of like that idea." She reached out and boldly stroked his fly.

"Okay, that does it." Abandoning the washing machine plan without a single regret, he picked her up and carried her, protesting every step of the way, to his bedroom. "You're the one who wouldn't take off your clothes. Now, deal with it."

"But your quilt!" she shrieked as he tossed her down and unzipped her jeans.

"It washes." He pulled off her jeans and her panties in one swift movement, scattering dried mud and smearing the wet mud everywhere. He didn't care. After what they'd both been through, they needed this connection, and that trumped getting dirt on his quilt.

The glory of paradise awaited him between her soft thighs, and he trembled at the thought of burying his cock there. He'd meant to take this slow and treasure every second, but she'd goaded him, and by God, a man had his limits. Maybe she'd meant to push him past those limits because she was desperate, too.

He shoved his jeans and briefs to the floor, stepped out of them, and grabbed a condom from the bedside table drawer, aware that she watched his every movement as he put it on. "Am I shocking you with my lack of subtlety?" He braced his arms on the mattress where she lay sprawled across it, breathing hard.

"Yes. And I love it."

"Good answer." Grasping her hips, he pulled her to the edge of the bed, lifted her, and pushed in deep. He saw no need for foreplay, no reason to make sure she was ready for him. Her teasing words and the flame in her blue eyes had told him all he needed to know.

Knees braced against the mattress, he held her there, anchored by his cock, and closed his eyes for a brief moment of gratitude. Rain pounded on the roof with a frenzied beat, as if urging him on. He'd hoped, he'd dreamed, but he'd never known for sure this would happen.

Then he opened his eyes to find Astrid looking up at him with excitement shining in her blue gaze.

Her lips were parted and her breath came fast. "Do me," she murmured.

"Oh, I plan to." Holding her steady for his thrusts, he began to move. Focused on her expressive eyes, he glided in and out, loving her as he'd longed to for months. Her pupils widened as pleasure claimed her.

She responded as he'd known she would. Clutching handfuls of the quilt, she arched toward him, telling him without words that she wanted all he had to give. He wished he'd taken off her bra so he could see her breasts quiver each time he rocked forward.

But she'd tempted him beyond all endurance, and he'd skipped steps so that he could arrive at . . . this . . . pounding into her over and over, feeling her tighten around his cock, knowing that she was close . . . and closer still.

"Fletch . . ." Her plea was rich with passion. "Fletch, I'm . . ."

He dragged in air. "Hope so." He kept stroking, holding the rhythm steady, relentless. "That's the idea."

She whimpered, and then she came apart with a wail of surrender. That sweet sound would stay with him for a long, long time. He exulted in her climax, pumping faster to bring her higher, and higher yet.

Then his control snapped, and he drove in once more

with a groan of satisfaction. Pulsing within her, he touched heaven and knew that from this moment forward, he'd never be satisfied with anything less than making love to Astrid.

Drifting in the hazy afterglow of her climax, Astrid listened to the rain and wallowed in bliss. That, she concluded, was how a real man made love—with confidence and complete disregard for little things like mud on the quilt. After he'd eased away from her, he'd made sure she was settled comfortably on the bed before walking into the attached master bath.

He was a wonderful combination of masterful gestures and gentle consideration. She'd never found that before in a lover, but then, she'd never been in bed with a cowboy. She wondered if the nature of his work, caring for animals that depended on him to be both strong and empathetic, brought out those qualities.

Maybe, but she also thought he was naturally that way, which was why he'd been drawn to raising horses. Her work required the same qualities, and normally she reveled in taking charge. But letting someone else do that, someone she trusted, felt amazing. For the first time in ages, she was completely relaxed.

After disposing of the condom, Fletch returned and climbed into bed. He wrapped his arms around her, ignoring any leftover mud. "This needs to come off." Unfastening her bra, he tugged it free and tossed it over his shoulder onto the floor.

"Mm." He cupped her breasts and lazily brushed his thumbs over her nipples. "I hope we get to do this again sometime, because I have plans for these."

Tired as she was, she still responded to his touch with a tightening deep in her belly. His hands were calloused by hours of hard labor, which made his touch unlike any she'd known, and more exciting because of that. "We can probably do it again . . . when you're up to it."

"Better not say that." He looked into her eyes and smiled. "I might be up to it sooner than you think. And you need rest."

"You do, too." She should probably be considering the long-term ramifications of having sex with him instead of agreeing to more of it, but she didn't want to think about the future now. Living in the moment had far more appeal.

Clichéd though her response might be, his heroism and his take-charge attitude made her feel feminine and cherished, and she wasn't willing to give that up yet. Denying both of them this incredible pleasure would be straying into martyr territory, and she'd never been a fan of martyrdom. Plus the guy had an amazing package. There was that.

She ran her finger down the side of his jaw. "You've been awake as long as I have. And you had to drag me through the water while I just hung there doing nothing."

"You were breathing. That was all I cared about."

She cupped his face. "But you must be exhausted."

"I should be, but when I look at you, I get a second wind."

"You're high on adrenaline." She brushed her thumb over his cheek. His prominent cheekbones and deep-set eyes hinted at Native American ancestry. Just looking at him was a pleasure. But she noticed weary lines around those eyes. "We should sleep."

"Probably. Anyway, I'm not making love to you again until I've shaved off the stubble." He continued to caress her. "Your skin is like silk. I don't want to hurt you."

"Maybe I like the manly scrape of your beard on my breasts." She was certainly enjoying having his hands there.

"But it wouldn't be just your breasts." He held her gaze. "Eventually I'd move on, and you'd feel the manly scrape of my beard between your thighs."

Tension coiled within her. "I see."

"And once I get into that program, I like to make it last. So I'll shave first, so I can settle in and do the job right."

That reminded her of his agile tongue, and lust grabbed her in predictable places. "I think you know exactly what you're doing by talking to me this way."

He smiled. "What am I doing?"

"Making me hot."

"Is that so?" He slid one hand over her belly, tunneled his fingers through her curls, and began to explore while still massaging her breast. "You are pretty hot, at that."

She drew in a breath. "I thought we were going to rest."

"We will." He slipped his fingers in deeper with devastating effect. "In a minute."

She began to tremble. "This is crazy. I just—"

"That's what's so fun about ladies. They can come a lot. Guys, not so much."

She was in no position to argue about whether she could come again so soon, because she was about to. He understood exactly how to stroke her, how to make her whimper and shiver as her climax approached.

"Let go, sweet Astrid." He began pinching her nipple in the same rhythm. "Come for me."

She obeyed his command, arching her back with a wild cry of release. Afterward she lay with her eyes closed and a smile of pure joy curved her mouth. "Awesome," she whispered.

"Yes, you are."

Her eyes fluttered open. "It's you, Fletch. You're the awesomeness."

"It's us." He combed her hair back from her face and kissed her lightly on the mouth. "It's us."

Five

The last thing Astrid remembered was hearing the rain as Fletch traced the curve of her cheek with the tip of his finger and urged her to sleep. She must have done that instantly. When she woke up, she was on her side in the same position, so she hadn't moved at all. She'd been just that tired and just that relaxed.

But there were two changes to her situation. Fletch wasn't in bed with her anymore, and he'd obviously covered her with a blanket at some point. The light had shifted, and if she were to guess, she'd say it was afternoon, although it was hard to tell because the rain continued to fall.

Fletch had made coffee. She could smell it. Climbing out of bed, she noticed that none of her clothes remained in the room, either. She glanced around, taking in the room's décor for the first time. She'd seen the rest of the house briefly during visits to tend his horses, but never his bedroom, obviously.

The bedroom mirrored the other rooms, in that it looked like a decidedly heterosexual man had chosen everything without advice from a woman. The dark wood furniture—the bed, a dresser, and a rocking chair—were straightforward pieces without embellishments. The colors of the fabrics in the bed linens and the curtains were earth tones of green and brown.

The walls provided the most interesting element of the room—colorful vintage posters, all professionally framed. She wasn't an expert, but she recognized Elvis, which suggested the rest were of that era, too. Fletch had mentioned that his mother had loved classic rock, and Astrid wondered if the posters had belonged to her.

The aroma of coffee was joined by the tang of onions sautéing in butter. Her mouth watering, she wrapped herself in the light cream-colored blanket and walked out of the bedroom. It didn't matter what Fletch was cooking. She was starving and would eat anything.

The one-story house had a basic design. The master bedroom and attached bath were at one end, with the great room and kitchen in the middle. A second bedroom and attached bath, which now functioned as Fletch's office, was at the far end of the house.

She'd always liked the simplicity of the house. Although it wasn't particularly large or luxurious, it had some nice touches like granite countertops, hardwood floors, and good-sized windows. Most charming of all, Fletch had paid extra for a wood-burning fireplace made of native stone. Her first visit here had been during winter, and he'd had a fire going.

She hadn't stayed to enjoy it with him, because that wouldn't have been the professional thing to do. But she'd wanted to. She even thought that he'd wanted her to.

The image of sharing a cozy fire with him was lovely,

but winter was several months away, and projecting that far into the future wasn't a good idea. She was here now, and Fletch stood in the kitchen dressed in a clean white T-shirt and jeans. His back was to her as he stirred onions in the frying pan. The browning onions crackled enough that he obviously hadn't heard her bare feet on the wooden floor.

She took a moment to watch him cook before announcing her presence. In her world of privilege, guys didn't cook. They ate in restaurants or hired someone to cook for them. Normally, Edna would be here to cook for Fletch, but he'd obviously learned the skill at some point. She wondered if there was anything the guy couldn't do.

His dark hair was damp from a recent shower. If he'd showered and shaved in the master bath, she *really* must have been zonked. She suspected he'd gone to the other end of the house to clean up so he wouldn't disturb her. That would be a Fletch move.

A center island with stools on the living room side separated the kitchen from the rest of the large space. She slid onto one of the stools and cleared her throat. "You're being observed, Mr. Chef."

He turned, spatula in hand, and grinned at her. "I'd tell you what you look like wrapped in that blanket, but it would be politically incorrect."

"It was all I had. Someone stole my clothes."

He laughed and went back to stirring his onions. "Yeah, well, someone kept yammering about turning on the washer earlier this morning, so I decided to take care of that so I wouldn't hear about it when she woke up."

"What time is it?"

"A little past two. Not very late."

"You would have eventually come in to get me, right? You wouldn't have let me sleep for twelve hours or anything, would you?"

"No." He reached for a bowl with a whisk leaning in it, whipped the contents a few times, and dumped what looked like scrambled eggs in the pan. "I would selfishly have made you wake up so we could have sex again."

That made her giggle. "You're impossible."

"Impossible to forget, I hope."

"That, too." She leaned her chin on her hand. She could sit here watching him for a very long time and not get bored. His broad shoulders, slim hips, and excellent buns were worth the price of admission.

"Want coffee?"

"Love some."

"Want sex?"

"Eventually, but I want food first."

He abandoned his eggs and poured her a mug of coffee. "I anticipated that," he said as he brought her the coffee and set it on the island. "That's why I'm slaving over a hot stove, so I can provide you with enough fuel to become a tigress in the bedroom."

She looked into his brown eyes. "You are so full of it, Grayson."

"Yes, ma'am." He winked at her. "And I want to give it all to you. Now drink your coffee, and in a jiffy I'll have some scrambled eggs for you. And toast."

"What kind of toast? I'm particular about my toast." She couldn't believe how much fun she was having. She'd never kidded around with her boyfriends like this.

"It's cinnamon-raisin or nothing, sweetheart."

"Lucky you. That's my favorite."

He glanced over his shoulder. "Somehow I knew that. Don't ask me why."

"Why?"

He groaned. "You really are a pain in the ass. But I'll reveal my secret, because if I don't, you'll badger me until I do."

"You've got that right."

"A couple of months ago, you told me about a bakery in Dallas that makes amazing cinnamon-raisin bread. I think the mother of one of your friends works there."

"That's right. Melanie's mother."

"So the next time I was in town, I checked it out. Now I'm hooked. I buy in bulk and freeze it."

She took a minute to absorb the news that a chance comment from her had prompted him to change his shopping and eating habits. But she was no different. Ever since learning that he was into classic rock, she'd tuned in to a station that played that, which was how she knew who Buddy Holly was when he'd announced the foal's new name.

"Don't put too much importance on that." He opened a cupboard and took down a couple of plates. "I'm always looking for local businesses to support."

"Oh, I didn't," she said, lying through her teeth. "I do the same." She would never admit how she'd obsessed over him for the past six months.

"Yep. That's the value of talking to a variety of people." He dished out the eggs, took a couple of forks from a drawer, and brought the plates and forks over. "Here you go. Fuel up."

"Thanks, but you're making this sound like a pit stop at the Indianapolis 500. What exactly are you expecting of me?"

Grabbing his own mug of coffee, he rounded the island and sat down on the stool next to hers. He glanced over at her. "Nervous?"

"A little, yeah." Especially because she'd noticed that he'd shaved, and he'd made some explicit promises about what would happen once he'd rid himself of the bristle.

"Then let me ease your mind, pretty lady." He met her gaze. "Your clothes are in the dryer. They should be dry in another twenty or thirty minutes. If at any time you want me to take you home, you have only to say the word and it will be done."

"So I'm in charge?"

"As much as you want to be."

"Now, *that's* a loaded comment if I ever heard one."

His expression shifted from teasing to earnest. "Astrid, I've dreamed of having you in my bed ever since I met you. Forgive me if I'm eager to keep you there as long as I can. I won't be the one to call a halt. You'll have to do it. If I had my way, you'd stay . . . indefinitely."

It was quite an admission, one that made him vulnerable. Her heart ached, because she longed for that kind of simple attraction—a man and a woman who discovered how right they were for each other and allowed the relationship to progress naturally. But life wasn't that easy, and there were things about her that he didn't know, things that undoubtedly would change his perception of her.

But she kept the exchange lighthearted, for both their

sakes. "With only one set of clothes, staying indefinitely would involve way too much time in your laundry room."

He smiled. "Unless we forget about clothes completely."

"There's a thought."

"A most excellent thought. Now eat your breakfast before it gets cold."

"Yes, Mommy."

He laughed, and the potential for an awkward moment passed.

She dug into the breakfast he'd prepared, which was delicious. "Great food," she said between bites. "Where did you learn how to cook?"

"My mom taught me. She believed that a boy should be as handy in the kitchen as a girl. I had to do my own laundry, too, so you'll be happy to know I separate whites and colors."

"Excellent." She thought about her clothes. "I didn't have any whites."

"That helped. And for the record, your black lace bra and black panties are sexy as hell."

"So we're back to sex, are we?" She pushed away her empty plate and sipped her coffee.

"Don't I wish. But there's something I have to tell you. I wanted to wait until you'd finished."

Her chest tightened as she glanced over at him. "It's about the truck, isn't it?"

"The sheriff's department called. They found it."

"Where?"

"A long way downstream, a good twenty miles, at least. That water was moving fast."

"I know." She needed to hear this, but she didn't want to. Living in a bubble had been great. She'd pushed the accident to the back of her mind while she'd contemplated bedroom games with Fletch. No longer. An image of her truck being pulled from the stream, water spilling out of the cab, twisted her stomach into a knot.

"Damn. You look horrified. I didn't want to tell you at all, but I felt you needed to know."

"Yes, I do." She took a fortifying breath. "Was ... anything still in it?"

He shook his head. "Sorry. They think it was tossed against other debris. The tailgate is gone, and the driver's-side door. The cab and truck bed are both empty."

"So it's pretty beat up, I guess."

"Afraid so. They've towed it to a yard. I have the number if you want to call."

She recoiled at the idea. Eventually she'd have to deal with her wrecked truck, but maybe not today. "Did you say I would?"

"No. I told them you were still recovering from your ordeal and would be in touch when you got your bearings."

"Thank you."

His voice gentled. "Astrid, do you have good insurance? Is that what you're worried about?"

She glanced into his eyes, warm with concern, and thought how ironic it was that he was worried about the money. "I have good insurance. I'm just mad at myself for being careless. I shouldn't have driven over that bridge. I put myself and you in great danger and ruined a perfectly good truck, not to mention losing all those medical supplies."

"Don't be so hard on yourself." He slipped his arm around her shoulders. "We all have lapses. You'd been up all night. It's hard to be sharp when you're exhausted."

"I wish I could say that was the reason I didn't stop to look before I drove over the bridge. The fact is, I was fantasizing about you."

He blinked. "Me?"

"You, naked."

He seemed torn between horror and delight. "I'm not sure how I'm supposed to take that. Are you saying it's all my fault?"

"No! It's my fault for reliving that kiss when I should have been paying attention to the road. But if you weren't so damned sexy, then none of this would have happened!"

He was quiet for a moment. "Do you wish it hadn't?"

"No." She said it in a small voice, but honesty made her admit the truth, however damning.

"That's a relief. For a minute there I thought you were going to say that sex with me wasn't worth nearly dying and losing both your truck and everything in it." His mouth twitched, as if he wanted to smile but didn't dare.

But she saw the glint of amusement in his eyes, and the tightness in her chest loosened. "I was determined not to have sex with you, you know."

"I do know. And I was just as determined that you would, but I figured it would be a long, arduous campaign."

"Instead it was a short, arduous campaign." Her smile trembled a little. "I'll bet you've never had to go through so much trouble to get a woman into bed before."

"Can't say that I have." He squeezed her shoulder as he held her gaze. "But you are so worth it."

"So are you."

"Apparently I am, considering I make up for those missing supplies, a totaled truck, and potential loss of life."

Her smile became a grin. "Don't let it go to your head, Grayson."

"Too late. The more I think about your confession, the more I like it. An intelligent, beautiful woman drove blindly onto a dangerous bridge because she was mesmerized by the thought of seeing me naked. That's an epic tribute to my package."

"Good grief. I've created a monster."

"I mean, think about this for a minute. You lost all sense of self-preservation under the influence of that vision. I need to use my sexual powers more responsibly from now on. For example, don't ever have sex with me and then try to operate heavy machinery. You might—"

"Fletch!" Laughing, she grabbed his face in both hands. "Get a grip. You're good, but you're not *that* good."

His eyebrows rose. "Is that a challenge?"

Too late, she saw the warning light in his eyes. "No, I just—"

"I think it was a challenge, and this ol' boy never backs down from a challenge." With lightning speed he scooped her off the stool. The blanket fell away as he hoisted her over his shoulder, her bare bottom in the air.

"Put me down!"

"Not a chance." He carried her, squealing and pounding on his back, toward the bedroom.

"Stop this! I need a shower first!"

"You'll need a shower afterward, too, so let's not worry about that now, shall we?"

With no more ceremony than he'd shown her this morning, he tossed her down on the bed, but this time he followed her there, pinning her to the mattress with his large body. "Not that good, huh? We'll just see about that."

Six

Fletch wasn't about to let Astrid blame herself for what had happened on the bridge, especially after he understood why it had happened. If anyone should take the blame, he should, for kissing her in the first place. But because they were alive and frolicking on his bed, he didn't plan to wallow in guilt over that, either.

She wanted him, apparently far more than he'd ever imagined, and that was the best news he'd heard yet. She no longer mentioned the stumbling block that he was a client. As he kissed his way down her warm, silky body, he was fairly sure she didn't think of him as a client right now.

When he reached her moist triangle of blonde curls and used his tongue to find that all-important spot where her orgasms lived, he doubted she was thinking of anything. That's exactly what he wanted, to distract her from the scary events of the morning and remind her of the pleasure they could enjoy in this bed. Judging from her moans and the pressure of her fingertips against his scalp, he was succeeding.

He gave her one quick climax to lay the groundwork, and then he nestled more securely into the cradle of her thighs and slowed the action. He loved taking his time on the second go-round, loved building the pressure and backing off, increasing her excitement and easing back. The erotic taste and scent of her hardened his cock, but his cock would have to wait. This was all about giving her the orgasm that she'd begged for, one that had been promised for so long that when it arrived, it would rock her world.

When she began to thrash around, he knew he was achieving his goal. Her moans grew louder, and she even—this made him smile—started to swear. She saved the begging for last, with a few threats thrown in.

He hoped she'd make good on them, because he enjoyed this game, too. He wouldn't mind having her full mouth give him some payback for what he was doing to her now. In fact, he was counting on her need for revenge, because in this case, revenge would be sweet for both of them.

But he was struggling with his own needs, too, and finally he burrowed in and gave her what she'd pleaded for, because he couldn't wait much longer for his own climax. She yelled as she tumbled over the edge, and then yelled some more as the spasms rolled through her. Breathing hard, she collapsed on the bed.

While she lay gasping, eyes closed, he worked fast to unzip and grab a little raincoat out of the drawer. He didn't bother taking off his clothes. This one would be fast. Moving over her, he knelt between her thighs.

"My turn," he murmured. His mouth, flavored with her passion, settled over hers as he slid home. He'd thought she was wrung out, but she lifted her hips and squeezed his cock in welcome. Then she wrapped her legs around his, locking him in. Her arms came around his back, and he felt the imprint of her fingers.

Okay, then. Maybe she could come again. He revised his plan of quick and easy. Her tongue met his as he began stroking deliberately, shifting his angle, absorbing her response. Oh, yeah. She was right there with him.

Heat shot through his veins as he realized that he'd found a woman who could take what he had to offer and be ready for more, a woman with a sexual appetite for him that matched the one he had for her. He'd despaired of finding such a woman, yet here she was, her body moving in perfect rhythm with his. His climax neared, but so did hers. He could feel her tightening.

Lifting his mouth from hers, he looked into her flushed face. "Open your eyes," he murmured.

Her lashes fluttered, and she looked up at him. Her eyes were so dark they were almost navy. She gulped for air. "You are . . . that good."

"So are you, lady. So are you." Holding her gaze, he increased the tempo, and in seconds, they came, their triumphant cries mingling as they shuddered in each other's arms.

Slowly the rocking stopped, the trembling stopped, and he could breathe almost normally. But he couldn't stop looking at her, and she seemed equally focused on him. She opened her mouth as if to speak, and then . . . didn't.

He took the risk. "Okay, I'll say it. It's never been this good."

Gratitude shone in her eyes. "You're braver than I am.

It's never been like this for me, either, but ... I think you're more experienced than I am, and I wondered if maybe you always—"

"No." He shook his head. "Not like this. I've never felt so completely in tune with a woman as I do with you. That's why I wanted to see your eyes. I needed to make sure you knew it was me making love to you and not some anonymous guy."

She stroked his back. "You could never be anonymous. You're an amazing lover, Fletch."

"Careful. You know how easily I get an inflated opinion of myself."

"Justifiably so, too. You just changed my whole outlook by hauling me into this bed and having your way with me. I was on the blame train headed nowhere, and you derailed me. Thank you."

"You're welcome, but I had my own selfish motives. It's tough to have good sex with an unhappy lady."

She smiled. "Well, you've made me a very happy lady. You should probably patent that thing you do with your tongue."

"Thanks."

"How does that work, exactly?"

He chuckled. "Trade secret. But I'm glad you like it. And that you're happy. Ready for that shower now?"

"If you'll wash my back."

"I'll wash your back, your front, and everything in between." He waggled his eyebrows. "All the better to touch you, my dear."

"Something tells me this is going to be a very long shower."

*   *   *

They ran out of hot water before they ran out of fun things to do in Fletch's shower stall. Astrid loved the sexy play, which wasn't so much about achieving orgasms as it was about thoroughly exploring each other and splashing water everywhere. They cavorted in the spray like a couple of kids. She'd never seen this uninhibited side of him, and he brought out the silliness in her, too.

When the water turned cold, they dried each other off and mopped up the mess they'd made. She didn't realize until they were almost done that this morning's horror had faded during their long shower. Earlier today, water had been her enemy. How healing it was to reacquaint herself with water as a friend. She didn't know if Fletch had meant to do that, but she wouldn't be surprised. He had depths she'd suspected but never seen so clearly before in the months she'd known him.

She handed him a pile of soggy towels. "We should go see Janis."

"We should. That's a great idea. Herman sent me a text saying she was doing fine, but I'd like to check it out myself. I'll get your clothes."

And her clothes would be dry by now. Even though Fletch could be spontaneous, he also kept track of things, like knowing her clothes needed to go into the dryer before they took their shower. That kind of attention to detail impressed her and fostered her trust.

He returned quickly with her jeans, shirt, and underwear. He'd dried the bra, but she wasn't about to complain. A guy wouldn't think of air-drying anything, and they didn't have time for that, anyway. She was grateful for the warm, clean clothes.

"I won't be able to take vital signs for Janis or Buddy,"

she said as she pulled up her jeans and fastened the snap. "But I should be able to confirm whether all is well, even without my instruments."

"I look forward to hearing your professional opinion."

The huskiness in his voice made her glance up. He gazed at her bare breasts with a soft glow of desire in his eyes. On cue, her nipples tightened.

"Sorry." He looked away. "You're just so beautiful. I'm sort of obsessed with your naked body. Hope you don't mind."

"I don't mind, but under the circumstances, you probably shouldn't try to operate heavy machinery."

He laughed so hard he had to wipe tears from his eyes. "You are a kick, Astrid Lindberg."

"I am?" She'd never thought of herself that way. Intelligent, yes. Reasonably good-looking. Efficient. But no one had ever accused her of being a kick. She liked it.

"You absolutely are. I never know what's going to come out of that luscious mouth of yours." He snapped his shirt. "That reminds me that during certain events this afternoon, you made some dire threats against my person."

Arching her back, she fastened her bra. "I did, didn't I?" She tried to be nonchalant about it, but remembering the circumstances under which she'd made those threats caused her to throb with longing. Moisture gathered between her thighs, and her nipples ached.

"So what I want to know is . . ." He paused to tuck his shirt into his jeans. "Were those idle threats or serious ones?"

"Very serious ones."

"Thank God, because if you want to know my overriding fantasy, it involves your mouth and my cock."

She sucked in a breath. "You're a terrible tease, Fletcher Grayson."

"So they say." He didn't seem worried about it.

"We're headed down to the barn to check on your mare and her foal. You know damned well I'll think about that the whole time we're down there."

"You will? That's awesome. And bonus, you won't be called upon to operate any heavy machinery."

She grabbed her shirt and stuck her tongue out at him.

"Wow, a preview. Now I'm really excited."

She finished buttoning her shirt and started toward the door. "Not me. I'm cool as a cucumber."

"Liar. Even though you're wearing a bra and a shirt, I can see your nipples poking out."

She glanced back at him. "And I can see the bulge in your pants, hotshot. Shall we go, or can you walk?"

"I can walk just fine." He winced, but he kept his stride steady as they left the house and stepped outside. The afternoon had been cooled a little by the rain, but some late sunshine had made the air muggy.

Astrid glanced around as they walked the short distance from the house to the barn, which was three times the size. Fletch had put the bulk of his money there, which made sense because he was only one guy who didn't need much space, and his future success was tied to the horses he housed in the barn. "Where is everybody?" she asked. "The place seems deserted."

"We feed early on Sunday so everyone can take off and have time for personal business."

"That's a nice thing to do for your hands, but I'll bet you stick around and keep an eye on things."

"It's my ranch." He said it with pride.

"Guess I'll need to come out and visit you on Sundays, then." That would suit her better, anyway. Better for her to hang out with him than the other way around.

His glance was quick and intense. "You'll do that?"

"Yeah, I'll do that."

His smile took her breath away. "Good."

She felt a pang of guilt. No telling where this was going, but she could tell they were both becoming invested very quickly. Maybe eventually she'd be able to tell him about her background, and he'd be okay with it. Maybe her parents would understand that he was not a fortune hunter, and they wouldn't subject him to the third degree.

And maybe none of that would work out, and the relationship would crash and burn. But she couldn't give him up. Not yet. They might tire of each other, and that would solve everything. Fat chance. She was as likely to tire of Fletch Grayson as Janis was likely to win the Kentucky Derby.

He fished a key out of his pocket and opened the padlock securing the double doors into the barn. He left the doors open so the late-afternoon sun could light their way as they walked back to the foaling stall. Astrid thought of all that had happened since she'd left this barn mere hours before. She couldn't regret any of it.

Mother and son lay in a bed of clean straw. Janis was awake and alert, and Buddy was curled against her side, fast asleep. His coat looked good, and his breathing was even.

"Hey, girl." Fletch spoke to Janis. "Nice kid you got there."

Janis nickered, but she didn't get up, as if she didn't want to disturb her sleeping baby.

"I have the feeling she's ready to settle in for the night," Astrid murmured.

"Me, too." Fletch slipped his arm around Astrid's waist and drew her close to his side. "Messing with them now seems wrong. Janis has it under control."

"She looks calm. No signs of distress."

"That's what Herman said, but I like seeing for myself. Look at those identical white socks on her and Buddy. I'm stoked about that."

"They'll be a photogenic pair." Wrapping her arm around his waist, Astrid snuggled against him and enjoyed the shared moment of contemplating mother and foal. "I'm surprised you haven't piped rock tunes into the barn."

"Don't laugh. I thought about it. But the hands are into country. I could get away with some crossover tunes, but they'd rather have Johnny Cash than Fats Domino. I decided to scrap the concept for now."

"Except you're the boss. You could pipe in whatever you wanted."

"Well, yeah, but what's the fun in that? It's tough to get good work out of unhappy ranch hands."

"So your goal is to make everyone happy so they'll perform better?"

"Yep. Not very complicated. But you have to remember that my parents were both teachers. I grew up on behavior-modification techniques."

"It's a smart approach, Fletch. I predict great things for the Rocking G."

He glanced down at her. "That means a lot to me."

She met his gaze, and the atmosphere crackled. Maybe one day they wouldn't look at each other and feel this sexual tension, but that day hadn't arrived. His lack of inhibition had made her bolder, and she licked her lips. "Hey, there, gorgeous. Any dark corners in this barn?"

His throat moved in a slow swallow. "Could be."

"Care to direct me to one?"

"I'd be a fool not to." With his arm securely around her waist, he pulled her away from the foaling stall and guided her down the aisle to an empty stall shrouded in darkness. "Will this do?"

"Looks perfect." She reached out and unlatched the stall door. "Come with me, cowboy."

Moments later, she knelt in the fresh straw and drew his zipper down. "About those threats . . ."

His breathing rasped in the silence broken only by the restless movement of horses. "Lady, you're full of surprises."

"Gonna stop me?"

"Not on your life."

Seven

Among the new experiences Fletch had discovered with Astrid, getting a blow job in the privacy of his barn was high on his list of favorites. He'd never look at this particular stall the same way again.

But the ecstasy he'd enjoyed in the barn was short-lived. As they walked back to the house, arms around each other, cozy as could be, he asked her what she wanted him to cook for dinner.

"I should probably go home."

The joy seeped right out of him. "Why?"

She laughed. "Because I live there."

"I know, but you could spend the night here and I'll drive you back in the morning. We can leave as early as you want."

Even though she'd alluded to coming back to visit him on Sundays, that was a week away, and so much could happen in a week. She could change her mind, for example. He didn't want her to leave yet. One more night in his bed would solidify their relationship a little more.

"I'm tempted to stay." She snuggled closer as they reached the steps leading up to his front door. "But tomorrow will be crazy. I'll have to rent a vehicle, cancel the appointments I can't keep, get the insurance paperwork rolling, order new sup—"

"I have a truck you can borrow. In fact, you can take mine and I'll drive the clunker until you get wheels." Wow, was he a genius or what? Loaning her his truck would keep them connected.

"That's extremely generous, Fletch, but there's a small problem. My driver's license is somewhere downstream."

"Oh. Right. You'll need someone to take you down to the DMV tomorrow. If you need—"

"I'll ask my friend Melanie to take me. She can also drop me off at the rental place later."

"You're sure you don't want to borrow my truck instead?" It was a last-ditch effort, and he knew she didn't really need the truck. Her insurance would cover a rental.

"Thanks, but I'll be fine. I just need a ride home. I hate to make you go all the way to my clinic and back, especially because you'll have to take the long route, but I don't have much choice."

"I don't mind." He turned her to face him. "But I sure wish you'd stay tonight. You won't be able to accomplish anything until tomorrow morning, anyway. Like I said, I'll take you back nice and early. Nobody has to be the wiser."

She sighed. "I realize that, but I still think it's better if you take me back now."

"Why? Who will know when you pull in?"

"Me."

He blew out a breath. "I'm beginning to understand. If you leave now, you can explain your activities with a clear conscience."

"Exactly. I'll make the obligatory calls to family and friends tonight. I'll say it took a while for me to recover from almost drowning, which is true. Then you drove me home. I won't be telling the whole truth, but I won't be lying, either. If I stay tonight . . . well, I can't make those calls, and explaining where I've been all this time would be . . . awkward."

"I take it you'll have to do some explaining?" He wondered who she answered to. Her parents? Another man? His gut clenched. "Astrid, if there's a guy in the picture, I deserve to know that."

"No guy. Just friends and family."

"And they would disapprove of you spending the night with me?"

She didn't answer right away. "Maybe," she said at last. "In any case, you said yourself that this is our business. That's why you didn't tell Herman I was coming back home with you, remember?"

"Yeah, I remember." He'd wanted to protect their privacy then, when everything was new and tenuous. He hadn't been sure how things would go between them. But they'd had a terrific time, both in and out of bed, and now he didn't care who knew they were involved.

But she did. Although that might have to do with him being a client, he couldn't shake the suspicion that her caution stemmed from something else. If he kept probing, he might find out, and he might not like it.

Pushing the matter now didn't seem like a good idea. They'd had some good times, and now she wanted to leave. He had to let her go and hope that when they met again, they'd be on the same footing as they had been today.

He released her. "Guess I'd better get the keys and a couple of rags. The seat's still a mess."

The ride back to her clinic and the apartment she'd had the contractor build above it was largely silent. Fletch wasn't happy with her decision to keep their relationship secret, and she didn't blame him. He'd saved her from drowning, and something that dramatic eliminated any vet-client barriers between them. No one would condemn them for forging a bond over that life-threatening episode.

Consequently, she couldn't trot out that excuse anymore, which left her with no obvious reason to conceal her liaison with Fletcher Grayson. She'd boxed herself into a corner and wasn't sure how to get out without causing pain for both of them. She could deal with her own pain, but she hated the idea of inflicting it on him.

For six months she'd allowed him to believe that she was a struggling veterinarian much as he was a struggling horse breeder. Now that they'd become lovers, she didn't know how to tell him that she was the daughter of one of the richest families in Dallas. Or that her parents wouldn't be overjoyed that she was seeing a rancher who operated on a slim margin of profit.

She could imagine the conversation she'd have with her parents. Her mother would advise her to end the relationship before things got sticky. Her father, an overbearing man who assumed he ruled the world, might take it upon himself to pay Fletch a visit to explain why he should give up this romance. Medieval though the gesture might be, her father was capable of offering Fletch money to stay away from his daughter.

She shuddered at the indignities Fletch might endure because of her. He had no idea, and that was entirely her fault. She wanted to protect him, at least until she figured out what she was going to do. Somehow, some way, she had to tell him the truth about her background, and she didn't know how on earth she'd do that.

When he pulled up in front of the clinic, a light shone from her upstairs apartment. She'd put a lamp on a timer so that she wouldn't walk into darkness. That lamp was a Tiffany style that probably cost more than Fletch cleared in a month.

The rest of her furniture was equally pricey. But common courtesy dictated that she should invite him to come up, and she just had to hope he didn't notice that she was surrounded by expensive items. The apartment was relatively small, so maybe he wouldn't think much about what was in it.

She'd grown up with nice things, and had been taught to have expensive taste. She hadn't thought twice about buying a high-quality sofa and chairs, along with a gorgeous cherry dining set. The art on her walls was original, and her china Wedgwood and her glassware Baccarat.

As she led Fletch up the interior stairway to her apartment, she told herself that guys usually didn't notice such things, especially if they weren't used to seeing them. Last year she'd dated a commodities trader with a hefty bank account, and he'd commented on everything in her apartment. Then he'd proven that although he knew how to make money, he had no clue how to make love.

Astrid's mother and father had heartily approved of

the commodities trader, who'd kissed like an oxygen-deprived trout and had cold hands and a scrawny chest. All the money in the world wouldn't make up for that combination in her bed on a chilly winter night. She'd said as much to her mother, who had promised to help her find a billionaire who was a good kisser, had warm hands, and sported a manly chest.

Meanwhile Astrid had discovered a rancher who had all those attributes and even more important ones—like compassion and honesty. He was only minus the hefty bank account, so her parents would assume he was after her money. Acceptance would be very slow in coming, if it ever came at all. Meanwhile Fletch would be subjected to scrutiny he didn't deserve.

"I'll make us some coffee," she said as she topped the stairs. "And I have some shrimp in the refrigerator, and some leftover risotto. We could make a quick meal out of that."

"Fancy eats." He climbed the stairs behind her, his boots noisy on the wooden steps. "But you don't have to feed me. Coffee's fine. I could use a little caffeine for the drive back."

This was the point at which she should invite him to stay, but if she did that, her plan to call friends and family tonight would go out the window. And she'd be forced to disguise her behavior even more.

"At least stay for some food," she said. "You fixed me brunch, so let me offer you a little dinner." She walked into the apartment, flicking on lights as she went. "It's the least I can do."

"Maybe you should just give me coffee."

His tone suggested she might want to take stock of

the situation. He stood in her small living area, feet planted, his Stetson shading his eyes, his hands at his sides. He looked tense.

She had a good idea what was bothering him, but she asked him anyway. "Why not stay for some dinner?"

His chest heaved. "We're alone in this apartment. I don't have my hands on the wheel, so I want them to be on you."

Heat washed over her. "I don't have any . . . I'm not prepared with . . ."

His laugh was rough with desire. "You think I left that to chance?"

"No, I guess you wouldn't." She swallowed. If she brought a real man into this apartment, she could expect that he'd act like one, with no hesitation whatsoever. That thrilled her right down to her toes.

"So the way I see it, we have two choices. You can make some coffee and I'll pretend that I'm not thinking of stripping you naked and taking you on the first available surface, or you can heat up the shrimp and risotto, and we'll settle in for the night. Up to you."

"Or . . ." She walked around the sofa to stand in front of him. "You can strip me naked and take me on the first available surface, and we can have shrimp and risotto later."

With a groan, he swept her up in his arms with such force that his hat tumbled to the floor. "Where's your bedroom?"

"First door on the right." Once again, she was being carried to bed, and she was growing fond of the custom. A night-light from the attached bath filtered in just enough that he could find the bed without stumbling.

He didn't toss her down this time. He laid her on the comforter with great care. She sensed that he wouldn't be as reckless when it wasn't his house.

Then he undressed her slowly, interspersing the process with many kisses. He did it well, but then, he knew the territory and he knew the clothes. He'd laundered them himself earlier today.

When he was finished, he stood and made short work of removing his own clothes, but not before he fished a condom out of his jeans pocket.

As the wrapping crinkled, she couldn't help laughing. "And I thought you went to fetch your keys and cleaning rags."

"A condom doesn't take up much room in a guy's pocket." The latex snapped as he sheathed himself. "And tucking one in there for good measure is never a bad idea."

"No." She opened her arms and welcomed him. "It's not." And then he was there, filling her the way only Fletch could do. His warm body covered hers, and she wondered how she'd ever imagined sending him away with nothing more than a cup of coffee.

He settled into the sweet rhythm they'd discovered worked for them, and she rose to meet him as glorious tension filled her with anticipation. For this, she would risk most anything. But she didn't want to risk Fletch's pride.

His breath warmed her ear as he thrust deep. "Way better than coffee."

"Yes." She arched into his embrace. "Way better." And she came with such abandon that she surprised herself with her wild cries.

"I like that," he said, breathing hard. "I like when you go a little crazy. It makes me ... go crazy ... too ..." Pumping fast, he found his orgasmic bliss and cried out as he shuddered against her.

She held him fast for long moments after that and wondered how she'd ever imagined they would not make love here. The passion between them ran too deep. Besides, Fletch had a need to position himself in her world, and this was an obvious way to do it.

That need worried her, because it would put him on a collision course with reality. She had to find a way to tell him about the money, the incredible wealth, but she wouldn't come out looking very good during that confession. She wanted to keep his good opinion of her, and that seemed impossible.

So she put off the telling and fed him shrimp and risotto, along with good strong coffee, and sent him back to the ranch with many lingering kisses. The sex and the food seemed to have distracted him from his surroundings, and she gave thanks for that.

When his truck pulled away, she watched from her second-story window as the red taillights disappeared. Then she crossed to her landline phone, speed-dialed her mother, and prepared to give a very edited version of her weekend.

Eight

Astrid had known from the minute she called Melanie to beg for some chauffeur service that she'd spill her guts about Fletch. Melanie Shaw was one of Astrid's two best friends in the world, the other being Valerie Wolitzky. They'd joined the same sorority in college, and because they were all only children, they'd bonded like the true sisters they'd each always wished for.

Their personalities complemented each other and they became inseparable. Big-hearted Melanie, with wide gray eyes and hair she described as plain brown, was the nurturer in the group. Astrid was the driven one, out to prove that she was more than a rich socialite, while redheaded Val was the brain who'd gone on to law school.

After graduation they'd all remained in the Dallas area, which meant they could continue to see one another often. Melanie had grown up on a small ranch and continued to work for her dad, but she'd recently become engaged to billionaire Drew Eldridge. Melanie was the perfect person to give advice about how to navigate financial inequality in a relationship.

"Maybe your rancher guy would be fine knowing you're rich," Melanie said as they waited their turn at the DMV.

"Maybe. But I wish I'd told him in the beginning." Astrid sighed. "I didn't, though. In fact, I took pains to disguise it. I'm afraid that if I tell him now, I'll seem dishonest."

"You have to tell him, though." Melanie's gray eyes filled with compassion. "I know it won't be easy, but if you really like him . . ."

"I really like him."

Melanie smiled. "You should see how you light up when you say that. In all the years I've known you, I haven't seen that expression when you talked about a guy. I'm excited for you."

"My parents won't be. So let's say I manage to admit I'm wealthy without driving him away. You know what comes next. I have to introduce him to my mom and dad."

"But he's a hero, right? He saved you! They must want to meet him."

"Oh, they do. They want to give him money. He'd be so insulted. Before I take him over there, I have to convince them not to do that, or it will be a complete disaster."

"I agree." Melanie nodded. "Ixnay on the oneymay."

"As I said, they're excited to meet him, but as my rescuer. If I introduce him as my boyfriend, they'll roll up the red carpet immediately."

"Okay, I know something about this scenario. Drew's parents weren't thrilled with our engagement, either. But here's the bonus. Drew stood strong in the face of their disapproval. If I hadn't been in love with him before, I would have fallen like a ton of bricks when he proudly told his mother and father that he was the luckiest guy in the world to have me as a fiancée. Because he really feels that way, his folks are coming around."

Astrid thought about that. "It's a good point. I guess they mostly want me to be happy."

"That's right, and when you demonstrate how happy Fletch makes you, and they get to know him and realize he's not after your money, everything will be okay."

"I hope so. I swear, if my father makes one snide remark—"

"Don't let him get away with that. Be strong." Her gaze was steady. "It's your life."

Astrid regarded her friend with new respect. "That trip to Paris stiffened your spine, didn't it, girlfriend?"

"It did. I wish you and Val had gone like we'd planned, but—"

"Then you wouldn't have discovered your own strength, or met Drew. It worked out the way it was meant to."

"And this will, too."

Astrid groaned. "I still don't know how to tell him I'm wealthy. And after I do, even if he seems okay with it, will there be awkwardness?"

"Like what?"

"Well, in your case, you can just move into Drew's elegant home. If Fletch and I decide to be together, then how do we handle the fact that I'm used to pricier digs than he is?"

"I do like Drew's home and I was happy to move there. But how do you want to handle it?"

Astrid thought about Fletch's house—the simple

lines, the rock fireplace, and especially his big bed. She smiled as the truth dawned. "I could be very happy in his house. Sure, I have expensive furniture, but I don't *need* expensive furniture. It's more habit than anything."

Melanie laughed. "I know. You've never been a snob. I can't imagine why you're worried about different life-styles. You live way below your means. Your parents don't, but who cares? It's your—"

"It's my life. I get it. I get it!"

"Yay! Problem solved! The two of you can have a blast shopping at big-box furniture stores."

Astrid winced. "Maybe not."

"Okay, estate sales, then."

"That's more like it. But there's something else. He operates on a very slim profit margin. Sometimes he goes without one thing so he can afford another. I could change all that, and I'd want to help him prosper, but how will he feel about accepting money from me?"

"One way to find out." Melanie chuckled. "Astrid, you can bat this around for as long as you want, and look at it six ways to Sunday, but until you actually talk to him, you'll have no idea how he'll react. My advice is to just do it."

"It's good advice."

"So when will you talk to him?"

She took a shaky breath. "Once everything's straightened out from the accident."

Melanie looked as if she wanted to say something, but she held her tongue.

Astrid had known her long enough that she could guess what her friend wasn't saying, though. Mel didn't think putting off the conversation was a good idea. "I have to get this stuff under control, Mel. I don't even have a phone yet. I couldn't call him if I wanted to."

"Do you know his number?"

"As it happens, I do." She hadn't memorized many phone numbers, but somehow his had stuck in her mind. Imagine that.

"I have a phone. You could arrange to meet him for lunch."

Astrid's stomach churned as she contemplated putting everything on the line right away. She wasn't ready. "Twenty-four hours isn't going to make that much difference. Then I'll have my ducks in a row, at least mostly, and I can think more clearly about how I want to broach the subject."

"All righty." Melanie gave her a quick hug. "It's your life."

Janis and Buddy were in great shape. Herman and the other two hired hands had everything under control at the Rocking G. The insurance adjuster had evaluated the collapsed bridge and the paperwork on that was in process.

Although Fletch could always find something to do—a horse that needed exercising, a fencepost that wobbled, some research online as he mapped out his breeding program in more detail—nothing seemed pressing enough to demand his immediate attention. He knew exactly why that was. He was still focused on Astrid and wondered how she was progressing with all her issues.

He'd thought about calling, but she might not have picked up a new cell phone yet. Besides, he didn't want to appear needy, even though he was, a little bit. He told himself she'd contact him and set a time to see him, at least by next Sunday . . . but that seemed like forever. By Sunday he might be a raving lunatic.

Yesterday he'd been convinced they'd eliminated any obstacles to having a relationship. But today he wasn't at all sure about that. Her manner told him obstacles still existed, and if he had to guess, he'd say her parents' opinion constituted at least one of them.

He couldn't imagine why, unless they were extremely conservative about sex before marriage. After giving the matter more thought, he decided that must be it. She hadn't wanted to discuss her parents with him, possibly out of loyalty to their beliefs, and maybe because she wasn't honoring those beliefs.

So he'd help her work around that issue, but in order to do that, they had to discuss it. In order to discuss it, he had to talk with her, preferably face-to-face. He hated to think that wouldn't happen until Sunday.

Astrid was the only person he could talk to about their relationship, since he'd promised to keep it quiet. That promise had boxed him in more than he'd realized when he'd made it. He had a couple of close friends from high school and either one of them would gladly listen to him rant about his frustration, but he'd told Astrid he wouldn't do that.

By early afternoon he was desperately seeking an outlet for his restlessness. Finally he came up with one, grabbed his keys, and climbed in his truck. He was curious about the condition of her truck, and the sheriff's department had given him the name of the yard where it was being kept. He'd drive over and check it out.

As he navigated the muddy back roads he was required to take because of the collapsed bridge, he told himself visiting the yard was a good idea. She'd probably been attached to that truck. He certainly was to his. Seeing it all beat up would upset her, and if he'd seen it, too, he'd be better equipped to understand and console her.

Damn, she'd probably need consoling, too, especially when she first saw the truck. He hoped she wouldn't go to the yard by herself. That would be really depressing, and he wanted to cushion the blow.

She hadn't asked him, though. It hadn't escaped his notice that she hadn't asked him to help her at all. She'd called on her friend Melanie, and that was okay, but he would have liked to have been involved.

When he located the yard, he parked his truck next to the high chain-link fence and climbed out. He was no stranger to yards like this. A guy in need of a replacement bumper or fender could often find one at a reasonable price in these establishments. That kind of search had the excitement of a treasure hunt built in.

Today, though, he was looking for a wrecked truck that had been in fine shape early yesterday morning, and that produced a whole different feeling. Now that he was here, he wasn't as interested in viewing the damage as he'd thought he'd be. He'd do it, though, for Astrid's sake.

"Can I help you?" A thin guy wearing a white T-shirt, worn jeans, and a baseball cap walked out of a small shack near the entrance to the yard.

"I wanted to take a look at a truck that came in yesterday. White crew cab, went into the water up by the Rocking G."

"Oh, yeah." The guy glanced at the side of Fletch's

truck, obviously noticing the Rocking G brand. "Were you there?"

"I was."

"You just missed the owner. She was here not thirty minutes ago."

Fletch swore under his breath. If he'd followed his instincts sooner, he might have met her here. Then again, she might not have appreciated that. God knows he didn't want her to think he was turning into a damned stalker.

"The insurance adjuster's been out, too, but that doesn't surprise me. After all, she's a Lindberg."

"Excuse me?"

"A Lindberg." The guy peered at him from under the brim of his cap. "Apparently that doesn't mean anything to you."

"Not really, other than it's her last name."

"I might not know about the family, either, except a few years ago her daddy wrecked a Lamborghini and they towed it here."

"Did you say *Lamborghini*?" Fletch didn't know much about luxury cars, but he recognized that name.

"Yep. Worth more than a million bucks. Totaled. Man, I hated to see that fine piece of machinery all torn up. He was lucky to walk away from it. Anyway, a car like that makes an impression. Now the name Lindberg rings a bell whenever I hear it."

"I'll bet." A million bucks. For a car. His mind made such a sharp U-turn that he felt a little dizzy. Her parents weren't conservative people who disapproved of premarital sex. They were filthy rich, which meant Astrid was filthy rich, too.

Now everything made sense. He'd known she was hesitant about committing to their relationship. After learning this critical bit of information, one she'd failed to impart, the reason had become painfully obvious. She was rich and he was not.

Anger sat in his chest, hard and hot, burning away all the tender feelings he'd had for her. What was he to her? The equivalent of a pool boy? Oh, she'd liked the sex well enough. He didn't doubt that. She might have figured that a once-a-week romp would be fun for a while. But she'd had no intention of letting it go beyond a casual affair.

"Still want to see her truck?"

Fletch stared at him. He'd forgotten the guy was standing there. "No." He glanced up at the sun and estimated the time to be about three. "I need to get going."

"You're sure? It's just right over yonder." He gestured toward the fence.

Fletch looked, and sure enough, he could see the front half of the truck. It was sitting behind a bashed-in yellow van. "Yeah, okay. Why not?"

"I mean, you drove here, so you might as well." The guy unlocked the gate and led the way through it. "She told me she jumped free."

"Yep." The image flashed through his mind and clutched at his heart. It probably always would when he thought of it. From now on, he'd do his best not to.

"Good thing she jumped. You get trapped in the vehicle when it goes in, you're done for. Maybe she has her old man's luck when it comes to things like that."

"Could be."

"I'm sort of surprised that she's a vet, though. You'd think she'd go into finance, like her daddy."

"She would hate that." He hadn't meant to say the words out loud.

"So you know her pretty well, then?"

"She's my vet." Or at least she used to be. He planned to fire her, right after he gave her a piece of his mind.

"So you must be the guy who pulled her out of the water."

"That's me."

"You could be in for a reward, then. Her parents must be plenty grateful. You probably saved her life."

Fletch shrugged. "Maybe."

"Listen, take my advice. Don't be shy. The Lindbergs are loaded, and if they offer you a reward for saving their only child, why not accept it? Unless you already have more money than you know what to do with."

"Nope." He laughed at the irony of it all. "I'm just a regular working stiff, trying to make ends meet."

"That's what I'm saying. Take the money."

"I'll think about it." He should, too, if a reward came his way. His knee-jerk response was that he didn't want their stinkin' money. Accepting money for doing what was right wasn't his style.

But he had so many plans for expanding his ranch, and if a cash reward would help him do that, he shouldn't let stupid pride stand in his way. Yeah, he'd take the money. Just so long as Astrid wasn't the one who delivered it. After he'd tracked her down this afternoon, or tonight, or whenever he got his chance to say his piece, he never wanted to see her again.

Nine

By five o'clock, Astrid was able to head home in her rented truck stocked with some basic medical supplies so that the next day she'd be able to catch up on the appointments she'd had to cancel. She had a new phone, and her insurance adjuster was on the case. She didn't have to wait for insurance money to buy a new truck, but she wasn't up to doing it today.

Instead she was looking forward to a warm bath, a glass of wine, and, eventually, a phone call to Fletch. She was still debating when and where to meet him tomorrow, but she'd figure that out while she soaked in the tub. He'd be expecting a call from her, anyway. He'd want to know how she made out with all her errands, and she missed talking to him.

Seeing his truck parked in front of her clinic startled her. He hadn't tried to call. She'd had her phone activated since early afternoon. Yet here he was.

As she approached, he got out, closed the cab door, and leaned against the front fender, arms crossed. His Stetson shaded his face, so she couldn't read his expression, but his body language was clear enough. He was angry.

Her heart began to pound. Only one thing could cause that kind of response. Somehow he'd found out about the money.

Mouth dry and pulse racing, she stopped her truck. Her hand shook as she turned the key, shutting off the motor. What now? Could she make him understand why she hadn't told him?

Saying a little prayer that she could appeal to that gentle, caring side of him, she climbed down from the rental truck and walked toward him. When he didn't come to meet her, she understood just how angry he must be. He'd always been so glad to see her.

Not now. The closer she came, the more she realized how rigid his body was. Finally she gazed into his eyes, and her spirit shrank. He'd never looked at her like that, with eyes so cold that she shivered.

"Fletch, I can explain."

"Really?" His tone was as cold as his eyes. "I'll be fascinated to hear what you come up with. Were you ever going to tell me? Or were you just stringing me along until you got tired of the sex?"

She gasped, the breath going out of her as if he'd punched her in the stomach. "That's what you think? That all I cared about was sex?"

"Obvious, isn't it? I know you liked that part, but whenever I tried to establish something more concrete between us, you shied away. At first you claimed it was because I was a client. Was that ever true, or just a ploy?"

"It was true!" Her heart cracked right down the middle. "I value my professional reputation."

"I can't imagine why it matters. You don't need the money."

Her hand connected with his cheek before she realized she was going to slap him. She stepped back, horrified that she'd done such a thing. But her work was so important to her, and he'd implied she didn't really care about it.

A red mark on his cheek branded him, but he didn't act as if he'd felt a thing. "You're a good vet," he said. "I'll give you that. But you're no longer my vet."

"Fletch, don't do this. I was going to tell you. I just didn't know how. Everything happened so fast."

"I knew you for six months before that *everything* took place. You could have given me a hint, some little sign, so that I wouldn't make a fool of myself worrying about whether your business stayed in the black."

"I don't like to advertise it, and I made a point of not telling anyone in my practice. You were no different."

He flinched for the first time. "Apparently not. Except that I'm good in bed, so that came in handy."

"Stop! It's not only sex between us! Don't say these awful things. We've shared so much!"

"I thought so, too, but where was it going, Astrid? I'm not in your league, and you knew that from the start. You could have told me so. All I can figure is you wanted to satisfy your curiosity and scratch that itch."

"No! That's not fair. I told you I'd decided not to go to bed with you. You were the one convinced it would happen."

"Yeah." He sounded more weary than angry now. "But I was operating on false information. The thing is, I *knew* something wasn't right, and I ignored the warning signals. My bad. It doesn't matter. It's over."

"Don't say that. I was going to call you tonight and set up a meeting for tomorrow. I was going to tell you then."

"So you could give me the brush-off? Hey, I've saved you the trouble."

"You're furious with me, and I understand that, but I wanted to tell you. Like I said, I couldn't figure out how."

He gazed at her, his expression blank. "Now I know."

"How did you find out?"

"Not that it matters, but I went to the yard to see your truck. I thought it might help if I—well, never mind that. The guy at the yard told me about your dad's Lamborghini. After that, the puzzle pieces fell into place."

"You went to see my truck?" She'd never dreamed he would do such a thing.

"Crazy, isn't it? I had some idea that seeing the damage would help me to comfort you. I thought you'd be upset. Stupid of me, but I wasn't in the know."

"I *was* upset."

"Why? You can replace it without batting an eye."

She stared at him, and her own anger rose to meet his. "You're like everyone else, assuming that just because someone has the money to replace things, they don't care if they're destroyed. You're spouting the same clichés I've heard all my life. Well, screw you."

"I think you already did."

"That's crude."

"I feel crude at the moment. So sue me. But you won't get much. As you know, I don't have a lot of ready cash."

"Okay, then! Be a jackass and let this money thing

come between us! I thought maybe you'd be different, but you're not."

"Nope." He unfolded his arms and pushed away from the fender. "I'm just your average guy." He walked around to the driver's side and opened the door.

"You're not average! You saved my life!"

"I would have done that for anyone." Closing the door, he started the engine, backed the truck out, and drove away.

She stood in the parking area, her arms wrapped tight around her body. Her chest hurt so much that she had trouble breathing. Apparently this was what heartbreak felt like. She'd always laughed when people said money couldn't buy happiness. It had been her friend for a long time. But it wasn't her friend now.

Fletch spent the first half of the drive home nursing his righteous anger and listening to Chubby Checker, turned up really loud. He spent the second half in silence, haunted by the devastation in Astrid's blue eyes. He'd been so harsh, but damn it, she'd *used* him.

Hadn't she?

Well, it was true she hadn't come on to him. He'd been the one who'd kissed her. Yes, but she could have told him then. She could have said *Fletch, there's something you don't know about me. I'm one of the richest girls in Dallas.*

He tried to picture her saying such a thing and couldn't. She wasn't the type. Although she might have more money than God, she didn't act like it.

Which should have told him that the money wasn't all that important to her.

But it was there, and it wouldn't melt overnight or be absorbed in some Ponzi scheme so that she'd suddenly be on the same financial footing as he was. That would be ridiculous, anyway. She might be using that money to finance her clinic, and for all he knew she did a lot of pro bono work because she didn't have to make a huge profit.

She wouldn't tell him that, of course. That might be what wounded him most of all. She hadn't trusted him with the information about her wealth, as if she thought he'd go off the deep end if he found out.

Which he had.

She'd told him he was no different from everyone else. He believed all the clichés about rich people. He'd demonstrated that prejudice beautifully tonight, hadn't he? He'd found out she was rich and had assumed the worst.

By the time he pulled up in front of the ranch house, his anger had drained away and he felt like crap for beating up on her like that. But the truth was, he didn't really know how she felt about him. She'd planned to tell him, she'd said, but would knowing have made any difference really? She still might have viewed their affair as temporary fun. She'd said nothing to contradict that.

He didn't feel like going into the house, so he left his truck and walked down to the barn. Horses had always calmed him. Even though he associated Janis and Buddy with Astrid, he drifted toward the foaling stall. Maybe he was a glutton for punishment.

Janis was munching her evening oats, and Buddy came over on his stiltlike legs to investigate Fletch. Fletch stroked the sweet baby's nose and told him what a great stallion he would become someday. Astrid had made this birth possible, and Fletch couldn't forget that as he scratched Buddy's soft coat.

Another vet might have pushed for a C-section, which would be more costly—more profit for the vet—and might result in all kinds of complications. Astrid had hung on for the natural approach, letting Janis work it out herself. Fletch realized that could have backfired, but he'd been with Astrid on that. If the decision had been wrong, they would have shared the blame.

We've shared so much.

They had, and none of it had to do with being rich or poor. It had been all about the love of animals and a general optimistic belief that if left alone, the animals would figure out the best course of action. It was, he realized, a philosophy of animal management, but it was also a general philosophy of life. Don't push extreme measures. Wait and see. Let things unfold naturally.

Had she been trying to do that with their relationship? Then they'd been thrown into a high-pressure situation, and the natural timetable had been skewed by her plunge into the stream. He remembered that she'd driven across the bridge while thinking about him.

Janis finished her oats and came over for some petting. "What do you say, girl?" Fletch brushed her forelock out of her eyes. "Am I an idiot?"

Janis snorted and bobbed her head.

It was a typical horsey gesture, not to be interpreted in any special way, but Fletch laughed. "Could be I am. You're the expert on these things. There's no finer treatise on it than Janis Joplin's 'The Rose.'"

He was officially getting slap-happy, but talking to the horses was better than wandering up to the house and facing that empty king-sized bed. He looked for reasons to stay, and ended up straightening tack and sweeping the wooden aisle between the stalls.

That's where he was when Astrid walked into the barn. He saw a movement, glanced up from his sweeping, and saw her standing under an overhead light, a blonde angel who made his heart leap. He dropped the broom.

"I couldn't leave it like that between us," she said.

He took a breath. "I was mean."

"Yes, you were. I didn't know you had it in you to be that mean."

"Neither did I." His chest tightened. "Apparently you get to me."

"Likewise." She stayed right where she was, not advancing, but not retreating either.

He hoped she wasn't a figment of his imagination, but she looked real enough. "For the record, I'm not automatically prejudiced against rich people."

"That's nice to hear." She took a deep breath. "But if being rich is a problem to you, I'd rather give away every penny if that would ... would ..."

She wasn't going to move, but he did. He closed the distance between them in three strides. Stopping in front of her, he looked into her eyes. "Would what?"

She swallowed. "Would allow us to love each other."

That was all he needed. He swept her into his arms. "Loving you has nothing to do with money." Then he kissed her and poured all that he felt for her into that kiss.

With a moan, she responded, telling him without words how much he meant to her.

She'd told him all this before with her kisses, and he

hadn't been willing to listen. No one surrendered like this without love in her heart. She'd cared all along. He'd been the fool who hadn't recognized it.

He kissed her, and kissed her some more. "I'm so sorry," he murmured between kisses. "I'm so sorry I doubted you."

"I'm so sorry I gave you reason to doubt." Then she wrapped her arms around him as if she would never let go.

At last he raised his head and looked into her eyes. "I love you, Astrid, and I intend to marry you. Is that a problem?"

She smiled. "No, it's a solution. If you didn't love me, I would be heartbroken, because I love you, too."

"What about your parents?"

"A very dear friend gave me some wonderful advice. She said that once they see how happy you make me, they'll come around."

"I intend to make you so happy that they'll come around really fast."

Her expression sobered. "I wasn't kidding, Fletch. If you're uncomfortable with the money, I'll get rid of it. It doesn't matter to me."

"Let's not get carried away." He hugged her tight. "If you're determined to divest yourself of your fortune, I have a suggestion for where to put it."

"Into your breeding program?"

"Yep."

"That's wonderful! I thought you wouldn't take it."

"That would be dumb, now, wouldn't it? What idiot turns his back on the prospect of making a dream come true?"

"Not me." She cradled his face in her hands.

"Not us." And instead of kissing her, he scooped her up in his arms. The barn might be great for stolen moments, but he had some serious lovemaking in mind. For that, he intended to take the love of his life inside and make use of a sturdy king-sized bed. This time, they wouldn't even have to worry about mud.

Epilogue

Wanting to share her joy with her friends, Astrid called for a girls' night out at their favorite watering hole, Golden Spurs & Stetson in downtown Dallas. Melanie and Val were waiting for her at their customary table near the front door when she hurried in.

They both leaped up to hug her and exclaim over how happy she looked.

"I'm beyond happy." She beamed at her friends as they settled into their chairs. "I didn't know a feeling this great even existed!"

Melanie practically bounced in her chair. "I knew it! I knew he was right for you!"

Val reached over and squeezed Astrid's hand. "Good for you, getting away from the bad kisser and going for the guy who knows how."

Astrid grinned. "Yes, ma'am, he sure does."

"Look at you." Melanie regarded her with pride. "You're positively glowing."

"And we need drinks!" Val said. "The waitress was just here, but it's busy tonight. I'd better go find her."

After she left, Astrid glanced at Mel. "It was a close call with Fletch. I should have followed your advice and told him about my family sooner. Thank God he didn't stay angry with me."

"He didn't because he loves you. And you love him."

"I do. I can't believe how much." She lowered her voice. "So how is Val taking this? Is she still determined not to date anyone?"

"Yes, and I'm worried about her. That fire at the concert was horrible, I know, but she's not getting over it. I wish she'd see a therapist, but she keeps putting that off. Her paranoia is ruining her love life, and I get the feeling it's affecting her job, too."

"That's bad. I mean, when we're forced to sit at the front table every time we come here, just so she's near the door . . ."

"Right. Here she comes."

Val flashed a smile as she pulled out a chair. "Talking about me, weren't you?"

"Yes." Astrid met her gaze. "We both think you should see somebody."

"I see lots of people!" Her determined smile grew brighter. "The law office is chock-full of them. People everywhere."

"I mean about your issues." Astrid refused to let Val joke her way out of it. Her friend's funky clothing choices and trendy haircut made her look like a confident woman of the world. Instead, after breaking her arm during a mob scene at a concert, she'd become a scared rabbit. "This overly cautious person is not the Valerie Wolitzky I remember from college."

"That's for sure," Melanie said. "I still think about

that epic trip to Six Flags our senior year. God, that was fun. We should do it again."

Val's face grew pale. "We could," she said quickly, "but you have so much to do getting ready for your wedding to Drew, and all signs point to Astrid launching into wedding planning soon, so maybe—"

"It's okay." Astrid touched her arm. "We wouldn't drag you there. Not until you're ready. But seriously, would you at least start researching therapists?"

"Sure." Val nodded. "I'll do that." But she glanced up with obvious relief when the waitress arrived to take their drink orders. Then she changed the subject.

Astrid let her, because beating her over the head about the situation wouldn't help. But she hated that Val wasn't living life to the fullest.

Now more than ever, Astrid understood how important that was. Thanks to Fletch, she was alive, in every sense of the word. She wanted that kind of joy for Val, too. If only something, or someone, would come along and jolt her out of the miserable rut she was in.

Their margaritas arrived, and Val raised her glass. "Here's to Astrid and Fletch finding each other."

"At long last," Melanie said with a smile.

"It was truly a miracle." Thanking her lucky stars, Astrid clinked glasses with Melanie and Val and sipped her drink. Then she raised it again and glanced at Val. "Here's to going for the gusto."

Val laughed. "All right, all right. I'll find a therapist. Geez." And she touched her glass to Astrid's and Melanie's.

Astrid wished she could get a time commitment on that promise but decided not to push tonight, which was supposed to be about celebrating, not soul-searching. Astrid had much to celebrate. She had great friends, a wonderful career, and she'd been lucky enough to find a guy who was everything she'd ever wanted. He wasn't the billionaire she'd always assumed she'd marry, but she'd learned that, for her, a cowboy was the perfect man.

Safe in His Arms

VALERIE

One

One minute Valerie Wolitzky was drinking margaritas with her two pals, Astrid Lindberg and Melanie Shaw, in their favorite Dallas watering hole, the Golden Spurs & Stetson. The next minute an alarm shrieked, and Val leaped from her seat, knocking over her chair and her drink. She had to get out. *Now.*

Panic buzzed in her ears as she charged the front door. She had to beat the mob of people. If she didn't, she'd be trapped . . . just like before.

Wham! She hit a solid wall of muscle and staggered back. A cowboy blocked her way. She shoved him hard. "Let me out!"

He grabbed her shoulders. "Hold on, there, ma'am. What's the problem?"

Was he an idiot? With adrenaline-fueled strength, she pushed him aside and barreled through the door, almost knocking down a second man who was right behind him. But she got out the door.

Safe! She was safe! Shaking, she leaned over and braced her hands on her knees as she gulped for air. The warm breeze of a summer night touched her wet cheeks. She swiped at them as she slowly straightened. She needed to sit down, but there was nowhere to—

"Val!" Astrid's shout penetrated the buzzing in her ears, and she turned. Her two friends burst through the door of the bar and rushed toward her.

Relief that they were okay was followed by hot shame. She hadn't thought of them, hadn't even tried to save them. She'd only thought of herself.

"Omigod, Val." Melanie, brown hair flying, reached her first and hugged her. "It's okay. Some smoking oil set off the smoke detector in the kitchen. It's okay. It's okay."

Filled with gratitude for her friend's safety, Val hugged her back without paying much attention to what she was saying.

Astrid joined the huddle and rubbed Val's back. "Easy, girlfriend. Take it easy. Everything's fine."

Gradually Valerie's heartbeat slowed, and the grip of fear eased. She took a quivering breath and wondered why she wasn't hearing sirens. She stepped out of Melanie's embrace and looked around. "Where are the fire trucks?"

"There's no fire." Astrid continued to stroke her back. "Just a little smoke."

"Did they evacuate the building?"

"No, sweetie." Melanie gazed at her with compassion. "They shut off the alarm right away and came out of the kitchen to explain the problem."

Valerie's heart started pounding again. *Dear God.* "I was . . . the only one who ran out?"

Both Melanie and Astrid nodded.

"Well, except us," Melanie added. "We took off after you."

"Oh, no." Val covered her face as embarrassment flooded through her, scorching her cheeks. She'd overreacted. Caused a scene. Involved her friends in her craziness. Slowly she lowered her hands and stared at them in misery. "I'm so sorry," she whispered.

"Don't worry about it." Astrid squeezed her arm. "But Val, it's time to get serious about—"

"Ma'am? Are you all right?" The cowboy Valerie had smacked into when she fled now walked over to her, trailed by the other guy, who wore a business suit. They both looked worried.

Val thought of the old cliché and wished the sidewalk really would open up and swallow her. "Yes, thank you." She wished the words didn't sound so wobbly and uncertain.

"You don't look all right." The cowboy kept coming. He had a purposeful, John Wayne stride, and he towered over the other man. "You're shaking like a newborn foal. What happened in there?"

Melanie put a protective arm around Val's shoulder. "Thanks for your concern, but she'll be fine."

He paused and tipped his Stetson back with his thumb. "I'm sure she will. I just . . . was it the smoke alarm that spooked you? I heard it go off right before I got to the door."

He seemed like a nice guy who only wanted to help. Val couldn't fault him for that after she'd tried to knock him down in her full-out panic mode. He must have seen the terror in her eyes. "I'm afraid I overreacted." She cleared her throat and summoned her lawyer's voice. "I apologize for plowing into you and yelling. That was rude."

"No worries." He glanced at Astrid and Melanie standing on either side of her. "I'm glad your friends are here." He hesitated before bringing his attention back to Val.

His eyes were gray. Not a gloomy, dark sort of gray, but light, almost silver. They shone with kindness. "Listen, I don't know you at all, and I'm probably butting in where I have no business, but I understand a little something about post-traumatic stress." He turned to the man who'd come up behind him. "And my buddy Will wrote the book on it. Literally." He looked at Val again. "If you need—"

"To see someone?" She managed not to choke on the words. "I appreciate the thought, but I have that covered." She had nothing covered, because she was determined to handle the issue herself, despite what her friends thought she should do. But he didn't have to know any of that.

"Good. That's good. But if you need a second opinion, I highly recommend Will. Say, Will, you have any cards with you?"

"I think so." The man reached inside his suit jacket. "Yep. Here's one."

Val stepped back, away from the outstretched business card. If she ever decided to go that route, she'd find her own shrink. Locating the right person would require lots of research. A chance meeting on the sidewalk didn't qualify as an intelligent method for hiring a professional therapist. "Thanks, but I—"

"I'll take it." Astrid reached for the card. She looked

at the name printed there before tucking the card in her jeans pocket. Then she exchanged a glance with the cowboy.

Val figured that the wordless message between Astrid and the cowboy was along the lines of *I can handle it from here.*

As if to confirm that, the cowboy touched the brim of his hat, a classic farewell gesture. "We've kept you ladies long enough. I'm glad you're all right, ma'am. You three have a nice evening." Both men turned and headed back toward the bar.

Val swung to face Astrid. "I know what you're up to, but I'm not making an appointment with some guy I met on the street."

"Oh, yes, you are." Astrid's blue eyes flashed with determination. She was small and blonde, but anyone who underestimated her because of that would be making a huge mistake. "He's not just *some guy*. He's Will Bryan, who's appeared on lots of talk shows because of his book on PTSD. I've seen him on TV, but somehow I missed the fact he's from Dallas."

"So he's famous? Then I'll bet he's booked solid." That should take care of that.

Melanie spoke up. "If he's booked solid, he would have said so instead of handing over his card. Anyway, that cowboy seems to be his good friend, and he suggested you contact this Will guy. If you mention to Will that you were the tall redhead he met outside the Golden Spurs and Stetson, I'm sure he'll work you in."

"Yeah, and charge me a million bucks now that he's so well known." Another excellent reason why she wouldn't be calling him.

Astrid's jaw firmed. "Being prominent doesn't necessarily mean he charges more than anyone else. And if his fee is really high, then I'll—"

"No, you won't, Astrid Lindberg. I've never taken money from you, and I won't start now." Val, Astrid, and Melanie had been sorority sisters. Fortunately Astrid's wealthy background hadn't been a barrier to their friendship, even though Melanie and Val had scraped through school with scholarships and student loans and Astrid had sailed along on her parents' considerable money.

"You can pay me back later."

"No." Val shook her head. "Look, I don't need a celebrity therapist."

"Maybe not, but you need a therapist, and you're making no progress toward getting one." Astrid pulled the card out of her pocket. "It's been months since the concert hall fire, and you're not getting better on your own. This guy showing up right when you had a meltdown seems like it was meant to be."

Val's stomach churned. Until that awful night of the fire and the stampede, she'd prided herself on her self-sufficiency and emotional stability. Now she freaked at every little thing. She hated feeling so out of control these days, but the idea of allowing some stranger to probe into her vulnerability made her break out in a cold sweat. "I just need time."

"No, you don't." Melanie put her arm around Val's shoulders again, and her grip was tighter than before. Melanie's curves made her look soft, but she had a backbone of steel. "You've had time, and nothing's changed. This is a fabulous opportunity, and you're going to see this therapist . . . even if we have to hog-tie you and haul you there ourselves."

Astrid sighed in obvious relief. "Well said, Melanie. So here's the deal, Val. We're your best friends, and we can't stand by and watch this train wreck any longer. You've stopped dating. You've turned down a promotion at the law firm. You insist on sitting at the table by the front door when we go out anywhere. Enough."

Val looked from one determined expression to the other. The thought of doing what her friends demanded scared the shit out of her, but they were right. She was stuck in a prison of her own making. And now she'd dragged them into it. "Okay." She swallowed. "I'll do it."

Nine in the morning, and already the sun felt like a branding iron on Adam Templeton's shoulders as he walked toward the barn. On most days, heading down to see his horses calmed him, but not this morning. What the hell had he gotten himself into?

Will thought it was hysterically funny that Adam was nervous about working with Valerie Wolitzky, especially since Adam had been the one to prompt Will into providing his card outside the Golden Spurs & Stetson. *You've dealt with battle-scarred soldiers who are a thousand times more traumatized than she is,* Will had said. *She'll be a piece of cake compared to them.*

Oh, yeah, she'd be a piece of cake, all right. Sweet and tempting. Of course, she could be married or seeing someone. That would help. His divorce from Elise was only fifteen months old, and Adam felt battle-scarred, himself.

He'd mentioned to Will that all the folks he'd worked

with thus far had been men. Will had told him that wouldn't always be the case. Female soldiers came home with PTSD, too. If Adam was serious about this new direction in his life, he'd need to help women as well as men.

Well, yeah, point taken. And Adam was serious about this venture. He hadn't resigned his position as CEO of the family corporation and turned it over to his younger brother so that he could *play cowboy*, as Elise had termed it.

He'd never enjoyed the corporate world, but his little brother loved it. Nate was thrilled that Adam had bucked tradition and given him control of the family's holdings. For years, Adam had unquestioningly followed the path laid out by his father and grandfather, a path Elise and her parents had approved of. None of those people could dictate to him now.

His grandfather and father had both died in their fifties of heart attacks, and Elise had married another billionaire, so even the alimony payments weren't an issue anymore. He'd taken inventory of his situation and decided he had enough money to last several lifetimes. He had the luxury of doing what he loved and making his brother Nate happy at the same time.

After consulting with Will, a close friend since high school, Adam had returned to his first passion—horses and ranching. He'd bought the Triple Bar and enough registered quarter horses to start a breeding operation. But the breeding was more of a hobby and not Adam's primary purpose in buying the ranch.

Equine therapy was catching on in the mental health community, and Will was a strong proponent of using animals to connect with tortured individuals. Adam loved the idea that this ranch, which he'd bought to satisfy his own yearnings, also could be a healing place for those who'd been battered by war and other calamities.

He was only about six months into it, but so far, the process had been rewarding. Apparently teaching people how to care for and interact with horses was a good companion activity to Will's therapy sessions. Adam had watched several vets regain some peace of mind through interacting with his animals.

Intellectually he'd known his charges wouldn't always be men, although up to now they had been. But why did the first woman have to be a scrappy female defiantly hiding her vulnerability? She'd obviously prefer to go down in flames rather than admit she needed help. Her friends must have done some serious arm-twisting to get her into Will's office.

That type of personality never failed to trip the switch on Adam's protective instincts. On top of that, she was a long-legged redhead with porcelain skin and green eyes, a knockout who would interest any man with a pulse. He hadn't explained any of that to Will, but they'd been friends for a long time. He wouldn't put it past Will to have sent her out here on purpose.

It would be just like him, and he had a legitimate right to interfere in Adam's social life. Will had suffered through countless rants during Adam's messy divorce from Elise. Will, a lucky cuss who'd found the right woman right off the bat, had strongly suggested that Adam should get back in the game and stop hiding. He thought Adam still had his own demons to slay, and he was probably right.

But Adam didn't feel ready to engage in that battle

just yet. So what if he was attracted to the lovely Miss Wolitzky? He'd control himself. He was here to help her bond with horses and resolve her fears, whatever they might be. Because of patient confidentiality, Will never discussed specifics with Adam.

Valerie had instructions to meet him at the barn. Will had told her that Adam was the same guy she'd run into when she'd dashed out of the bar in such a panic. According to Will, she hadn't been particularly happy about that because the incident had embarrassed her no end.

That hardly surprised him. So maybe they were even. He was worried about having her come to his ranch, and she didn't want to be there. But she had a problem, and Will believed the horses could help her solve it.

The barn wasn't air-conditioned, at least not yet. Adam could easily afford to do it, but an air-conditioned barn, one with doors and windows permanently closed all summer, wasn't part of his ranching fantasy, so he'd held off. Heating the place in winter didn't bother him, but he'd balked at air-conditioning.

Instead he'd installed fans in the rafters, and they worked reasonably well. The hands had been through the barn already this morning, mucking stalls and spreading clean straw. Adam took a deep breath, enjoying the blended aromas of fresh straw and aged wood.

It was an older structure, but huge. He planned to preserve the ambiance and add a few things, like open-air enclosures outside most of the stalls, especially the large ones where he'd house his brood mares. He'd wanted this ranch life since he'd been five, and now he had it.

All the horses had been turned out into the pasture except Rocket Fuel, the gelding Adam had designated as the horse Valerie would work with, and a mare and her new foal. The bay mare, Saucy Lady, promised to be a valuable brood mare. Her mostly black colt, Naughty Boy, had been sold before his birth to a Dallas-area stable.

Adam was on his way down the concrete aisle between the stalls to check on Saucy Lady and Naughty Boy when he heard a car pull up outside. He glanced at the barn clock. Nine-fifteen. If that was Valerie, she was right on time.

Retracing his steps, he grabbed a clipboard off the wall. She'd have to sign a waiver before he let her near any of his horses. A billionaire was a juicy target for lawsuits.

As he approached the open barn door, he mentally prepared himself to be friendly yet businesslike. Damn it, he'd never had this kind of anxiety when welcoming Will's other patients. But no matter how he'd tried to reframe this meeting, it felt exactly like a date, and he was sadly out of practice for those.

He walked into the sunshine and found her standing beside her jaunty little black sports car. She looked anything but jaunty, though. She stood ramrod straight, arms at her sides, her expression an unyielding mask, her eyes hidden behind large sunglasses.

Her jeans looked new, and so did her brown Ropers. She wore a plain white T-shirt tucked in, which emphasized her narrow hips and long legs. The pristine straw cowboy hat dangling from her slender fingers had obviously never seen service.

She could have been a mannequin in a store window except for her hair. Boyishly short and tousled, it blazed in shades of deep orange and seemed to radiate energy. He couldn't stop looking at that hair, which provided the only evidence of her inner fire, a fire he knew existed. He'd been on the receiving end when she'd erupted.

He dragged in a breath. Keeping his distance from Valerie Wolitzky was going to be a challenge.

Two

He was at least as tall as Valerie remembered, maybe an inch or two taller. Not many men made her feel petite, but this one did. Adam Templeton, quarter-horse breeder, former corporate raider, rich dude. Will hadn't told her any of that, but once she'd learned the name of the cowboy who would be helping her become better acquainted with horses, she'd Googled him. What she hadn't discovered on the Internet, she'd learned from her friends.

Between Astrid, who had many connections among Dallas's wealthiest citizens, and Melanie, who was engaged to Dallas billionaire Drew Eldridge, Val had found out about Adam's divorce and his recent decision to leave the corporate world. Now he raised horses and helped Will rehabilitate returning vets.

But in his shift to a rural lifestyle, he'd spared no expense. Driving in on a freshly paved road, she'd glimpsed an elegant two-story house on a rise overlooking a ranching operation that had to be worth millions. Sleek horses with glossy coats grazed in pastures bordered with sparkling white fences. All the numerous outbuildings had a fresh coat of tan paint.

She'd noticed two cowboys on horseback crossing one of the pastures. Another was inside one of the corrals exercising a horse with the use of a long line that allowed the horse to trot in a circle, and yet another cowhand was raking an empty corral near the barn. She hadn't seen a single weed growing anywhere.

The owner of all that perfection stood before her looking like a good ol' boy in his worn Stetson, faded jeans, and scuffed boots. She wasn't fooled. Anyone who took note of his body language would recognize a man who wielded power. His broad shoulders were thrown back, his stance was slightly open, and his square jaw was firm. Intelligence gleamed in his silver eyes.

And something else flickered briefly in those eyes, something that made her jumpy nerves fizz even more — sexual interest. He doused the flame immediately, but not before she felt an unwelcome response in her own traitorous body. A girl could be forgiven for that, she supposed. The guy was, after all, gorgeous.

But she'd sworn off men for the time being. The last one she'd trusted had abandoned her to the crush of bodies trying to escape the concert hall. Intellectually she knew that not all men were cowards and not all crowds would turn into mobs, but that logical conclusion hadn't filtered into her subconscious, which remained on red alert.

She adopted the tone she used on the phone with new clients. "Good morning, Mr. Templeton. Thank you for fitting me into your schedule."

"Good morning, Miss Wolitzky." A trace of humor laced his words. "Do you think we could loosen up enough to call each other by our given names?"

"I can if you can . . . Adam." He had an honest, solid name. She didn't know anyone else with that name, so using it shouldn't affect her one way or the other. Yet just saying it out loud established a greater sense of intimacy, at least for her.

"Then that much is settled . . . Valerie." The telltale flicker was back in his eyes. He extinguished it and held out the clipboard in his hand. "Before we get started, I need you to sign a waiver."

"Naturally." Will had told her about this, and she would have been suspicious of anyone who didn't require it. As a lawyer, she liked to find evidence of legal clarity. Stepping forward, she took the clipboard and glanced over the standard waiver that absolved him of any responsibility for her fragile self.

She signed the waiver with the pen attached to the clipboard with a string. Considering what this guy was worth, she was surprised he didn't have his lawyer standing by to witness it.

He gestured toward the barn. "Come on inside and I'll introduce you to Rocket Fuel." He stood aside to let her go in first.

She planted both feet and stayed where she was. *"Rocket Fuel?"* She'd heard of cowboys who delighted in putting greenhorns up on the meanest horse in the barn. She'd just signed a waiver giving him carte blanche when it came to her personal safety. She wasn't about to climb aboard a horse named Rocket Fuel.

The corner of his mouth kicked up in a smile. "His racing days are over, I'm afraid. At one time he could launch himself from the starting gate with blinding speed, but now he just makes a good saddle horse."

She wasn't convinced. "Did Will happen to mention anything about my riding experience?"

"Nope. He deliberately tells me as little as possible about his patients. Figures it's up to them to say whatever they care to. Assume I know nothing about you except your name."

She peered at him. "I knew he wouldn't reveal the personal things we talked about during our sessions, but the horse stuff isn't exactly privileged information."

"Maybe not, but he believes it's better if I start with no preconceived ideas about what you can and can't do, or what you will or won't do, for that matter. He leaves it up to you to fill me in."

"Oh." She debated just how honest to be. God, this was hard. She hated being out of her depth in any situation. "Well . . . I'm not used to being around full-sized horses."

"Ponies, then?"

She nodded. Hell, she might as well lay it all out. "As in pony rides, the kind where they're hitched to spokes and you just go round and round." She waited for him to laugh, or at least chuckle.

He did neither. Instead he gazed at her the way he had after the embarrassing incident outside the bar—with kindness. "Okay. Did you like it?"

"Not much. It was boring. I'm sure it was even more boring for the ponies."

THE PERFECT MAN 229

"No doubt. So how do you feel about getting acquainted with a full-sized horse?"

Her first impulse was to say it would be no big deal. Both of her best friends were good riders. Melanie had grown up on a small ranch and had ridden practically since birth. Astrid could ride both English and Western, and she was now a large-animal vet.

Melanie and Astrid had been extremely enthusiastic about Will's suggestion that Val try working with horses as a way to calm her fears. Horses didn't scare either one of them, and they'd assumed she wasn't afraid either. She'd never contradicted that belief.

"I could probably ride one," she said.

"You probably could," Adam said. "But let's start with grooming the horse. Rocket Fuel loves to be brushed. He'd be in seventh heaven if you'd spend some time this morning doing that."

"Okay." She heard the relief in her voice and winced. But all the way out here she'd wondered what this horse interaction involved and whether she'd be expected to get on a thousand-pound animal she had no idea how to control and gallop off into the sunset.

Will had been vague about the process and had said that Adam tailored it to fit the individual. She'd told him she wasn't much of a rider, but he'd assured her that wasn't important.

Because she wasn't stupid, she knew Will was sending her into an unfamiliar situation on purpose so that she could have a chance to move out of her comfort zone in a relatively safe environment. He obviously trusted Adam Templeton a great deal.

But could she trust Adam? She barely knew him.

Will's good opinion of him was helpful, but Will was one of his best friends and might be giving Adam more credit than he deserved.

Brushing a horse sounded innocuous enough, though, so she stepped inside the barn. Once out of the sunlight, she had to take off her shades or risk tripping over her own feet. That possibility was even greater because this was a first outing for her boots and she wasn't used to them yet.

Propping her shades on top of her head, she accompanied Adam past a row of stalls. The scent of hay reminded her of a high school hayride and making out with her teenaged boyfriend. She'd bet Adam Templeton was a great kisser. Confident men like him usually were because they had nothing to prove.

She, however, would not be finding out about his kissing abilities. Even as she thought that, she couldn't help sneaking a sideways look to check out his mouth. He had a full bottom lip, which was often a good beginning to a hot kiss. Not that she'd ever find out if his mouth lived up to its potential.

Wow, this was one long-ass aisle. "How come all the stalls are empty?" she asked.

"We turn the horses out in the pasture unless the weather's lousy. It's not good for them to stay cooped up in the barn."

"Makes sense. So Rocket Fuel had to stay behind because of me?"

"Yes, but you can make it up to him with a good grooming session."

Right then a horse with a white blaze down its face

stuck its head over a stall door and stared at them. Those big brown eyes looked friendly.

"Is that Rocket Fuel?" Valerie asked. If so, he wasn't quite so scary.

"No, that's Saucy Lady."

"Why isn't she out in the pasture?"

"She foaled yesterday, so we're keeping them both close for a while."

"A baby horse?" Now, that was more like it. She could deal with a baby any old day. "Could I brush the foal, instead?"

"Maybe another day you can. Saucy Lady doesn't know you yet, and she's protective of her foal. We'll be better off with Rocket Fuel."

"Understood. Do you think she'd let me peek in the stall?"

"Sure, if I'm there, she should be fine. Hey, Saucy Lady, I have someone here who wants to admire your son. Want to show him off a little?"

The horse lifted her head and snorted.

"Is she saying yes or no?"

"She's saying maybe, if I happen to have a piece of carrot in my pocket, which fortunately I do."

Valerie was fascinated by Adam's indulgent tone. He might be a billionaire, but this horse was more than a moneymaking animal to him. He obviously loved her.

She hung back as Adam walked over to Saucy Lady. He murmured softly, saying things Valerie couldn't hear as he stroked the mare's nose and scratched behind her ears. Saucy Lady nuzzled him as if returning the affection.

"Come on over," he said as he dug in his pocket. "I've told her she can trust you. Just stay relaxed and don't make any abrupt moves." He fed the horse a chunk of carrot and continued to murmur sweet nothings in her ear.

Valerie approached slowly. "Have you always loved horses?"

"As long as I can remember." He pulled another piece of carrot from his pocket. "Hold out your hand. Keep it flat and let her take it from you."

"Will she bite me?"

"Not on purpose. So keep your hand flat and don't get your fingers in the way."

Valerie would have preferred not to feed the horse, but she was here to conquer her fears, so she accepted the carrot and held it in her palm, fingers as straight and flat as she could manage. Saucy Lady lowered her head and soft lips played over the surface of Valerie's hand. The sensation gave her goose bumps. Then the carrot disappeared, and the horse chewed, crunching it between her enormous teeth.

"Perfect." Adam's voice was warm, and close. "Now that you've made a friend, take a look at her foal."

Valerie had been so intent on offering the carrot without getting bit that she'd temporarily forgotten why she was doing it in the first place. Sticking her hands in her pockets in case Saucy Lady mistook a finger for a carrot, she peered over the stall door.

There, lying curled up in a bed of straw, was a baby horse. He was coal black except for a white blaze like his momma's. He was so precious that she couldn't help sighing with pleasure. "Does he have a name yet?"

"Absolutely. He's a registered quarter horse. Officially he's Saucy Lady's Naughty Boy, but we won't use the entire handle around the barn. We call him Bubba."

"Bubba? He's too little to be a Bubba."

"He'll grow into it."

"Is his daddy black?"

"Yes, ma'am."

"Do you own the father, too?"

"No. Saucy Lady was pregnant when I bought her, which sent the price up considerably. I was more than happy to pay it, though. She's a proven brood mare. And a sweetheart, besides."

Valerie had a million questions, most of them revolving around his decision to chuck his former career and go into the horse-breeding business. But asking those questions would reveal that she'd checked up on him before coming out here, and she wasn't willing to let him know that.

Instead she settled on making comments that might encourage him to talk about it. "I can see why raising horses would be appealing. They're beautiful, and this little guy is adorable."

"I can't even begin to describe how much pleasure I get from owning this ranch and working with quarter horses. It's satisfying work and I love it."

Which seemed to say that he didn't consider his former job satisfying. She gave him points for figuring that out and doing something about it. Not many men would give up a position as head honcho of a family empire in order to pursue a different dream.

And he was also donating his time and resources to the rehabilitation cause. "By the way, I think it's great that you're donating your time to help Will's patients." She'd asked if the ranch visits would cost extra, but apparently Adam wouldn't take money for any of it.

"Don't make me out to be too noble." Looking uncomfortable for the first time since they'd entered the barn, he stepped away from Saucy Lady's stall. "I get a tax deduction out of the deal."

"For me, too?"

He smiled. "No, not for you. Just the vets."

"So I should be paying you for this if I'm not a deductible expense."

"No, you shouldn't. You're a special case. I'm the one who pushed you in Will's direction, and if he thinks hanging out with my horses will help you, I'm happy to see what I can do."

The idea of being a special charity case didn't sit well with her. "I *can* pay. I'm a lawyer and I make decent money."

He nodded as if she'd just confirmed something he'd been puzzling about. "I figured you'd have a job that took brains."

"Why did you think so?"

"The way you spoke to me outside the bar. You had a commanding presence. It makes perfect sense that you're a lawyer."

"You should know. I'm sure you've worked with your share." That comment had slipped out, and she wanted to bite her tongue.

His silver gaze sharpened. "Been checking up on me, have you?"

She started to apologize. No, damn it. She had a right to know who she was dealing with. "Yes, I have."

He crossed his arms over his impressive chest. "That gives you quite an advantage. I know next to nothing about you. I'm guessing you found a boatload of stuff about me."

"Maybe that's because you're more interesting than I am."

"Not by a long shot. I'm just more visible."

"And newsworthy."

He stared at the floor for a moment before looking into her eyes. "None of it matters for what you and I need to accomplish."

"Not necessarily. I checked you out because I need to know whether I can trust you."

He studied her for several long seconds, his expression unreadable. "You can," he said at last. "I give you my word on that. But I suspect you're not into trusting guys these days."

She thought of Justin, the man she'd dated for a few months and even slept with. When the chips were down, Justin had left her to save his own skin. But was she any better? She'd run out of the bar the other night without considering the welfare of her best friends.

The threat hadn't been real, but at the time, she'd thought it was. She needed to forgive Justin, but still, she wished he'd stayed to help protect her. "I have been disappointed," she said, "but courage is sometimes hard to come by."

His voice was gentle. "I know. I've had to fight for every ounce of it I have. But for the record, I admire you for coming here when you clearly didn't want to."

"You're right. I didn't want to come. But you know what? I've fed a carrot to a horse. Now I have a little sliver of courage I didn't have before. I'm already ahead of the game."

He smiled. Even his eyes smiled. "Valerie, I do believe we're going to get along."

She liked that smile. A little tug of awareness caught her off guard, but she quickly suppressed it. She wasn't in the market. "I'm sure we will."

Three

Adam felt the subtle shift that told him she'd just re-treated a little. She was protecting herself, and he under-stood that completely. He'd learned from Will that people reacted to personal trauma in many different ways.

Some tried to block the fear through mind-numbing substances. Others used sex for the same purpose. Apparently Valerie's coping mechanism involved hiding in a carefully constructed shell. They were alike in that.

And it boded well for her success here at the ranch. Once she conquered her anxiety about horses, she'd love how they calmed her jangled nerves. He certainly did.

He glanced at her. "Ready to groom Rocket Fuel?"

"Yes." She took a deep breath. "Lead on."

"He's down at the far end on the left. You go on ahead. I need to grab the supplies." He'd sent her by her-self on purpose. Rocket Fuel was the friendliest horse in his stable, which was why Adam often used him for the first session. Discovering that the horse wanted to greet her without Adam coaxing him into it should boost her confidence.

He took his time fetching one of the plastic caddies they used to hold brushes and currycombs. Then he grabbed a lead rope. They'd be doing this outside.

When he finally made his way to the far end of the barn, the sight of her tentatively stroking the gelding's nose tugged at his heart. She was talking to him, too, although her words were pitched too low for Adam to hear. But Rocket Fuel's ears had swiveled forward to catch the sound of her voice.

That was another thing Adam liked about her. When he'd first laid eyes on her, she'd screeched at him, which hadn't been pleasant, but her normal voice had rounded, bell-like tones. He enjoyed listening to it.

She appealed to him more than any woman he'd met since his divorce. Hell, *no* woman had appealed to him since his divorce. Will had accused him of shutting down his libido, and apparently he had.

In any case, it was wide-awake now. Valerie made a sweet picture as she got acquainted with Rocket Fuel, but she was also sexy as hell in those tight jeans. Slim as she was, she still had curves that sent a message straight to his groin.

He stopped staring at her cute little ass and focused on the interchange between her and Rocket Fuel. "Looks like you've made a friend."

She ran her slender fingers down the chestnut gelding's nose. "I'll bet he flirts with all the girls."

"He does, but he likes some better than others. He seems quite happy right now." Adam would be, too, if she stroked him like that. He mentally gave himself a shake, exasperated by his one-track mind. This wouldn't be an easy situation, not easy at all.

"His coat already looks shiny." She moved away from the horse. "Are you sure he needs grooming?"

"If you were to ask him, he'd tell you he wouldn't mind being groomed twenty-four-seven. Horses enjoy being touched as much as people do." But until this very moment, he hadn't realized how deprived he felt in that regard.

Like most men, he'd counted on sex to satisfy the need to be touched. Because he wasn't having sex these days, he'd cut out that opportunity for human contact. He'd put his sensual needs on ice, but apparently they were starting to thaw.

She glanced at him, apprehension shining in her green eyes. "Will I be grooming him in the stall?"

"No." He should have explained that from the get-go, but he'd been distracted, damn it. "I'll lead him out back and tie him to the hitching post. That gives you more room to maneuver."

"Oh. Good." She still didn't seem relaxed, but some of the fear had left her eyes.

"You can carry this." He handed her the caddy for the grooming tools. "I'll bring him out for you." Eventually he'd like to have her feel comfortable going into the stall with the horse, but that would be for another day.

She backed away as he unlatched the door and walked inside, all the while talking to the gelding. Rocket Fuel was such a great horse, up for anything. Adam had bought him for sentimental reasons because nobody wanted a gelding that couldn't race anymore. But Rocket Fuel had turned out to be perfect for working with PTSD patients.

Adam clipped the lead rope to the horse's halter and

led him out of the stall. Valerie stood clear across the aisle. She'd put on her hat and tucked the earpiece of her sunglasses in the neck of her T-shirt. She held the caddy in front of her like a shield. Apparently petting Rocket Fuel when he was safely confined in a stall was a whole other thing from confronting him up close and personal.

He decided a little coaching might be in order. "I'll walk on his left and you can walk on his right."

"How about I just follow you out?"

"When working with a horse, it's best to walk beside them. They can see you then, and they like that better. Horses are prey animals, and we're predators. They have more reason to fear us than we have to fear them."

She nodded, although her expression told him she didn't really buy that. She followed his suggestion and walked alongside, but she put as much distance between herself and the horse as possible. Rocket Fuel's hooves clicked rhythmically on the cement floor.

"Is it true they can smell fear?"

Poor woman. She was really frightened. He could hardly wait until she realized how gentle this horse was. "I don't know about that, but I'm sure they pick up on our moods."

"Will I make him nervous?"

"Don't worry about Rocket Fuel. He's the steadiest horse on the planet. Believe it or not, he seems to know it's his job to help people get used to him. You two will be buddies before you know it."

"You think?"

"I know. I've seen it happen." He led the gelding into the sunshine and over to the hitching post.

Valerie followed, but maintained her distance.

"I suggest starting with the brush." Adam kept his voice nonchalant. "I like to go front to back, neck to tail, kind of like washing a car. Then you can come around and repeat the process on the other side." He tied the lead rope to the cross rail of the hitching post.

"Have you ever washed a car?"

It was a fair question. Guys like him usually didn't wash cars. She was a smart cookie who knew that. "Matter of fact, I have washed a car. Will's, not mine. We used to hang out at his house because . . . I guess because we could do things like wash his car in the driveway. It was a novelty for me." He rested his hands on Rocket Fuel's back and gazed at her. "Ready to get started?"

"Ready as I'll ever be." She set down the caddy and pulled out a brush before slowly approaching the horse. "Would you mind staying right there for a little while? Just until I get the hang of it?"

"Be glad to."

With the brush in her left hand, she stroked Rocket Fuel's neck so lightly that it probably tickled him. He snorted, and she drew back. "I'm doing it wrong."

"Use a little more pressure. He's a big guy. He can take it."

"Okay." She stepped closer and put some muscle into it. She had a cute habit of poking her tongue into her cheek while she concentrated on her work.

"That's great. Perfect. So you're left-handed?"

"No. This is the arm that was broken, and my physical therapist told me to use it whenever I could, since my natural tendency is to use my right."

"Broken?"

She hesitated. "Maybe I should tell you what happened. It's not a big secret or anything."

"You're not required to." Although he did want to know. Some of the soldiers didn't want to talk, which he understood, but knowing the nature of the trauma helped him work with them. The horses, instinctive creatures that they were, didn't need to know a damned thing, but Adam was only human.

"It might help if you know where I'm coming from."

Will had cautioned him not to counsel without a license, and to be up front about that with the people who came to his ranch, so he delivered the usual disclaimer. "Just remember I'm no therapist, just a guy with a ranch and some horses."

She glanced up at him, a gleam of humor in her eyes. "I'll keep that in mind." She returned her attention to the horse. "Should I do his legs?"

"Sure. Brush everything except his privates."

A quick smile put a dimple in her cheek.

She was a beautiful woman, and a plucky one, too. She crouched down to brush Rocket Fuel's fetlocks, putting herself close to his hooves. Maybe she was beginning to believe this horse wasn't out to hurt her.

When she didn't continue with her story, he thought maybe she'd decided against telling it, after all.

But then she spoke. "Remember the fire that broke out during a concert a few months ago?"

His heart stalled. "You were there?"

"Yes. I got caught in the crush and knocked down. I was lucky that I only ended up with a couple of broken ribs and a broken arm. But it scared the bejeezus out of me. People were . . ." She swallowed. "Crazy."

He had the impulse to walk around the horse and hold her, but he didn't think that would be a wise move. "I guess you must have gone alone." He'd met her two friends, and they would have fought that crowd tooth and nail to make sure they all got out unscathed.

"I went with a guy."

Adam sucked in a breath. He tried to remember if anyone had died in that mob scene. He wasn't sure. "Did he . . . was he . . ."

"Oh, he's fine." She brushed Rocket Fuel's foreleg again and again. "He used to run track, so he vaulted over people on his way to the exit. I tried to follow him, but that didn't work out."

"He *left* you?" Adam's muscles bunched in an instinctive response to that horrific news. Good thing Mr. Track Star wasn't standing here, or he would no longer be *fine*.

"Yes, but I can't talk, can I?" She kept her attention on her task. "I thought the bar was on fire and I ran out on my two best friends."

"That's different."

"No, it's not."

"It is, and I'll tell you why. At the bar, you responded that way because of your previous bad experience. I doubt the track star had that excuse when he ran out on you. Also, when a man escorts a woman somewhere, he's in charge of her safety. Case closed."

She looked up at him without speaking, but her eyes said plenty. They started off with a soft glow that grew brighter, and brighter yet. Apparently she'd really liked hearing him say that. "Thank you, Adam."

"For what?"

"Being a stand-up kind of guy."

His conscience pricked him. "Don't make me out to be a hero. I've done plenty of things I'm not proud of."

"But you wouldn't abandon a woman to a crazed mob."

"God, no. I'm sorry if you like the guy, but that's despicable. You could have been killed."

"Fortunately I wasn't." She stood. "But since then I've been a little . . . edgy."

"No doubt."

She started in on Rocket Fuel's flanks. "You don't have to babysit me now. I'm getting into this."

"Okay." He stepped back. "When you get to his rump, just come around that way to this side, but stick close to him. He's not a kicker, but it's better to learn good habits. When walking around behind a horse, either stay out of range, or move in close so he can't get any momentum."

"Have you ever been kicked?"

"Once, and I'm sure it was an accident, plus I wasn't paying attention like I should have been. I had a football-sized bruise on my thigh for a good while, but no broken bones." He hoped telling that story hadn't been a mistake. "I don't mean to scare you, but I want you to be safe."

"You've made that very clear. And I appreciate it."

"Common sense takes care of most things with horses, especially if they're raised right, like Rocket Fuel. I can't take any credit for him. He was a sweetheart when I got him."

"Mm-hm." Her answer was soft, almost indistinct.

He no longer heard the sound of the brush whisking over the horse's coat. When he peered over Rocket Fuel's back, he discovered her head was down, her face obscured by the brim of her hat. She rested the hand with the brush against Rocket Fuel's rib cage, and she'd propped her other hand right next to it. Her shoulders quivered. She was crying.

Shit. What was he supposed to do? The guys didn't cry. They swore a lot, but not a one of them had cried. He couldn't just stand there and let her cry all by herself. She'd had one guy desert her in her hour of need. He'd be damned if another one would.

Moving quickly to her side of the horse, he spoke her name so she wouldn't startle. Then he wrapped an arm around her shoulders.

With a sob, she turned and buried her face against his chest, knocking her hat to the ground. He wrapped her in his arms and held on while she soaked his shirt with her tears. She was a fairly noisy crier, and he thanked God for Rocket Fuel, who remained calm and stoic in the face of her misery.

Adam wasn't so stoic. He wanted to find the asshole who had left her to be trampled by a mob. Adam had a strong urge to rearrange the guy's face. Accidents happened, but she wouldn't be sobbing in his arms if the slimeball had stuck by her.

Thank God she'd plowed into him the other night and he'd had the presence of mind to get Will's card to her, or rather, her friend. Valerie couldn't do better than Will for a problem like this. But she was crying so hard, and all he knew to do was hold her and tell her everything would be okay. He doubted that she even heard him.

Eventually she ran out of steam, but she kept her face pressed against his damp shirt. "I'm so embarrassed."

"Don't be."

"I am. I don't even know you."

He rubbed her back. "Sometimes that's better."

"Maybe." She sniffed and kept her face buried. "I'm supposed to stay for a whole hour, but if it's okay with you, I'd like to hang it up for today."

"Whatever works for you."

"I'll be back."

"I hope so." He *really* hoped so.

"I didn't know brushing a horse would turn me into a faucet."

"Like I said, Rocket Fuel has his own methods for getting to know folks."

"He's a great horse."

"Yes, he is."

She took a shaky breath and finally lifted her head. "Don't look at me. I'm sure my mascara's smeared and my eyes are red."

"So's your nose." He wasn't about to obey her command not to look at her. She was beautiful even when she wasn't.

"You weren't supposed to look." She gave him a wobbly smile.

"I like looking at you, Valerie."

"Stop that. You'll make me cry again. How come you're so great?"

"I'm not."

"Yes, you are." Rising on tiptoe, she pressed a quick, but very warm, kiss on his lips. "Thank you."

He stood there in stunned silence. That's something else the soldiers never did. Should he kiss her back? No. She'd expressed gratitude, not passion. His mouth tingled and he felt a little dizzy. Then he realized that could be due to lack of oxygen, and he dragged in a breath.

But it had been a long time, more than a year, since any woman had kissed him on the mouth, and he savored the sensation. No doubt about it, whatever emotions he'd locked away during the divorce proceedings were working loose. That would be good news if he had an outlet for those feelings, but as he did not, he was on the road to Frustration City without a detour in sight.

Four

Originally Valerie had been scheduled to spend an hour each Saturday morning at the Triple Bar, but she wrangled an extra hour from work midweek so she could go out more often. The senior partners at the law firm seemed happy to give it to her.

She'd told them she was in therapy to get over her PTSD, something she'd never talked about in the office before. They were delighted. Apparently everyone she knew had been hoping she'd get herself help, and she'd had no clue they were paying that much attention.

As she drove out to the ranch for her third Saturday session, she hummed along with the radio. Three weeks ago she'd made this trip with a sour ball of anxiety in her stomach. Today she felt as if the sun was shining in her heart, even if it wasn't shining outside.

Rain had been falling off and on ever since she'd left her apartment. She didn't know how that would affect her work with Rocket Fuel, but Adam hadn't called to cancel, so apparently they were still on. That made her very happy. The hours spent at the ranch had become her favorite thing.

She loved watching the new foal, Naughty Boy, aka Bubba, who was now big enough to romp outdoors with his mother. After she'd finished grooming Rocket Fuel, she'd walk over to the fence and the curious foal would run up to check her out. She'd stroke his silky neck for a few seconds and then he'd bound away again.

Grooming Rocket Fuel wasn't scary anymore, either. She'd even tried leading him around the corral a few times, and she'd learned how to put on and take off his halter. She looked forward to gazing into his liquid brown eyes and running her bare hands over his solid warmth.

Sometimes, she got a little teary when she did that, but she'd never completely lost it like the first time. That morning she'd clung to Adam as if he were the mast of a ship in a storm-tossed sea and if she let go for an instant, she'd drown.

They hadn't spoken of that moment since then, but she thought about it constantly. Her tears had come without warning. She'd always prided herself on controlling her emotions, especially in front of others, but she'd been helpless to do it that day.

When she'd felt the warmth and strength of his arm around her shoulders, she'd allowed herself to let go. And he'd come through like a champ. The memory of his solid warmth and his soothing words remained clear three weeks later.

Another sensation remained clear, too—the velvet touch of his lips against hers. Later that day she'd blushed to think that she'd been so bold, but her embarrassment had faded since then. In fact, she'd been tempted to try it again. Or maybe not.

She'd debated the wisdom of that during the days when she wasn't at the ranch, days when she missed Adam a lot. Judging from his casual comments, he hadn't dated anyone since his divorce. But she'd caught him watching her a few times with a gleam in his eye.

If he'd been alert, he might have caught her doing the same with him. His gentle, yet firm, approach to his horses was sexy. She liked his loose-hipped, confident stride, and she'd learned to read his mood by the way he wore his hat. Nudging it back with his thumb meant he was curious about something and about to ask a question. Pulling it low over his eyes indicated intense focus, or even anger.

She wondered if he knew that he'd jerked down the brim of his hat when she'd told him about Justin leaving her at the concert. His anger, coupled with his emphasis on keeping her safe, had been one of the reasons she'd started blubbering. Add in Rocket Fuel's patience with her lame attempt to groom him, and she'd been an emotional wreck.

Three weeks later, she felt stronger. Sirens still made her slightly nauseated, and she took the stairs at work instead of riding in the elevator with a bunch of folks. She'd promised herself to take the elevator on Monday, though.

Last night she'd met her friends for drinks at the Golden Spurs & Stetson, and she'd suggested sitting within view of the door, but not right next to it, like before. She also gave herself points for overcoming her humiliation enough to go back in there. Baby steps, but important ones, in her estimation.

Melanie and Astrid had asked her how she was getting along with Adam. That was a complicated question, so she'd dodged it. Knowing her friends, they hadn't been fooled. They'd figured out she was interested. But they hadn't pushed for more information, for which she was grateful.

She hadn't worked out her own feelings for the guy. But when she drove up and saw him standing just inside the barn door out of the rain, her heart did a little summersault of joy. He obviously was waiting for her.

When she stopped the car and climbed out, he smiled and motioned to her. "Get on in here. And watch out for the mud."

"What, you're not going to spread your cloak over that puddle?" She left her hat on the passenger seat. She wouldn't need to shade her eyes from the sun today.

"This is a working ranch, lady, not the streets of Elizabethan England." He grinned at her as she made a dash for the barn. "Was that a test to see if I'd heard of Sir Walter Raleigh?"

"I wouldn't presume to test you on trivia." She fluffed her hair with her fingers. "I'll bet you had a grander education than I did."

He thumbed back his hat. "You didn't Google that information?" Apparently the guy wore his hat rain or shine.

"Actually, I did Google it, so I know how fancy your education was, but now I'm kind of embarrassed about snooping."

"Don't be." His silver gaze was warm. "I would have done the same thing in your place."

"I'll bet not many ranchers around here have degrees from Harvard."

He grimaced. "Family tradition. My grandfather went there, and my father went there, so of course I had to go there." Then he blew out a breath. "Listen to me, whining because I was forced to attend an Ivy League school. What a brat."

She was touched that he'd confided in her. He usually kept his personal remarks to a minimum. "I don't think it's the school so much as not having a choice."

His eyes widened. "Exactly! My path was mapped out for me and I didn't think I could change it. Will's the person who finally convinced me I could."

"I'm glad he did. You seem totally at home here."

"I am." He sighed with obvious satisfaction. "My mom's starting to accept my decision, which is nice. She was upset about the divorce, but Elise would never have adjusted to ranch life. She told me she'd married a guy who wore tuxes and three-piece suits. She had no interest in living with John Wayne."

Valerie didn't know if the coziness of the dry barn had encouraged him to talk about himself, but she welcomed the chance to know him better. Poor guy. Neither his family nor his wife had valued the real Adam Templeton.

"For what it's worth," she said, "I think you're a vast improvement over John Wayne."

"You mean because I'm alive?"

She laughed. "Well, there's that, but I—"

"Wow. That's the first time I've seen you laugh."

"It is? That can't be right."

"You haven't laughed the whole time you've been coming out here. I would have remembered if you had."

She wondered if he realized how much he'd revealed with that one remark. He'd been paying attention to her, all right. Very close attention. The implication of that sent a shiver of pleasure up her spine.

He cleared his throat. "So I guess you're making progress, huh?"

"I think so. I plan to tackle riding in the office elevator on Monday."

"Great idea." He hesitated. "Want me to ride it with you?"

"That would be silly." But she had to admit the task would be much easier with his solid presence. "Comforting as it would be to have you there, I can't ask you to come downtown just to ride an elevator with me."

"Then we'll throw in lunch."

Her chest tightened. He was asking her out. She hadn't accepted a date from anyone since the fire because she hadn't wanted to risk an embarrassing meltdown. But he'd already seen her lose control. He knew all about her issues.

"We don't have to have lunch," he said quietly. "I could just ride the elevator with you and leave."

She realized then that the invitation wasn't all about her. If she'd guessed right, he hadn't asked a woman for a date since before he was married. He might be rich, and he might be confident when dealing with his finances or with his horses, but that didn't mean he wasn't vulnerable in this area.

"I'd love to have lunch with you," she said. "And I'll save my elevator ride for when you show up at my office. We'll go down together."

"Okay." He still seemed uneasy. "I'm not trying to push you into anything, though. It's just lunch."

She met his gaze. "I like you, Adam. I like you a lot."

His response was velvet-soft. "Likewise, Valerie." Heat flared in his silver eyes for a brief moment before his expression changed and he was all business. "We'd best get started on today's project before the hour gets away from us."

"Right." She took a deep breath and tried to regain her mental balance. She'd suddenly pictured how the hour could really get away from them if he moved even one step closer. "What's on tap for today?"

"Since it's raining, we could work with Rocket Fuel in his stall, if you're up to it. Might be good practice for the elevator ride."

"Sure." During her last session she'd walked into the horse's stall, clipped the lead rope onto his halter, and led him out to the hitching post. Grooming him in the stall shouldn't bother her.

"The caddy's all set to go."

"I'll get it." She walked into the tack room and grabbed the plastic container. The barn had become a familiar place to her, and she loved feeling at ease there.

As they walked down the aisle, she noticed heads poking out from most of the stalls. "You have a full house today."

"Pure laziness on my part. They'd be willing to go out and run around in the rain, but then we'd have to clean 'em up again. Bubba's owner is coming out to pay a visit tomorrow, and I'm prideful enough to want all the horses looking good."

She stopped walking. "Wait a minute. Bubba's *owner*? That's not you?"

"No. A racing stable had already contracted for the

foal when I bought Saucy Lady, assuming it was a live birth. It was, so they'll take him once he's weaned."

"That's terrible!"

His gaze was stoic. "That's the horse business. I knew I wouldn't get to keep him when I bought his momma."

"But ... but you're a wealthy man. You could buy him back."

"I did offer, but they won't sell. They agreed to amend the contract for a price, though, so Bubba goes to them on the condition he won't start his training until he's two. He was born late in the year, so theoretically they could take him out early because of it, sort of like a kid who's enrolled in school before he's ready. They could ruin him if they do that."

"Let me get this straight. You had to pay them to do the right thing for a horse that doesn't belong to you?"

"Yes, and that might sound like a stupid financial decision, but I couldn't let that little guy go without protecting him."

"It doesn't sound stupid. It sounds humane." She wondered how many times he'd been chastised for such impulses when he was younger and being groomed to be a hard-headed businessman.

"I'll be watching them like a hawk, too. If they show any signs of trying to race him too soon, my lawyers will slap an injunction on them and I'll sue to get him back." He tugged the brim of his hat down over his eyes.

"You're a good man, Adam."

He shook his head. "Like I said before, don't go making me out to be something I'm not. I've made some business decisions I wish I could do over."

"In the past."

"Yeah, but the repercussions extend into the future." His jaw tensed.

"If you'll excuse my saying so, you're pretty hard on yourself."

"Now you sound like Will. He keeps telling me not to beat myself up over things I can't change."

"Smart guy." She hesitated. "Can we make a detour and go see Bubba before we head down to Rocket Fuel's stall?"

He glanced at her. "I was afraid of that. You're getting attached, aren't you?"

"And you're not?"

"I . . ."

"Adam Templeton, you are a big old softie and it'll tear you up inside when Bubba leaves, so don't get all macho on me and pretend otherwise."

That made him smile. "Okay, I won't. Let's go see that little guy."

When they arrived outside the stall, Valerie set down the grooming caddy so she could lean against the stall door and peek in. Adam joined her there, his hips mere inches from hers. She could hear him breathing, and the scent of his aftershave tantalized her. She was developing a massive crush on Mr. Templeton.

Bubba was nursing.

Valerie couldn't imagine separating mother and baby. "I suppose he'd have to be weaned, regardless of whether he stayed here."

"He would. Don't worry. It'll be a gradual process. I won't ship him off until he's used to being on his own."

"But he'll lose his home as well as his mother."

He glanced over at her. "I love these horses, but I'm

in the business of raising them for sale. If I tried to keep them all, I'd go through a hell of a lot of money in a very short time. I'm not focused on the bottom line the way I used to be, but I'd rather not lose money on this venture if I can help it."

"I know." She gazed at him. "I didn't mean to sound judgmental." But she had sounded that way, and he'd been judged his whole life and found wanting. "I'm sorry. Of course you have to sell horses to keep the ranch going. I was out of line to make that comment."

"It's okay, Valerie. You can always be honest with me and tell me how you feel. I'm being honest with you in describing how this operation works."

"And I get it. I do. I promise to take that into consideration from now on. How soon will he be weaned?"

"Not for a long time. Four or five months from now, maybe longer."

She relaxed. "Oh, good." She wondered what their status would be four or five months from now. She'd never discussed the duration of these sessions, either with Will or with Adam. But at some point, she hoped she would be cured of her phobias. And then what would be her excuse for coming to the ranch?

"Don't worry," Adam said. "I'll take it slow and easy. The new owners may want to get their hands on him, but they don't want a neurotic mess because he was weaned too early."

"No reason to rush it." Or to rush her treatment. Ha. She knew exactly why she wanted to drag it out. She was looking for an excuse to keep seeing him. But they were having lunch on Monday. That would change the dynamic.

Her mind leaped ahead as she thought of where they'd go and what she'd wear. She'd never dated a billionaire before. But as she stood next to him watching Bubba nurse, she realized he wouldn't show up looking like a billionaire.

No, he'd walk into her office in jeans, Western shirt, boots, and Stetson. He'd look the way he always did. She'd be the one in a whole different costume. And after appearing in plain old jeans and T-shirts for three weeks, she had the purely feminine urge to knock his socks off.

Five

On Monday morning, Adam parked his truck in a garage a block away from Valerie's law office. He'd chosen a café close by, one that advertised quick lunch service. Although he would have rather taken her somewhere more atmospheric, he wasn't sure what her schedule was. She might have so many appointments that she wouldn't be able to linger.

This whole setup was new to him. His dating years had involved debutantes with plenty of free time and a taste for luxury. But he was at a different point in his life, and as a result he'd asked a working girl to lunch. His usual approach of champagne and caviar wouldn't fit the occasion.

To say he was nervous would be grossly understating the case. He'd called Will yesterday and asked him point blank if he'd hoped for a romance between Adam and Valerie. Will had admitted the idea had crossed his mind, which in Will-speak meant he'd planned the entire thing.

Adam couldn't be upset with the guy. Valerie was terrific, and something might actually come out of Will's meddling. Will had asked to meet for a drink after work today so he could find out how lunch had turned out. That meant Adam had to stay in town for the remainder of the day, so he'd made an appointment with his lawyers to go over the amended contract for Bubba and make sure it was ironclad.

But that was all later. First he had to manage this date, for that's exactly what it was. Despite the offer of helping Valerie handle her first elevator ride since the fire, he'd also invited her to eat a meal with him. Anyone with the slightest bit of common sense would classify that as a date.

He was familiar with the building. His grandfather had owned it, and made a killing when he sold it. Adam had grown up hearing about those spectacular financial victories, but that kind of challenge held no interest for him now. Truthfully, it never had.

Walking inside the tasteful lobby, Adam located the directory and the law firm of Meacham and Daniels, where Valerie worked. When Adam had been married to Elise, he'd attended social functions with the senior partners, Stan Meacham and Robert Daniels. He'd liked them both. Valerie had chosen a good firm when she'd hired on here.

He rode the elevator to the fourth floor and listened for any alarming rattles or squeaks in the mechanism. The elevator seemed smooth, and the posted certification said it had been recently checked out. He hoped the damned thing wouldn't malfunction.

Thinking about the elevator had distracted him, but once he was walking down a carpeted hallway to the law offices, his chest grew tight. What the hell was he doing?

Was he ready for this? He'd tossed the lunch idea out in a moment of insanity when he hadn't been able to imagine her riding the elevator alone, at least not the first time.

Now he was committed to an actual date, and most women expected that would be followed by a second date, right? He had no trouble imagining himself in bed with the gorgeous Valerie Wolitzky. He'd fantasized that many times, and his dreams about her had become super-erotic. But this dating thing sucked. He was woefully out of practice.

Too bad. It was game time. He opened the door to the suite of offices and walked over to the receptionist's desk without hesitation. He wasn't going to let some cute blonde who didn't look more than twenty, max, see him sweat.

"I'm here for Miss Wolitzky."

She smiled, revealing even white teeth. "You must be Mr. Templeton. If you'll have a seat, I'll tell her you're here."

He didn't want to sit, but pacing the reception area would send the wrong message. So he levered himself onto a brown leather sofa and picked a magazine from the ones arranged across a glass coffee table. He didn't bother to look at the title.

When he realized the magazine he'd grabbed— *Career Woman's Weekly*—he put it back. He wasn't going to be found reading *Career Woman's Weekly* when Valerie walked into the reception area. Inspiration hit and he pulled out his phone. He could check his messages. Brilliant.

Except he had no messages. Earlier this morning he'd

deleted everything he didn't need, and no one had texted or emailed him since then. There was a time when he couldn't keep up with his messages, but ever since he'd changed direction, he had no trouble whatsoever.

Normally he loved that. Not having a ton of messages was evidence that he had indeed taken control of his life. But while he sat in the reception area waiting for Valerie, he would have liked to have some messages to answer.

"Adam?"

He glanced up from his messageless phone and leaped to his feet. *Wow.* He hadn't expected her to come out of her office in jeans and a T-shirt. He wasn't sure what he'd expected, but the short black skirt, paired with an emerald green blouse and black jacket, was a knock-out. That wasn't even taking into account her sexy heels and silver jewelry.

She hadn't worn jewelry to the barn, which made sense, but the silver teardrops looked great with her short hair, and the layered necklace emphasized her slender throat. Several silver bangles jingled when she moved her arm. He couldn't stop staring at her.

"Ready for lunch?" She adjusted the strap of her black shoulder purse and gave him a quick smile.

That's when he really looked into her green eyes and saw the anxiety there. She might be dressed like a confident professional, but she was afraid to get in that elevator. Thank God he was here.

"Yep, we're all set," he said. "I've found a little place that should get us in and out fast, in case you have an early-afternoon appointment."

"Thanks for that, but I built some extra time into my schedule today."

"That's good." He tucked his phone in his pocket. "Let's go."

"You two have fun," the receptionist called after them.

"Thanks, Carol!" Valerie sounded breezy and carefree.

But when Adam rested a hand against the small of her back, he could feel her trembling. "You'll be fine," he said in a low tone as they walked out of the office.

"I'll be better, now that you're here. It's such a small thing, but I've been worried about it since we made the plan on Saturday."

She reminded Adam of the skittish horses he'd worked with at the ranch. "Let's not get on the elevator yet." He slipped a hand around her waist and guided her down the hallway toward a window that looked out on the street. "Let's talk for a minute."

"I thought a nervous person was supposed to dive straight into something before she has a chance to think about it."

"Too late. You've been thinking about this elevator for nearly two days. Now you need to think about something else."

"Like what?"

He wracked his brain for a way to distract her. Finally he settled on the only thing that he could come up with. At the end of the hallway, he took off his hat and drew her into his arms. "This." Before she could protest, he lowered his head and took firm possession of her mouth.

She went rigid with surprise. Clearly she hadn't expected him to make a move like that. But she didn't pull away, and he took that as a sign that she wasn't totally opposed to the idea of kissing him for real, and not just the butterfly kiss she'd given him three weeks ago.

Slowly her resistance melted, and she nestled against him. He couldn't help groaning at the pleasure of it. That seemed to excite her. Wrapping her arms around his neck, she parted her lips and offered him . . . paradise.

He sank into the kiss, surrendering to a hunger he'd barely acknowledged until now. Cupping the back of her head, he buried his fingers in her soft curls and held her steady while he tasted, shifted his angle, and tasted again.

She was the perfect combination of sweetness and sin, carefree joy and dark desire. Her enthusiasm for the kiss fueled his, and he lost track of time and place. If someone had told him they'd been magically transported to a tropical island, he would have believed it.

Then a phone played the first notes of "The Yellow Rose of Texas" and broke the spell.

Valerie pulled away, her breathing uneven, her eyes dark with passion. "That's Astrid. She probably . . . wants to know about . . . the elevator."

Adam released her and dragged in air as he put on his hat. Holy hell. What if her phone hadn't rung? How far would he have taken that kiss? How far would she have let him take it?

She fumbled in her purse and came up with the phone. "Hey." She sounded normal as can be. "Nope, not yet." She glanced at Adam. "He's here and we're about to get on. Thanks for thinking of me. Sure. I will. 'Bye." She disconnected and started to put her phone back when the theme from the TV show *Dallas* chimed.

Valerie rolled her eyes. "Melanie." Answering the call,

she had a similar conversation before disconnecting. "They worry," she said.

"Because they care about you."

"They do, and they're both thrilled that you offered to ride the elevator with me. If you hadn't, they would have, but they think—" She flushed. "Never mind what they think."

"I'd very much like to know what they think." If he planned to get involved with Valerie, and that seemed likely, he needed to know more about her best friends.

"They think you're better suited to the job."

"Why me? They're your best friends. They know you better than anybody."

Her flush deepened. "Astrid said that a gorgeous hunk in a Stetson is exactly what I need to take my mind off my fears. Melanie dittoed that." She glanced up at him. "Happy, now?"

He couldn't help grinning. "Yes, ma'am. But I can't help wondering what *you* think." He was fishing for a compliment, but he didn't care. Being admired for his new persona was plain fun.

She met his gaze. Her cheeks still flamed, which made her green eyes sparkle even brighter. "I think my friends have excellent taste."

"Thanks." That comment warmed him clean through.

"You have a little lipstick ..." She reached up and rubbed his lower lip with her thumb. "That got it."

Looking into her eyes, he caught her hand and kissed the tips of her fingers. Heat shimmered in her gaze.

She gently disengaged her hand from his. "Let's go conquer that elevator before the urge to kiss you again overwhelms my good sense."

"You bet." This was quickly turning into one of the best days of his life.

As Valerie stood beside Adam in front of the bank of elevators, he took her hand, threading his fingers through hers. His grip was warm and firm. Even better, touching him reminded her of the way he'd kissed her. She couldn't think about that sizzling kiss and worry about the elevator at the same time.

His solution had been a brilliant one, but she didn't know if he'd done it mostly to calm her nerves, or if that kiss was the beginning of . . . what? That kiss created more questions than answers.

Yes, they had chemistry. She thought he'd be more than willing to take her to bed if the opportunity presented itself. But her hiatus from dating had taught her something. Before the fire she'd been focused on enjoying Mr. Right Now instead of searching for Mr. Right.

That was how she'd ended up with Justin, who'd never demanded any kind of deep connection. Neither had she, so maybe it shouldn't surprise her that he hadn't been willing to risk his life to save her. Before Justin had been Brent, and before him, Eric. Those superficial relationships had run their course and ended without much fanfare.

That kind of laissez-faire arrangement wouldn't work for her anymore. It was, she realized now, a waste of time, and time was a precious commodity. A person couldn't know how much of it they had left, and she'd already thrown away several years on dead-end love affairs.

But she had no idea how Adam viewed this attraction between them. He might be hoping to use it as a way to get his groove back after having his heart slammed by his divorce. If so, he'd have to find himself another woman to fill that temporary role.

She didn't know how to have that kind of discussion with him, though, because she'd never felt this way before. One thing was for sure—they wouldn't talk about it over lunch. She wondered what they would talk about when they didn't have a horse to focus on. Should be interesting to find out.

The elevator dinged and the doors slid open. Just her luck, it contained three people and a rolling cart piled high with file boxes. There was room for her and Adam, but just barely.

Adam squeezed her hand. "We can catch the next one," he murmured.

"No." Taking a quick breath, she stepped into the leftover space. She was through being a baby about this.

Still holding her hand, Adam removed his hat and followed her in. In typical elevator protocol, they all faced the door as it slowly closed. But as the opening narrowed, Valerie's chest tightened.

Breathe, she told herself, and she tried, but a steel band had wrapped itself around her lungs. She gripped Adam's hand and fought her rising panic. When he extricated his hand from hers, she made a little sound of protest.

Then his arm circled her shoulders and he pulled her close. Leaning down, he put his mouth close to her ear. "I'm here, Valerie," he murmured softly as he massaged her shoulder. "You're fine. Everything's okay." Then he pressed his lips to the tender spot behind her ear.

She closed her eyes and concentrated on the feel of

his mouth against her skin. So warm. Some of the tightness eased, and she took a shallow breath. And another.

He lifted his mouth and spoke into her ear again. "You're doing great," he said softly. "We're almost there."

The elevator jolted to a stop, and she opened her eyes in relief.

"Second floor," Adam said.

Two rather large men started into the elevator. "Squeeze in," one of them said. "We can make it."

"No, sorry." Adam stepped in front of Valerie. "We're full."

"Look, mister," one of the guys said. "We're running late. Just let us in. It's only one floor."

"Yeah, let them in," said someone in the back of the elevator. "We'll make room."

"No can do. Catch the next one." Adam reached over and pushed the button that closed the doors as the two men glared at him.

Valerie wrapped both arms around Adam's waist and gave him a hug. She stayed that way, pressed against him, until the doors opened on the first floor. Then she let go and followed him out, her heart full to the brim with gratitude.

He turned back to her with a smile of triumph. "Congratulations! You did it!"

"Thanks to you." Capturing his face in both hands, she pulled his head down and kissed him full on the mouth. She didn't care if the other elevator passengers got an eyeful. They probably already thought she and Adam were strange, not to mention unaccommodating.

It wasn't a long kiss, not like the one he'd given her, but she couldn't think of a better way to reward him for being such a hero. After she released him, she moved back and took a deep breath. "That was awesome."

"You actually liked the ride?"

"No. I hated the ride, but I loved the way you stood up to those guys who wanted to crowd in." She gazed at him. "You protected me," she said softly.

"Of course."

Looking into his eyes, she felt her heart lurch. She still didn't know how he saw their relationship, but for her, the jury was in. She'd fallen for him.

Six

Lunch went by so fast that Valerie was shocked when she glanced at her phone and discovered they'd been sitting there for more than an hour. Having something to talk about hadn't been a problem. Without the horses to distract them, they found out how many things they had in common—books, movies, music, even food choices.

But Valerie had shared common interests with the other guys she'd dated, too. This first lunch didn't seem like the occasion to ask the tough questions about whether Adam wanted kids and whether he ever intended to marry again. He might have decided against it, and his horses might have replaced any desire to have a family.

Until the fire, Valerie hadn't thought kids mattered to her, either, but lately she'd changed her mind. A kid or two would be nice. She could live without having them, but she wouldn't mind, if she found the right man—someone kind, nurturing, heroic. Someone like the guy sitting across the table from her at this cozy little café.

She'd been here before for lunch. It was close and reasonable, and she could usually get a table by the door. Yet today she hadn't minded where they sat. The hostess had given them a table roughly in the middle of the café, and Valerie hadn't once worried about the distance to the front door.

All her senses had been focused on Adam. Now every time she came in here she'd remember sharing a meal with him. Whether she'd meant to or not, she'd created memories with him that weren't likely to go away anytime soon.

"I saw you check the time." He put down his empty iced tea glass. "You should get back."

"Probably. But it's been fun."

"Sure has." His hat was tilted back and his smile was open and uncomplicated.

"You may not realize that it's significant, but we're sitting in the middle of the restaurant. I'm nowhere near the door."

"Shoot, I didn't think about that."

"Neither did I! That's what's so wonderful about it."

"I'm glad. I wish we didn't have to leave, but it's time for you to get back to work." He picked up the check and pulled his wallet out of his hip pocket.

"And for you to head back to the ranch."

"Actually, I'm not leaving until later." He set some bills on top of the check and returned his wallet to his pocket. "As long as I'm here, I decided to take care of some business. And I'm meeting Will for a drink at the Golden Spurs & Stetson after his last appointment."

"That's nice." She liked knowing he would be in town for a little longer, even if she wouldn't be seeing him.

They wouldn't be separated by so many miles. Yeah, she was definitely developing a crush on Adam Templeton.

She really needed to get a bead on how he felt about her. She thought about the old days, when fathers collared the men who were dating their daughters and demanded to know their intentions. She could use a custom like that right now.

Except it was totally impractical in this day and age. When she'd been in high school, her father had been more than happy to interfere in her love life, but she'd lived on her own for many years and that dynamic had gone by the wayside. She couldn't very well ask her dad to drive up from Houston and question Adam about his intentions.

She pushed back her chair. "Thank you for lunch. And give Will my best when you see him."

"Are you walking out on me?" He said it with a teasing grin as he stood.

"I wouldn't dream of it, but you said you have business to take care of, so I thought I'd get out of your hair." After standing, she took her purse from the back of the chair.

"My business isn't that urgent. I figured on walking you back and riding up the elevator with you, unless you don't want me to."

"Well, then, I'd love that." She wouldn't be seeing him again until Wednesday afternoon, so any added moments today would be a bonus. "I just didn't want to monopolize your time with my elevator phobia."

He paused. "It was a great excuse to see you, Valerie," he said quietly.

"Oh." Her cheeks warmed. "That's good to hear."

"Twice a week doesn't seem often enough."

Her breath caught. "It doesn't?" She cautioned herself not to read too much into that statement. A guy could say that kind of heady thing and still only be interested in a no-strings affair.

"No. In fact . . . will you have dinner with me tonight? I know it's short notice, but—"

"Yes." Well, she certainly wasn't playing hard to get, now was she? But she was impatient to find out if this flirtation would lead anywhere. She wanted him to be her knight in shining armor, but she didn't know if he wanted the role or not.

"Great." He smiled. "I'm meeting Will around five, but I'll hustle him off to his wife by six. I can pick you up around six-thirty."

"Okay." Anticipation shot through her, making her tingle all over.

"It won't be too fancy." He waited until she'd started for the café's front door, yet he somehow managed to get there in time to hold it open for her. "I didn't come prepared with a dinner jacket."

"I don't care about fancy." And the more she thought about it, the less she wanted to be waited on in a public place. And it had nothing to do with any concern that panic would set in. After today's lunch, she wasn't so worried about that.

But eating in a restaurant would mean more polite conversation about their likes and dislikes. Been there, done that. She was ready to take things to the next level. Until they did that, she couldn't broach the subject near to her heart, namely, his motives for pursuing her. What she required was a bit more privacy.

She wasn't a great cook, but she could manage spaghetti, and during their lunch conversation he'd already confirmed that he liked that. If she used one of the really good sauces in a jar and grated her own cheese, it should be decent. Add a bagged salad, a bottle of wine, and voilà!

They held hands on the way back to the office, and it seemed like the most natural thing in the world. In her heels, she was only a few inches shorter than he was. She wasn't sure if he matched his stride to hers, but they walked well together. That meant something, right?

"How did the visit with Bubba's owner go?" she asked as they approached her building.

"He worries me a little. That's why I'm checking with my lawyers this afternoon to make sure the amended contract will hold up."

She squeezed his hand. "You'll be able to protect that little guy. I have faith in you."

"Let's hope you're right."

In the lobby of her building, an empty elevator stood open. "Come on!" She hurried toward it. "We can make it."

He laughed and lengthened his stride. They dashed through the doors, barely making it before they closed.

Catching her other hand in his, he faced her as the elevator started up. "You okay?"

"Yes. Yes!" She launched herself into his arms and whisked off his hat. "I feel great. Kiss me, Adam."

With a groan he pulled her tight, and this time his mouth was more demanding. Gratifyingly so. The thrust of his tongue told her exactly what he was thinking, and he boldly cupped her bottom so that she could have no doubt about his immediate intentions.

Her plan for tonight was a *very* good idea. They'd get

down to the nitty-gritty and then she'd know whether to dive into this relationship headfirst or pull back. As the heat of their kiss intensified, he backed her against the elevator wall and pressed his thigh between her legs. The elevator pinged to a stop, and he released her with a soft curse.

Straightening her clothes and taking a deep breath, she looked into his passion-glazed eyes. "Don't make reservations for tonight. We'll eat in. I'll text you my address."

His sharp intake of breath and the searing glance he gave her provided all the encouragement she needed to follow through with that plan. When she walked out of the elevator, she knew he'd watch her leave. She deliberately twitched her hips and smiled at his moan of frustration before the doors closed and the elevator started back down.

She was playing with fire, and she knew it. She'd pretty much promised him sex tonight, which raised the stakes for her but might be simply a fun romp for him. But having sex was the only way she'd find that out. She'd know by his behavior afterward where she stood.

As for her elevator phobia, thanks to Adam and his sexy kisses, she had it on the run, perhaps forever.

"I figured you might like a report on how your match-making efforts are progressing." Adam studied his friend sitting across the small table.

"I wouldn't call it matchmaking, exactly." Will took a sip of his draft. "Sending her out to the Triple Bar was a logical move. I knew she was a good candidate for working with your horses."

"And a good candidate to draw me out of my shell?"

"Maybe. Do you like her?"

"No."

"I'm sorry. I thought you two would—"

"My feelings go way beyond *like*. She's the sexiest, most interesting woman I've met in a long time."

"See there?" Will sat back in his chair and smiled. "I had a feeling she'd appeal to you. And for what it's worth, I'm very encouraged by her progress. How did the elevator ride go?"

"You knew about that?"

"She told me today was the day, and then this morning she called to say you were riding with her. She wondered if she was wimping out, but I urged her to go with whatever worked. She needed to get on that elevator."

"Well, she rode it. Twice." He didn't dare think too much about that second time while he was sitting here with Will.

"That's great."

"After the first elevator ride, we went to lunch and sat at a table in the middle, fairly far away from the door. I didn't even think about it until she mentioned passing another milestone."

"Excellent." Will took another swig of beer. "You two could be very good for each other."

Adam nursed his beer. He was only allowing himself one, because he wanted to be completely sober when he arrived at Valerie's apartment. "There might be an issue, though."

"What's that?"

"She seems to think I'm some kind of hero."

Will laughed.

"Yeah, I know. Funny, isn't it?"

"No, it's not at all. I'm laughing at the way you said it, as if you couldn't possibly be any woman's hero."

"Hell, you of all people know I'm not hero material."

"Don't sell yourself short, buddy."

"Oh, come off it, Will. I should never have taken the CEO position and marrying Elise was a huge mistake. She had every right to kick me to the curb after I changed the rules of the game. Valerie's put me on a pedestal and I don't deserve to be there. I'm going to disappoint her, and then what?"

Will leaned forward. "Sure, you might disappoint her, but not in the ways that count. You've made mistakes, sure, but we all do when we're trying to figure out where we fit in the world. You're a good man, and that's what she values in you. She might be the first woman who sees who you really are and likes what she sees."

"I wish I believed that."

"I wish you did, too. I'm sure it's damned unfamiliar, unfortunately."

"I don't know, Will." Adam sighed and picked up his glass. "I just have the awful feeling she's built an image of me that I can never live up to."

"Maybe you already have lived up to it."

Adam shook his head. "Not a chance." Then he changed the subject, because that one was too depressing. He and Will talked sports and politics, but his mind never strayed far from thoughts of Valerie.

He planned to go to her apartment for dinner because he couldn't stay away. And he'd make love to her, because that was what she obviously intended, and he couldn't resist her. If he had any sense at all, he would resist, but he kept seeing that little twitch in her hips as she'd walked away from the elevator. Yeah, he would go to her apartment tonight. He could hardly wait.

Will, who was as perceptive as most therapists, picked up on Adam's underlying agitation. "Do you need to head back to the ranch? Is that why you're fidgeting?"

"Uh, no." He should have realized that meeting Will for a drink was a tactical error. The guy could read him better than any human on the planet. "Valerie invited me to her place for dinner."

Will's blond eyebrows lifted. "Did she, now?"

"She did, and I'll thank you not to comment on that fact."

"Wasn't planning to say a word."

"No, but you're thinking plenty. Should I cancel?"

Will held up both hands, palms out. "I'm not about to make that call. But I'm glad to hear she invited you over. It's a positive sign."

"Will, I haven't . . . I've been off the market for . . . well, you know."

"I do, and I think this is also a positive sign for you."

"You're looking entirely too pleased with yourself, buddy."

"All I did was put two people on the same path and let nature take its course."

"And if it all blows up?"

Will shrugged. "Life is messy. But you're both intelligent people with good hearts. I have faith that you'll be able to work it out."

"Just so you know, I told her I was having a drink with you tonight before I came over to her place."

"Then tell her I said hi."

"Will, what if tonight is a disaster and she refuses to come out to the Triple Bar anymore? How will that affect her progress?"

"First of all, I doubt tonight will be a disaster, and second of all, she's doing well. If she never came out to your ranch again, she'd still have sessions with me, and I have every confidence she'll recover. You can be proud of the help you've given her. She's going to be just fine."

"Good." Adam polished off his beer in three gulps. "That's very good." He didn't say that the idea of Valerie never coming out to the ranch again tied his stomach in knots. If going to her place tonight could ruin that, then he shouldn't do it. He shouldn't take that risk.

He pulled his phone out of his pocket. "I'm going to cancel. I can't take a chance that something will go wrong tonight and she'll give up on coming out to the ranch. She loves it there."

"Don't cancel."

"Why not?" Adam paused, the phone in his hand. "Give me one good reason."

"I could give you dozens, but I'll settle for what you just said. Did you hear yourself?"

"I can't take a chance on something going wrong."

"Not that. The last part. You said she loves it there."

"Yeah, she does. Her face lights up when she arrives, and she's really bonded with Rocket Fuel and Saucy Lady. I'm afraid she's attached to Bubba, too, but she understands about him. I'm hoping that soon I can get her up on Rocket Fuel and we can go for a ride. Not a long one, just a short little ride, to get her used to—"

"Adam, you've found a woman who loves your ranch. Why in God's name are you going to cancel your evening with her?"

"She loves the *ranch*, William. But the *rancher,* who would be yours truly, could end up being a huge disappointment to her. If I avoid that by backing off, then she can continue to enjoy the ranch she loves. Do you see what I'm saying?"

Will shook his head. "It must be hell to be you. Listen, I hate to be the one to tell you this, but you're screwed. If you cancel tonight, she'll be pissed, and you'll lose her. If you mess up tonight, she'll be pissed, and you'll lose her. So your best option is to head on over there and do your damnedest not to mess up."

"You're just a basket of rainbows and butterflies, Will."

His buddy smiled. "That's what they tell me. Now, get on your horse and ride over to Valerie's place."

"Right." Adam threw some money down on the table because it was his turn to pay. "If this doesn't work out, you owe me free counseling."

"It's always free, Adam."

He left the bar and prayed that he wouldn't end up sitting in Will's office next week, pouring out his troubles.

Seven

What had she been thinking? Valerie had arrived back at her apartment at five-forty-five after a mad dash to the grocery store. Adam would be at her door in forty-five minutes. She was about to risk having a man in her apartment again. More than that, she'd given him plenty of reason to believe they'd have sex.

Earlier she'd thought it was a fabulous idea. Now she realized that having sex involved giving up control, at least if you planned to do it right. For the past several months she'd been all about keeping things under control.

But she trusted Adam. He'd guided her through the process of learning to be comfortable with his horse, Rocket Fuel. He'd taken her successfully through her first elevator ride in months, and he'd protected her from suffering in a crowded elevator, which could easily have sent her into a panic.

She'd been fantasizing about him for three weeks, and their kiss during the second elevator ride had been hot enough to melt the buttons on the control panel. Inviting him to her place so they could explore this attraction on a deeper level was an obvious next move. Except she was having some of those pesky second thoughts.

Sometime this afternoon, when the glow from the elevator kiss had worn off, she'd started thinking about the fact that he wasn't just any cowboy. As they worked with the horses at his ranch, that was how she tended to view him, probably because she wasn't intimidated by a guy who wore faded jeans and scuffed boots. But he was also a billionaire.

This afternoon, Valerie had tried to convince herself it wasn't important. Adam shouldn't care what her apartment looked like or whether she'd cooked a gourmet meal. And he wouldn't, if he was the kind of man she thought he was, the kind she could get serious about. But they'd always met on his turf.

Correction, they'd always met in his barn. The barn was functional, not fancy. On her first visit to the Triple Bar, she'd paid attention to the obvious display of wealth in the pristine pastures and the elegant two-story house on the hill. After that, none of it had mattered because she'd focused on Adam and the horses.

But ignoring his wealth, especially if she envisioned a possible future with him, would be naïve. Tonight she'd find out how well he managed in a setting that was several notches down from what he was used to. That would be a good thing to know, right? If he was ill at ease, or if he patronized her, even a little bit, a relationship between them wouldn't work.

Therefore she shouldn't worry about how her place looked, but she wasn't that strong. The first thing that stood out in her initial survey was a smear of yellow paint on her white living room wall. Her landlord had given her permission to repaint, and she'd tested that cheery color with one ten-inch swipe of the brush. She wanted to cover it up.

Her bedroom closet yielded nothing but rolled-up rock band posters from her younger days. Then she spied her collection of scarves. Twenty minutes later, thanks to the scarves and some pushpins, she'd created a fabric wall decoration that looked . . . weird.

But she was out of time to worry about that, so she left it. Next she made a sweep of the area, grabbing up newspapers and magazines, straightening throw pillows, and blowing the dust off her coffee table. It would have to do. She still had to get dinner started, set the table, and change clothes.

Damn! She'd forgotten to buy wine. She had a half-bottle of Chardonnay in the refrigerator. Yeah, that would be classy. *Here's a glass of leftover wine. Hope you didn't want seconds, because that's all there is.*

Stopping in her tracks, she took several calming breaths. She could do this. Presenting a perfect scenario wasn't in the cards. No matter what she did, the ambiance wouldn't match what Adam had experienced while he was married to Elise.

Ah, there was her other hidden fear. While at work this afternoon, she'd Googled a picture of his ex, looking poised, blond, stunning, and dripping in expensive jewels. He might not want to be married to her anymore, but she was still the type he was used to. Elise would never offer him leftover wine and spaghetti sauce from a jar.

Screw it! Valerie rolled her eyes, impatient with herself. She'd taken this step, made this plan, and she might as well see it through. At six-twenty-seven, she turned on the burners under the pasta water and the pan for the spaghetti sauce. Then she ran into her bedroom and changed into a green and blue patterned dress that was on the slinky side and looked sort of hostesslike.

Her doorbell rang before she'd decided on shoes. Shoving her feet into some sparkly flip-flops, she took a deep breath, left her bedroom, and went to answer the door.

He stood in the hall holding a bottle of wine and a bouquet of flowers. His silver gaze was intent, his smile a little tense. She hoped to hell he wasn't having second thoughts, too.

Her heart thumped wildly. They were about to be completely alone for the first time since they'd met. So much hinged on tonight. So much.

He hoisted his gifts. "I know I'm a walking cliché, but—"

"No, it's sweet. Come in." She stepped back and he walked through her door, into her world. She was so nervous she could barely breathe. "Let me . . . Let me take those."

He handed her the bouquet and the wine. "You look beautiful, Valerie."

"It's just—" She caught herself before she dismissed his compliment. He'd made it with a soft reverence that told her it was more than an offhand remark. Even though he'd moved in circles where women wore designer clothes, her quickly chosen outfit had dazzled him. That touched her. "Thank you."

He took off his hat. "Where should I put this?"

"On the coffee table's fine."

He set it there without spending any time looking at the table, or the sofa and chairs, or any part of her living room, including her scarf wall art. His hot gaze came back immediately to rest on her. "Could you put those down for a minute?"

"Sure." Her heart beat faster as she laid the bouquet on the coffee table next to his hat and set the wine bottle beside the bouquet.

"I know you have dinner going. I can smell spaghetti sauce. But I need—"

"Me, too." She stepped into his arms with a moan of happiness. "Oh, me, too."

His hungry mouth on hers swept away her misgivings. He was desperate for her, and she was equally desperate for him. He crushed her to him, sending her racing pulse into overdrive. Yes, oh, *yes.*

Lifting his mouth from hers, he gripped her tight, as if afraid that ending the kiss would make her vanish. "Can dinner wait?"

She had no idea, but the ache building deep in her body answered for her. "Yes."

"Good, because I can't."

"Come with me." Wiggling out of his arms, she caught his hand and led him back to her bedroom. The sun hadn't set, and light filtered through her gauzy curtains, bathing the room in a golden glow. There would be no hiding in the dark this first time.

She didn't care. His obvious need for her made her bold. *And puts you in control*, whispered a little voice. She ignored it. Turning back to him, she pulled her dress over her head and tossed it aside.

He sucked in a breath. "Hold it. Don't move."

She paused, but she couldn't be completely still. She quivered in anticipation of what would come next, and what would happen after that, and how it would be when they finally . . .

"I don't want to forget how you look. You're outlined in gold, Valerie. You shimmer."

"Because I'm shaking."

"So am I. I want you so much that it scares me."

"I'm a little scared, too." She stepped toward him. "But the closer you are, the less I'm afraid." She rested her palms on his chest and felt the rapid beat of his heart.

His voice was husky as he wrapped his arms around her. "Then I'd better stay real close."

"Yes, please," she murmured. Holding his gaze, she began unfastening the snaps down the front of his shirt. "Otherwise, how can I undress you?"

Excitement flashed in his eyes. "You want to do that?"

"Very much." She finished with the snaps and pulled the shirttails out. "Remember on hot mornings when we'd both get sweaty?" She stroked upward from his waistband, massaging his sculpted abs and muscled chest.

He trembled beneath her fingertips. "I remember." His gaze locked with hers. "I'd watch a trickle of sweat slide into your cleavage and wonder how I'd ever manage to keep my hands to myself."

"And I longed for you to take off your shirt so I could see these manly pecs." She moved her hands in circles, loving the springy texture of his chest hair.

"You could've asked. I would have been happy to oblige."

"You could have touched me. I would have been thrilled."

"Maybe, but I couldn't make that move."

"You did today." She traced the strong line of his collarbone.

"I couldn't think of any other way to keep you from being scared."

"It worked. And now see what you've done." Reaching down, she unfastened his belt buckle. "I'm determined to have my way with you."

His throat moved in a slow swallow. "You know you're driving me crazy with this slow undressing routine. How about if I just take off my own clothes? Then you can have your way with me that much faster."

"It'll be more fun if I do it." Grasping the waistband of his jeans, she gave him a nudge in the direction of her bed. "In fact, I like the idea of you flat on your back, helpless to stop me from seducing you."

"I'm already pretty damned helpless to stop you, no matter what position I'm in."

"Humor me, Adam. Lie on my bed and let me play seductress."

He smiled. "A guy would have to be stupid to pass up an invitation like that."

"I'll take that as a yes." She walked him backward. When he reached the edge of the mattress, he let her push him down. "Excellent." She climbed onto the bed and leaned over him until her mouth was nearly touching his. "Prepare to be seduced."

"Valerie, sweetheart, I'm all yours."

Adam had finally figured out what was going on. He might be a little afraid of his intense feelings for her, but she was *really* afraid. She hadn't been intimate with a man since the fire, and obviously giving up control freaked her out.

So he stretched out on the bed, his booted feet still on the floor, his shirt on but unfastened, and prepared for the sweet torture of having her work him over as his climax hovered ever nearer. After giving him a kiss involving lots of tongue, she moved on to his chest. He hadn't thought his nipples were sensitive, but she proved him wrong about that.

Breathing became a real challenge as she eased him out of his jeans and briefs. She only pushed them to his knees. He realized that was all the undressing she needed for her purposes. She'd effectively hobbled him by doing that, which might give her an even greater sense of being in control.

When she wrapped her slender fingers around his cock, he didn't much care whether he was hog-tied by his jeans and underwear. He just hoped to hell he wouldn't come too fast. Between his lust for her and a long period of abstinence, he wasn't ready to bet on his staying power.

"You're . . . magnificent." Her comment was satisfyingly breathless.

He could live with heartfelt comments like that. "Glad I pass muster."

"Oh, you do." Still wearing her black bra and panties, she straddled his thighs while she caressed his pride and joy.

"FYI, I have two condoms in my jeans pocket, right side."

She cupped his balls and massaged gently. "Is that a hint?"

"Let's call it a request." He dragged in air. "Much more of touching me like that, and it'll become a desperate plea. It's been a long time, Val."

She smiled. "You called me Val. I like that."

"I'll call you anything you want me to if you'll grab one of those condoms." He was trying to let her be in charge, and if she didn't make a move soon ... But he wouldn't take over. That could be disastrous. She needed to direct the action.

"Pretty soon." With one last squeeze, she let go and reached behind her back. "I need to finish taking my clothes off."

He wanted to see her breasts. He did. He wanted to fondle them, too, and take them into his mouth. But sensory overload was a real danger in this situation.

She slipped her bra free and flipped it backward onto the floor. "That's better, don't you think?"

"Mm." He wasn't capable of coherent speech. The glory of her breasts beckoned to him. They hung there— full, round, and tipped with lush burgundy nipples. He reached for them.

"Easy, cowboy." She caught his wrists and leaned forward, pinning his arms to the bed as her breasts dangled inches from his mouth.

"You're diabolical."

"Just having fun."

"I dare you to give me a taste." He easily could have wrenched free, but he'd agreed to play her game, so he let her tease him. If this made her feel safe, then he'd go along. He had to admit the novelty excited him, but sooner or later, he was going to explode, and he worried it would be sooner.

"I never could resist a dare." Dipping lower, she allowed him to capture one tight nipple in his mouth. As he sucked, he felt his orgasm shouldering its way closer. But she wasn't immune to her needs, either. She moaned softly and rubbed the crotch of her panties against his thighs. The material was soaked.

He increased the pressure as he drew her breast into his mouth. She began to pant. Good. This torture could work both ways. He wanted her to be as frantic as he was.

Then maybe she'd abandon her need to control and surrender to the joy of the experience. He wanted that for her. He longed for her to trust him enough to let that happen.

Raising up, she deprived him of the plump breast she'd offered, but when she scooted back to rummage in the pocket of his jeans, he nurtured the hope that she was ready for the main event. He lifted his head to check on her progress. His cock was stiff as a fence post. "Now? Please?"

"Yes." She maneuvered herself out of her panties and threw those to the floor, too. Then she ripped open the condom package. As she rolled the condom on, her fingers shook, but she got the job done.

He gritted his teeth throughout the procedure. Coming in the midst of her condom application would not be cool. He was determined to last until she had an orgasm. She'd thrown down a gauntlet with her fooling around, and he was as competitive as the next guy.

But as she rose over him, he realized that sex was not supposed to be a competition. Or a battle for control. She'd turned it into one, and somehow, some way, he wanted to change that.

Then her warmth slowly enveloped him, and he lost whatever reasoning power he'd had left. As she sank downward, he lifted up, drawn in by the most perfect connection he'd ever had with a woman. So good. So incredibly good.

He gazed at her, hoping to see that same sense of homecoming in her expression. Her eyes were closed. Damn it, was she going to hide from him *now*? "Valerie," he murmured.

She shook her head and didn't open her eyes.

"Don't hide from me."

"I'm afraid to let go."

"Come here." He gripped her shoulders and tried to pull her to him.

"No."

But she was starting to contract around him, in spite of herself. He could feel it and knew that he wouldn't be able to resist those rhythmic pulses. "You're going to come," he said. "Let it happen."

"No. No!" And yet she erupted, and when she did, he couldn't hold back. With a groan, he surged upward. Their mutual climax should have been a moment of triumph, a moment of joy. Instead, as he shuddered in the aftermath, all he felt was despair. She didn't trust him, after all.

Then, like some cosmic joke, her smoke alarm went off. The minute it did, he knew what must have happened. She'd started supper, and it was burning on the stove.

With a shriek, she leaped from the bed and ran into the kitchen. He followed as soon as he rid himself of the condom and pulled up his briefs and jeans. The kitchen was filled with steam. She'd grabbed both pans, dumped them in the sink, and sprayed water on them.

The smoke alarm continued to screech. Adam grabbed a towel from a rack on the wall and waved it at the alarm, which gradually sputtered to a stop. He tried to tell himself this wasn't a disaster, but he knew it was.

Valerie turned to him, her expression stricken. "I guess I'm not ready, Adam. I'm so sorry."

"It takes time." His heart ached for her. "Don't give up on the basis of—"

"I know it's cowardly of me, but ... I want you to leave."

He took it like a shot to the gut. "Don't do this. Let's open the wine, order pizza. It'll be fine."

"No, it won't. Please go. I ... need time. Lots more time."

He couldn't very well force her to let him stay. Because he'd never been fully undressed, he could simply fasten his shirt, tuck it into his jeans, and buckle his belt. Walking into her living room, he picked up his hat.

Then he glanced around. He might never be here again, and he wanted to remember it. Her sofa and chair were slip-covered in practical beige, but she'd strewn colorful throw pillows everywhere. The art on her walls was bright, too, including ... what was that, anyway?

He peered at the whirligig of scarves tacked to the wall. He'd bet she'd made that, and it was inventive and pretty and filled with life, just like she was. Or how she could be, if she'd break out of this prison she'd constructed around herself.

He couldn't just abandon her. "Valerie, can we talk about this? Do you realize you didn't have a meltdown when the smoke alarm went off? You're making progress!"

"Not enough progress. I need to be by myself for a while. Good-bye, Adam."

He was dismissed. Will had warned him not to mess up. He'd tried his damnedest not to. Somehow, though, he had, and now she was kicking him out. With a heavy sigh, he left.

Eight

Although Valerie had expected to cry after Adam closed her front door, she didn't shed a single tear. Instead she wandered zombielike back to the bedroom and pulled a bathrobe out of the closet. As she belted it around her waist, she stared at the bed and wondered if she'd have to donate it to charity. Sleeping in it would be impossible after this.

She'd have to burn that maxidress, too, although at the moment she didn't have the energy to figure out how to do it without setting off the smoke alarm *again*.

You didn't have a meltdown when the smoke alarm went off. You're making progress. Adam's words came back to her.

Now that he was gone, she could admit that he had been right about that. The sound of the alarm had scared her, but not any more than that kind of noise had frightened her before the fire. Alarms were supposed to get the adrenaline pumping, so that people hearing them would take action.

She'd done that. After stupidly leaving the water boiling and the sauce heating, she'd headed into the bedroom with Adam. Smoke alarms were designed to keep carelessness from causing more serious harm, and everything had worked the way it was supposed to. She'd handled the smoking pans in the kitchen and they hadn't started a fire.

But that wasn't the main issue, and she knew it. Plopping down on the living room sofa, she gazed at the wine, and the bouquet lying on its side, gasping for water. The wine didn't need her attention, but the blue roses and baby's breath certainly did. Besides, blue roses cost the moon, and she couldn't let her foul mood ruin them.

As she found a vase for the flowers and filled it with water, she thought about her abysmal behavior in the lovemaking department. She'd imagined herself as a clever and sophisticated lady, taking charge like that. But underneath she'd been motivated by fear of losing control.

She might have gotten away with her ruse if she hadn't behaved like an idiot in the final moments. What normal woman rejects the idea of having an orgasm? She had, though, to her total embarrassment. Her body had surged ahead, demanding release, and she'd dug in her heels, as if she could keep it from happening.

No wonder Adam had been confused as hell. Any man would be. And now that she was thinking about Adam, she acknowledged that he hadn't said a single thing, veiled or blatant, that indicated he cared about the difference in their financial circumstances. Not an issue.

She'd certainly done her best to create other issues, though. He'd come here with an open heart, and she'd insisted on playing games. Had she learned nothing about honest communication during her sessions with Rocket Fuel? Apparently not.

If Adam had any sense, he'd give up on her as a bad job. To top it off, she'd created tonight's little drama on Adam's first date since his divorce. Wasn't that special? He might have hoped for a new start, and instead he'd been kicked in the teeth.

She didn't know how she'd ever repair that damage, but for now, she could at least clean up the mess in the kitchen. Maybe scrubbing those two scorched pots would bring her some kind of clarity. Pushing herself to her feet, she headed into the kitchen, rolled up the sleeves of her bathrobe, and ran hot water in the sink.

She was up to her elbows in soapy water when the doorbell rang. Glancing at the clock, she realized it wasn't that late. One of her neighbors could be dropping by to ask a favor.

The apartment complex didn't allow solicitors, and Astrid and Melanie both knew she'd asked Adam to come for dinner, so they wouldn't be showing up at her door. It had to be a neighbor. She could ignore them, of course, but it might be an emergency.

Or maybe they'd heard her smoke alarm and were worried about her. Goodness knows she'd be worried if she heard a smoke alarm in the building. Tightening the belt on her robe, she ran her fingers through her hair and went to the door.

Adam stood on the other side.

She stared at him. "What are you doing here?"

"Forcing the issue." He walked in without being invited.

She was so startled by his boldness that she stepped aside and let him in.

The minute she closed the door he spun to face her. "Listen, Valerie, you and I are closer to making a go of things than you think."

"We are?" She gazed at him, stunned by his sudden appearance. She'd sent him away. He hadn't stayed gone.

"Yes, damn it! Remember the elevator? You might have lost it if those two guys had wedged their way in, but they didn't, and you made it through that first ride."

"Yes, but an elevator ride is not the same as—"

"Sex? Why not? You were really close to enjoying yourself, but the last part, the climax, was too much for you. But you were almost there! You need to try it again."

She blinked. "When?"

"Now. With me."

"You can't be serious."

"I'm very serious. Every cowboy knows that when you fall off a horse, the best thing to do is get right back on."

She stared at him. "You're insane, Adam Templeton." But a tiny flame of hope flickered deep within her. If he hadn't lost faith, maybe she shouldn't, either.

"Maybe I am insane, but I've been driving around town thinking about you, and about us, and that whirligig you made with the scarves, and I—"

"The *scarves*? When did you notice the scarves?"

"As I was leaving. They are so you, the part of you that wants to be free of all this crap."

"Don't read anything into those scarves. I put them up right before you arrived to hide a smear of yellow paint. It took me about ten minutes."

He glanced at the scarves and back at her. "You just made my point, Madam Counselor. Look what happens when you let yourself do something crazy and spontaneous." He gestured to it. "A burst of beauty." He stepped closer. "That's what you're all about, Valerie. Don't give up on rediscovering who you are."

She began to tremble. Much as she wanted to deny what he was saying, it rang true. But was she brave enough to try again? What if she couldn't let go?

She stalled for time. "Listen, it's seven-forty-five and you haven't had dinner. You must be starving."

He shook his head. "I'm not starving." He took another step closer. "Come to bed with me, Valerie Wolitzky. If it works out the way I hope it will, we can order takeout later."

She shook so much she worried that her teeth would start chattering. "You're giving m-me a s-second chance?"

"I'm giving *us* a second chance."

"Why?" She held her breath.

"Because I think . . . I think we might have something special." His silver gaze searched hers. "And if I drive away from this apartment building without making love to you again, we might never find out if we do."

It was now or never. She felt like a skydiver at the open door of the plane. She gulped. "Okay."

"I have one condition, though."

"Wh-what?" If he didn't put his arms around her soon, she was going to shake herself apart.

"No games. No one-upmanship. Just . . . two people loving each other."

She nodded.

"Be brave, sweetheart."

She nodded again.

"And don't look so grim." He smiled down at her. "I think you're going to love this."

Adam hoped to hell she would respond to him. He wished she hadn't marched back to the bedroom like a condemned person heading for a firing squad. But at least she'd agreed to go. She hadn't thrown him out again.

The room was dim, and maybe that was for the best this time. She walked over to the bed, took off her bathrobe, and crawled under the covers. That was okay, too. She could have as much protection as she needed in the beginning.

She had a rocker in the bedroom, something he hadn't noticed before. He sat in it so he could take off his boots. He undressed as quickly as he could, because he had a feeling she was over there hyperventilating at the thought of letting down the barriers.

Knowing she was giving him another chance to make love to her was all the stimulation he needed to grow hard and ready. He put the condom on before he climbed into bed with her. Once he started this process, he didn't want to stop for anything. She might change her mind.

Poor thing, she was shaking so much. He gathered her close and began stroking her while he murmured words of comfort. She quivered less, and her skin began to warm under his fingertips.

Rolling her to her back, he moved over her and kissed her forehead, her closed eyelids, her cheeks, and finally, her mouth. He wasn't sure if she'd kiss him back, but she did. Sweet heaven, she did.

She began to touch him, too. Her hands trembled a

little, but perhaps it was eagerness now, not fear. Encouraged by that, he began an easy journey down her body, kissing and caressing her. When he reached her smooth belly, she tensed. He'd halfway expected that.

"Adam, don't . . ."

"Okay, I won't." As much as he'd love to taste all of her, he'd give up that pleasure for now. She wasn't ready to be that vulnerable. Not yet.

Instead he kissed his way back to her mouth as he continued to caress her hips, her thighs, and finally, that sweet spot he craved entrance to. She was wet. Very wet. His heart thudded with anticipation as he moved between her thighs.

Her expression was in shadow, but her sharp intake of breath told him to go slowly. He eased his cock in a little bit and paused. She grasped his hips, and for a moment, he thought she might try to stop him. But, no, she was silently urging him to go deeper.

With a groan, he sank into her. This was so right. They had to make it work between them. And he would do his level best to show her why.

Propping his weight on his forearms, he leaned down to feather a kiss over her lips. "Thank you," he murmured.

Her breath hitched. "I'm so much trouble."

"And so worth it." He drew back and slid in again as tiny arrows of pleasure shot through him.

"You should . . . have given up."

"I couldn't." Driven by his own needs, trying to keep his mind on hers, he began a steady rhythm.

She trembled beneath him. "I don't know why."

"Because . . ." The reason flowed through him in a river of certainty. "Because I love you."

"Oh, Adam." And she began to cry.

God, he'd messed up again. He couldn't force himself to break the connection, but he stopped moving. Buried deep within her, his cock twitched with impatience.

He kissed her wet cheeks. "I didn't mean to make you cry."

"I know." She sniffed. "Don't stop, Adam. Please don't stop."

"But you're crying."

"Because you're so *wonderful*." Her tears continued to flow. "Just love me," she said in a thick voice. "Please love me."

"I do. I started loving you the first day. I—"

"I mean *make* love to me!"

She sounded desperate, and as a matter of fact, so was he. He began to thrust, and this time she rose to meet him. She might be crying, but she was completely into this and reaching for her climax without hesitation, without fear.

Joy filled him as he moved faster. "That's it, Valerie! That's it!"

"I know . . . Adam . . . *Adam*." With a triumphant cry, she came, her body clenching around him as she both laughed and sobbed out her gratitude.

A second later, he tumbled into that brilliant, multi-colored world with her, and he held on for dear life. He would never let her go. Never.

Long moments later, he lay with his head on her shoulder and listened to the glorious sound of her breathing.

She wasn't crying anymore. Quite the contrary. Judging from the curve of her lips, she was smiling.

She stroked his back and sighed. "I hate to make you move, but—"

Instantly he pushed himself up. "I'm too heavy."

"No!" She wrapped her arms around him. "I want you right there, but you have to lift your head and look at me."

"Okay." He wasn't worried about her taking control now. Not after she'd been so thoroughly lost in his arms. They'd leaped that hurdle together. He hadn't messed up, after all.

"Maybe you should turn on the bedside lamp, although I warn you, my eyes will be red, so don't freak."

"We don't have to turn on the light."

"Yes, we do. Can you reach it?"

"Yep." Balancing himself on one arm, he stretched out the other and pushed the small switch. Then he blinked in the glare.

"I'll wait until your eyes adjust."

He blinked a few times. "I'm fine. And yeah, your eyes could use some saline drops."

"What a romantic thing to say."

He laughed. "That's me, Mr. Romance."

"I wasn't kidding. It is romantic, because you're such a caretaker. Of course you'd notice I need drops for my eyes. I cherish that about you."

"Well . . . okay. Thanks."

"I cherish lots of things about you, Adam. I wanted the light on so we could look at each other, because this is important. You see, I love you, too."

His chest tightened and his throat closed. Damned if he didn't feel a little misty-eyed, himself.

She cupped his cheek. "I think you liked hearing that."

"Yeah." He cleared the emotion from his throat. "I liked it a lot. I liked it so much, in fact, that you've given me an idea."

She smiled up at him. "What's that?"

"I was just wondering . . ." He gazed into her green eyes. "If you, Valerie Wolitzky, would do me the great honor of marrying me and making me the happiest guy in the world."

Her smile widened. "Yes. Yes, yes, a thousand times yes!"

"I have to warn you I'm not perfect."

"Maybe not, but you're the perfect man for me."

He thought his smile might be even brighter than hers. No doubt about it, this was the best damned day . . . and night, of his life.

Epilogue

Almost three weeks later, Adam walked toward the entrance to the Golden Spurs & Stetson with a very excited Valerie beside him. She'd come up with the idea of staging a private party at the bar for her girlfriends, their significant others, and friends and family. Adam considered it a sign of how far Valerie had come that she wasn't worried about being in a crowded venue.

And it would be crowded. Each of the six had invited a boatload of friends and relatives to share in their joy. Valerie's parents were driving up from Houston, along with two sets of aunts and uncles, plus a few cousins. She'd also asked everyone at her law firm.

Adam had included his mother, his former and current business associates, Will and his wife, and the ranch hands. Then he'd decided to ask some of his buddies from Harvard, and several were flying in.

Melanie and her fiancé, Drew Eldridge, had similarly long lists, as did Astrid and her guy, rancher Fletch Grayson. Adam would have footed the bill himself. He was just that happy. But Astrid, a woman with a fortune of her own, and Drew, also a billionaire, had insisted on splitting the costs among them.

Adam had to admit the idea was brilliant. And then Melanie had suggested something even more brilliant. She'd proposed that all three couples meet at the bar an hour before the other guests, so everyone could get acquainted before the onslaught.

Adam looked forward to it. He'd only seen Astrid and Melanie once, and that had been under difficult circumstances. He knew Drew Eldridge by reputation, and might have shared a table with him at a charity function, although he wouldn't swear to it. He'd never met Fletch Grayson and was eager to talk horses with another breeder.

Besides, he needed to get to know everyone in this tight circle. The women were best friends, which probably meant the guys would be seeing a lot of one another, maybe for years to come.

Valerie paused at the entrance and glanced up at Adam. "Just think how much our lives have changed since that night I plowed into you right here."

He squeezed her hand. "That was the luckiest night of my life."

"Mine, too." She looked into his eyes. "I love you, Adam."

He leaned down to give her a kiss. "And I love you right back, Valerie."

"Okay, okay, break it up!" Behind them, a woman laughed. "Quit blocking the doorway. Important people coming through."

They turned to find Astrid and Fletch both grinning as they approached the entrance.

Valerie hurried forward to give Astrid a hug. Then she hugged Fletch, too, although she did it carefully because he wore what looked like a brand-new Stetson. Adam recognized the style as one that he'd looked at just last week.

"Come and meet Adam." Valerie herded them in his direction.

Astrid enveloped him in a hug. "Well done," she murmured.

Adam didn't feel right taking credit for a transformation that had been a joint effort including Will and Rocket Fuel, not to mention Valerie's own bravery and determination. "I didn't—"

"You were a big part of it." She turned to Fletch. "I'd like you to meet my . . ." She hesitated. "Should I say?"

Fletch smiled. "That's up to you."

"Oh, heck. I can't stand it. We're engaged!"

Adam shook Fletch's hand and congratulated him while Astrid and Valerie shrieked and hugged.

"What, what?" Melanie hurried up, followed by a guy in a sport coat who had to be Drew Eldridge.

Valerie thrust Astrid's hand in Melanie's face. "They're engaged!" More hugging and shrieking followed.

Drew laughed as he navigated around the women and held out his hand to Fletch. "Congratulations. She's a wonderful woman."

"Agreed."

Drew then shook Adam's hand. "I recognize you, Templeton. You and I attended the same charity thing a couple of years ago. It's good to see you again."

"Same here. I'm glad you were on board with Valerie's idea."

"It's a terrific idea." Drew glanced toward the women, who were still in a huddle, and then looked at Adam and Fletch. "So, either of you into golf?"

Both Adam and Fletch shook their heads.

"I'm always up for a ride," Adam said.

Fletch nodded. "Me, too."

"Sorry," Drew said. "I'm not much of a rider."

Fletch adjusted the tilt of his Stetson. "Poker?"

"Poker works," Adam said.

"Excellent." Drew smiled. "My place. Next Wednesday night."

"Okay." Adam thought of Will, who loved a good poker game. He glanced at Drew. "Can I bring my friend Will?"

"Absolutely. The more the merrier."

"Wednesday night's great," Fletch said. "Astrid's got Melanie's bridal shower that night."

"Yeah." Adam had forgotten about that. "So does Valerie, come to think of it."

"My point exactly," Drew said.

"Hey, you guys." Valerie walked toward them and linked her arm through Adam's. "We were just thinking about next Wednesday night. We've got the shower, of course, but there's this antiques auction that we'll be missing, so we thought maybe you three—"

"Wish I could," Drew said, "but I have plans."

Fletch shook his head. "Sorry. I'm tied up, too."

"Yeah, so am I. What a shame." Adam sighed in feigned disappointment.

Astrid narrowed her eyes at them. "Why do I get the feeling that in the short time we left you three alone, you cooked up your own plan for Wednesday night?"

Fletch laughed and put his arm around her. "Just playing a little defense, sweetheart."

Melanie surveyed the group. "Well, ladies, we were worried that they might not get along, and they've already outmaneuvered us."

"This time." Valerie winked at Adam. "Hey, let's go inside. I think we have some serious toasting to do."

"Yep, we certainly do." Adam tucked Valerie in close as they walked into the bar. What a stroke of luck that he'd been in the right place at the right time that fateful night.

Will had told him it was meant to be. Then he'd sent Valerie out to the ranch. Adam had accused him of matchmaking, like that was a bad thing. It occurred to Adam that not only had it been a very good thing, but he'd neglected to thank Will properly. He'd do that tonight.

But Will was about to get his reward. Adam had found him a poker game. And Adam had never met anyone who could beat Will Bryan at poker.

Two hours later, Valerie returned from a quick trip to the ladies' room and paused to survey the crowd. Everywhere she looked, people were smiling and laughing. Some had arrived as strangers and all were from different walks of life, but sharing in the happiness of three joyous couples had made everyone instant friends.

Nothing else seemed important tonight—not social standing, and certainly not wealth or the lack of it. Seasoned ranch hands swapped stories with billionaires. Wealthy matriarchs talked earnestly with soccer moms. All around her, walls were coming down and stereotypes were being smashed.

Glancing across the room, she caught and held Adam's gaze. He smiled and gave her a thumbs-up. She'd been a little worried that this eclectic group wouldn't jell, but it had. And now she knew why. All that mattered, all that ever really mattered, was love.

Read on for a sneak peek at
Vicki Lewis Thompson's

CRAZY ABOUT THE COWBOY
A Sexy Texans Novel

Available in May 2015 from Signet Eclipse.

"Somebody should take a paintbrush to Sadie's left nipple." Vince Durant studied the six-by-ten mural on the far wall of Sadie's Saloon as he swigged his beer. "It's chipped."

A well-endowed nude reclined on a piece of red velvet Victorian furniture that he thought was called a fainting couch. Rumor had it that a local woman named Sadie had posed for the mural, but because the work was more than a century old, it was unconfirmed.

"Sadie's not the only thing needing a little TLC around here." Ike Plunkett was still behind the bar, which was reassuring.

Vince remembered Ike from seven years ago, and while the bartender's hair was a little thinner and his glasses a little thicker, he looked virtually the same. That couldn't be said for the town of Bickford, though. Except for the general store and this historic hotel, the place was pretty much dead.

Come to think of it, he'd seen no evidence of anyone staying there besides himself and his two friends who hadn't yet arrived. Even more troubling, the saloon was deserted, and that wasn't normal for a Friday afternoon. At the end of the day, cowboys in the Texas Panhandle enjoyed sipping a cold one. "I never realized how much the town depended on the Double J."

"I don't think any of us did until it was gone."

"You'd think by now somebody would have reopened it." Vince wouldn't have minded working there again. Turned out, he was good at wrangling greenhorns.

"Can't." Ike used a bar rag to wipe down the whiskey bottles lined up beneath an ornate mirror behind the bar. "Somebody torched it, probably for the insurance, and the land's tied up in a big legal hassle."

"Sorry to hear that." Vince polished off his beer and signaled for another. He was thirsty after the long drive from Fort Worth.

"Not half as sorry as we are."

"No, probably not." But he *was* sorry, and disappointed, too. He'd talked his buddies Mac Foster and Travis Langdon into having a reunion, figuring they could party in Bickford like they had during the year they'd all worked for the Double J. "I don't suppose you have live music this weekend?"

"We haven't had a band in here for a long time. Can't afford to pay 'em."

"That's depressing."

"Tell me about it."

"Oh, well. At least you have beer!" Vince lifted his bottle in the direction of the mural. "And Sadie! After a few of these, I might decide to repaint her nipple myself."

The street door to the saloon opened with the squeak of an unoiled hinge, and Vince turned to see if Mac or

Travis had come straight into the saloon instead of stopping by the hotel desk to check in like he had.

His smile of welcome faltered when Georgina Bickford walked through the door. He took some comfort in noticing that she seemed as disoriented by his presence as he was by hers. It made no sense, really. It wasn't like they had a history, although he'd tried his damnedest to charm her into going out with him. Maybe that was why he'd thought of her so often since then. She was the one girl he'd never been able to impress.

She didn't look particularly impressed to see him now, either. "Hello, Vince."

"Hello, Georgie."

Her voice was as cool as he remembered, and at least she hadn't forgotten his name. After seven years, that said something. He wasn't convinced it said something positive, though. A name could stick in a person's mind for both good reasons and bad.

"I'm surprised to see you here." She approached slowly, as if he had yellow caution tape draped around his barstool. "Just passing through?"

"Not exactly." He thumbed back his hat so he could see her better. She'd gotten prettier over the past seven years, but she'd always been great to look at, with her big brown eyes and honey-colored hair. He'd asked around and found out that she'd left college to run the general store after her dad had died. Vince had tried to be friendly, but she'd never given him the time of day.

She frowned. "If you're looking for work, there's not much to be had around here, I'm afraid."

"So I gathered." He hesitated. Oh, what the hell? "Can I buy you a drink?"

"No, thank you."

Shot down again, damn it.

"Georgie's first drink is on the house." Ike sent a glance of compassion Vince's way as he placed a glass of red wine on the bar. "All of the council members get one free drink per day. Bickford Hotel policy. It's the least we can do when they have such a thankless job."

"You're on the town council?" Then he wished he hadn't sounded so surprised. "I mean, I'm sure you're well-qualified and all. I just . . ."

She appeared to take pity on him. "It's okay. I'm the youngest member, but I also run the second-biggest revenue producer in town, so it's logical for me to be on the council." She smiled. "It wasn't a tough race. No one ran against me."

Hey, a smile. Progress.

"They wouldn't have dared run against you," Ike said. "What can I get you from the kitchen?"

"A barbecued pork sandwich would be great. Thanks, Ike."

The bartender glanced at Vince. "Want to order some food?"

"Not yet, thanks. I'll wait for Mac and Travis to get here."

"Fair enough." He opened the hinged section of the bar and walked back toward the kitchen.

"Mac and Travis?" Georgie picked up her wineglass but remained standing beside the bar instead of hopping up on a stool. "The same Mac and Travis who used to work for the Double J?"

"You have a good memory." She hadn't dated those old boys, either. Vince, Mac, and Travis had been the cutups of the group, and Georgie didn't approve of cutups. She'd made that clear seven years ago, and he doubted that she'd changed.

She took a sip of her wine. "Are you having some kind of Double J reunion?"

"In a way, but it's just the three of us."

Her brown eyes lit with curiosity. "And you're meeting here, in Bickford?"

"That's the plan." He liked her haircut, which was a little shorter than he remembered. It used to hang past her shoulders, but now it was chin length. The new cut made her look more sophisticated. Sexier.

"Why meet here?"

He shrugged. "It's where we used to hang out, but I hadn't realized the place had gone . . . uh, that it's not the same."

"If you were about to say it's gone to hell in a handbasket, you'd be on target. If you want to have a fun time, y'all might want to head somewhere else. Go on up to Amarillo, maybe."

"It'll be okay." He didn't remember her being quite so curvy seven years ago, either. She filled out the Bickford General Store's hunter green T-shirt, although he was careful not to be caught ogling. He'd noticed that her jeans fit mighty nice, too. Not that it made any difference whether she was a knockout or not. She hadn't changed regarding him. She showed no interest whatsoever.

"I can't imagine what you'll find to do around here," she said. "Sadie's doesn't heat up like it used to on the weekend. Anastasia and I might be the last two single women under thirty in Bickford."

"What about Charmaine?" He was surprised he remembered the names of her two stepsisters. Seven years ago, Anastasia and Charmaine had been too young to go out dancing at Sadie's, but Charmaine had snuck in one time, and Georgie had marched her back home.

"She's working in Dallas. She'd party with you if she could, but she isn't here, and Anastasia's not into that. Besides, even if she was, there's no live music anymore."

"Yeah, Ike said it wasn't in the budget. No worries. I haven't seen Mac and Travis since we left the Double J. Maybe it's better this way. We can drink beer and catch up."

"For the entire weekend?" She sounded skeptical.

"Well, no. We'll do that at night, but during the day we'll head out and round up the Ghost. Ike says he's still—"

"You most certainly will not!" She set her wineglass down with a sharp click and faced him, sparks of anger in her eyes. "Don't y'all dare go out there and harass that poor horse for your own amusement!"

He blinked in confusion. Seven years ago, the dappled gray stallion and his small band of wild horses had been fair game, a challenge for the cowboys who worked at the Double J. Vince and his buddies hadn't succeeded in roping him, mostly because they'd never been able to devote an entire weekend to the project. Now they could.

But Georgie was obviously ready to rip him a new one on the subject of the wild stallion. "There is no reason on God's green earth why you should go after him! He's not hurting anything, especially now that so few horses live in the area. Back when the Double J was in operation, I admit he tried to raid the corral a couple of times, but those days are over. There are four horses boarded at

Ed's stable, and they're all geldings. No mares. The Ghost leaves us alone, and we leave him alone!"

"But—"

"Is that why you decided to rendezvous here? To go after that stallion?"

"Partly, yeah. We always talked about capturing him, but we never did. Now seems as good a time as any."

Her eyes glittered in defiance. "You won't find him."

"Oh, I think we will. We have two whole days to look."

Ike returned from the kitchen, and Georgie wheeled toward him. "Did you tell Vince that the Ghost was still out there?"

Ike shrugged. "He asked. I wasn't going to lie to the man."

"Are you aware that Vince and his two cohorts are heading out on some macho quest to rope him?"

"I didn't know that." Ike looked at Vince. "You might want to reconsider. Georgie takes a special interest in those wild horses."

Crap. First he'd discovered that the town was deader than a doornail, and now Georgie Bickford was raining all over his wild-horse roundup. Maybe she was right and they should take this party elsewhere, but he'd craved the small-town experience, and he wouldn't get that in Amarillo or Lubbock.

Mac and Travis chose that moment to walk into the saloon. They'd shared a ride because they both worked at a ranch outside Midland. They sauntered in with wide grins, as if they owned the place. Vince left his barstool and went over to greet them. Much joking around and backslapping followed. Vince couldn't believe how happy he was to see those old boys. Until they arrived, he'd been outnumbered.

Mac and Travis tipped their hats and said hello to Georgie, who replied without smiling.

"So, where is everybody?" Mac glanced around. "Hey, Georgie. What's happened to this place?"

"We're experiencing an economic downturn." Georgie's jaw tightened. "I suggest you three mosey on to a place that's more suited to your needs."

"Nah, we don't need to do that," Travis said. "I assume Sadie's still serves beer."

"We do," Ike said.

"Then we're in business." Travis walked over to the bar and shook hands with Ike. "Good to see you. I'll have a longneck, like always."

"And I'll take my usual draft." Mac sat on a stool next to him.

"Coming up." Ike looked nervous, but he busied himself getting the beer.

Georgie cleared her throat. "I understand y'all are planning to round up the Ghost this weekend."

Mac nodded. "Yes, ma'am, we sure are. Isn't that right, Vince?"

For a split second Vince considered telling Mac there'd been a change of plans. Then his rebellious streak surfaced. By God, he'd organized this adventure, and he'd see it through. There was no law against chasing after that horse. He met Georgie's flinty gaze. "That's right, Mac."

Georgie's mouth thinned. "Over my dead body."

Also available from
New York Times Bestselling Author

Vicki Lewis Thompson

Werewolf in Las Vegas
A Wild About You Novel

Giselle Landry is in Las Vegas to haul her wayward
brother back home. But casino owner Luke Dalton is also
looking for her brother, who has run off with his little
sister. The two should join forces, but Luke is unaware
that Giselle's brother is also fleeing his duties as the future
alpha of the Landry werewolf pack—which includes his
Were bride.

Giselle can't let herself get close to Luke, even to solve
their shared dilemma. Still, the tension wears away her
resistance, and after a wild night with Luke, she is
shocked to find she's fallen for him. But Luke still doesn't
know Giselle's true identity. And once their siblings are
found, Giselle must return to San Francisco...

Can they overcome the odds—or will what happened in
Vegas stay in Vegas?

vickilewisthompson.com

Available wherever books are sold or at
penguin.com

S0547